THE SANTA GAMES

LEANNE TREESE

Moxie Publishing

Leanne Treese/Moxie Publishing LLC

P.O. Box 5323

Clinton, New Jersey 08809

Publishers Note: This is a work of fiction. Names, characters, places, and incidents are a product of the author's imagination. Locales and public names are sometimes used for atmospheric purposes. Any resemblance to people, living or dead, or to businesses, companies, events, institutions, or locales is completely coincidental.

Cover Design by JRC Designs/Jena R Collins

www.jenarcollins.com

inxti/Shutterstock.com HSTUDIO99/Shutterstock.com

PhotoJuli86/Shutterstock.com fotohunter/shu1erstock.com

Stock-Asso/shutterstock.com

ISBN print: 978-1-7358961-5-1

ISBN ebook: 978-1-7358961-6-8

❧ Created with Vellum

To my son, Kevin, who helped create this story during our many COVID dog walks

CHAPTER 1

 ndi

I TWIRL in front of the mirror in the padded dressing room, swaths of beaded white fabric billowing from my waist. My light brown curls, less unruly than normal, fall just above the beaded bodice. The dress shows off the curves of my fullish figure in the best possible way, accentuating the top, hiding the bottom.

"I'll leave you to think about it," the saleswoman says. Her voice is tight. Like she knows I can't afford the dress. Or anything else in the store.

Her heels click down the hall and Emma, my best friend from home, puts her hands on my shoulders. "Andi, it's perfect," she whispers.

"I think I love it."

Emma moves back. I shift right and left then angle my body

so I can see the fabric covered buttons and bow at the waist. "I definitely love it."

Emma leans down, grabs a handful of fabric from the skirt, and examines it. "Look at this detail. Can you imagine how long it takes to stitch on all those tiny beads?"

"Um, yes. Forever." I step back, still looking at dress in the mirror. "What do you think Cole will think?"

"Your fiancé?" She rolls her eyes. "It doesn't matter. It should be what *you* think. You're the bride." She pauses a moment. "Let me get the picture." She pulls out her phone.

It had been her idea for us to go to White House Bridal, an exclusive bridal shop in Manhattan. Find the dream dress, duplicate it for cheap. The plan was classic Emma; she was always looking for bargains.

I pose, hand on hip, engagement ring visible. She takes the shot and inspects it. "Perfect."

I lean over her shoulder. The image in the photo reveals a woman with a natural smile and light blue eyes fringed with dark lashes. Pink tinges her cheeks, curls frame her face. She -- the woman in the photo --looks so different from how I normally do in my paint-splattered work clothes, that, had I not physically seen Emma take it, I would not have believed it was me.

Emma punches at her phone. "Just sent it to you."

I give a final glance to the dress in the mirror. "Okay, as much as I love it, I'm pretty sure this dress cost more than I made last year." I think about my earnings as a freelance set designer for off-Broadway plays. "Possibly two years. I should get it off before something happens to it."

"Like?"

The saleswoman returns before I can describe all the catastrophes that might befall me while I'm wearing the dress in this drink-free, food-free room. "So?" the woman says, her voice saccharine sweet. "Yes to the dress?"

"I'll have to think about it."

"Of course." She purses her lips. I *know* she can't wait for us to leave.

We bundle up and leave the shop. Emma puts on a white beret she'd bought from a street vendor and pulls a pair of oversized sunglasses from a swingy purse (purchased from said street vendor). She angles her head in my direction. "Do I look famous?"

I smile. "Totally." I nod toward her hands. "Except you've got that pile of touristy brochures."

"Well, I don't want to miss anything." Though I'm the one who lives here, she'd planned this trip down to the minute. She'd even scheduled for bathroom breaks and crowds.

She walks at a slow pace, not a New York one, her eyes on the buildings and landmarks. With Christmas around the corner, there's a lot to look at. Storefronts showcase over-the-top holiday displays; giant decorated Christmas trees buttress the doors of nearly every skyscraper. Signs promoting discounts and deals are everywhere.

"I never understand how you live here. It's so different from home."

"Yeah. No pigs or cows or Amish buggies here," I say, thinking of the staples of our hometown back in central Pennsylvania. "But you get used to it. And I've been here almost two years." I point to a restaurant ahead, Grandin Bar and Grille. "That's Cole's favorite."

Emma nods but says nothing. I hate that she doesn't like him, that they don't like each other rather. In fairness, they are dramatically different. Emma loves chain restaurants, baseball games, and summer picnics with juicy watermelon chunks and thick burgers grilled over charcoal. Cole collects vintage wine and goes to art exhibits.

Wind blows at our backs. One of Emma's brochures tumbles down the sidewalk toward the restaurant. She bounds after it, red hair flying behind. She grabs the errant paper, stares a moment at the restaurant window before returning to my side. There's a shell-shocked expression on her face, different from the "I'm-not-in-Kansas-anymore" look she normally has when she's here.

I stop and move under an awning; crowds pass in front of us. "What is it? You look like you saw a ghost."

She shuts her eyes a moment then opens them. "I think I saw Cole at that restaurant. The one you said he liked."

"Grandin?" I tilt my head. Cole is the director of the West Riding Theatre. It's not far from here. But he'd had a meeting across town today with a production manager. It wouldn't make any sense for him to be at Grandin. "I don't think so."

I start walking again; Emma follows. The corner light turns green, and we make our way across the street, bodies smushed together by the crowd. "I'm sorry Andi but I think it was him."

I shrug. "All right. I'll text him." We reach the sidewalk and I pull out my phone.

Emma juts her hand out. "He looked like he was on a date," she blurts.

"What?"

"He was with a woman. They were drinking red wine."

I shake my head, annoyed. It's one thing not to like Cole, but accusing him of being with another woman? It's too much. "Cole doesn't drink red wine." I say this like it's a big gotcha, a glaring hole in Emma's argument.

"It looked like him," she insists. "You know, with the long hair."

She gestures past her shoulder, and I roll my eyes. I find it sexy, but both Emma and my mother *hate* Cole's long hair. Emma nicknamed him Fabio.

FAO Schwarz, next on Emma's itinerary, comes into view. I'm annoyed enough that I want to go back and check out the restaurant so, when Cole *isn't* there, I can come back and say, "I told you so."

"You know what," I say. "I'll go back and check." I gesture to the toy store. "Go in and I'll be back in a few."

"But what if it's him?"

"It's not."

I start back before she can say anything more, weaving through the crowds. I stand at the walkway across the street from Grandin, crane my neck toward the window. I can make out people, but not clearly enough to know if Cole is there. The light changes. I speed past a little boy with light-up Superman sneakers and a woman wearing a Statue of Liberty headband. I reach the sidewalk, duck behind a street cart featuring sausages. I peer around it, look toward the table in the corner, the spot Emma had said he'd been.

My heart lurches.

Cole is there.

He faces my direction, his tie loose around his neck. He rakes his hair and lifts a glass of red wine. He clinks it against hers, the woman. She leans forward; he flashes her the smile I love.

I take a deep breath. Okay. Okay. Just because Cole is eating lunch with a woman doesn't mean he's having a sordid affair.

My phone buzzes. I pull up a text from Emma. *How goes it?* Below her question is the text she'd sent earlier, the one featuring the picture she'd taken of me in the wedding dress.

I pull up the dress photo and stare at my princess-like image. In a snap decision, I forward the picture to Cole via text with the question *What do you think?* The swish of the message fills the air. I hold my breath, feel as if my heart is flying across the airwaves.

Cole shakes his head at his companion, reaches into his pocket, and pulls out his phone. He stares at the screen.

I wait for the broad smile, for him to turn the device around, show the woman, utter the words, "my fiancée."

Cole does none of those things. He looks at his phone with the same expression he might have had I sent him a text asking if he wanted to get Chinese food. After, he places the device on the table, facedown, and waves to the woman in a way that seems like an apology.

I stand, unblinking, trying to reconcile Cole's actual reaction with what I'd wanted to see.

The man in the sausage truck puts on new links and the sound of sizzling grease fills the air. He gives me a sideways glance. "You all right, lady?"

I don't answer, my eyes fixed on Cole. A server returns with a credit card. Cole tucks it in his wallet; they gather their coats and bags. He guides the woman toward the door, his hand on the small of her back.

"Lady?" the man repeats. "Are you okay?"

I step away from his cart, ready to bang into Cole in a pretend surprise meeting.

Then he kisses her.

CHAPTER 2

T hree months later
       Andi
       "So, this is it." I hold my arms out and do a quick spin on the snow-covered path. "I can't believe it took you so long to come."

Emma shoves her hands deep in her coat pockets. Her cheeks are pink from the cold. "Sorry."

"So?" I bug my eyes out. "You're my best friend. I'm dying here. What do you think?" I glance around Christmastown, the world's only holiday-themed amusement park.

The place where I now live.

Yeah.

That.

Okay. So, I don't live *in* the amusement park. I'm a caretaker for the man who owns it, Liam Quinn. Liam (and now I) live in a house adjacent to the property. Six weeks ago, his daughter, Bridget, hired me. Her parents had acquired a holiday-themed park several years before. They'd planned to renovate it, but her mom passed and her dad refused to sell or move. She was worried about him alone on the rambling property.

The money was good, the job was near home and, after the heart pummeling I'd endured from the Cole break-up, I needed something as dramatically different from the New York theatre scene as I could find. Working as a caretaker in a remote area of Pennsylvania? Yeah. That would work. Christmastown was the perfect place to hide out, figure out next steps, and mend my heart.

I didn't expect to love it so much.

"Well?" I glance at Emma.

She stands, mute.

I scan the area and, for a moment, see the space as Emma likely did. A street of neglected buildings leading to a man-made lake half filled with muddy water. Attractions reduced to twisted metal: chipped present carriages on the Ferris wheel, faded reindeer-and-sleigh cars on the Santa-themed roller coaster. Sky carts, designed to look like massive red and gold Christmas ornaments, sway on cables over our heads. Thick clouds overhead frame the sad picture.

"I know it looks awful. It'll be way better than this, obviously." I wave my hand around as if the gesture would make the mess disappear. "Come on. I'll show you the plans." I stride toward Liam's house on the outskirts of the property.

I turn back. Emma's standing still, eyes fixed on what had once been a heated ball pit, every ball a squishy Christmas ornament.

"We're not going to reopen that. Too germy." I walk back and direct my attention to the sad expanse of faded, weathered balls. "I'm thinking this might be a good spot to have a Christmas-themed playground. Or a bunch of firepits for s'mores. It'll be cold when the park is at its height." I gesture to an area where the booth might stand and wait for the expected response: "Great idea." "So imaginative." Or just plain, "fun!"

Emma kicks at a snow pile. "Your mom is worried about

you, Andi." She looks up, green eyes wide with concern. "I am too."

My eyes fix on the idle merry-go-round beyond the ball pit. The dormant Rudolph seems to jeer at me.

"I mean," Emma continues, "you leave New York. You abandon your job --"

"I was between jobs," I interrupt. This was true. The play I had worked on had just opened; the sets were complete.

"Okay, you were between jobs," Emma concedes, "but you have to admit this is all a bit random. Cole breaks up with you, and a month later you're a caretaker for an old man and spend all your time on his plans to restore this park." She gestures around. "Restoring a theme park is a huge undertaking. And this place is in bad shape." She picks up a faded candy cane decoration in demonstration.

I swipe the giant candy cane from her hand. It breaks in half with the effort, Emma holding the stem, me the crook. I stand, the crook in my hand like a festive weapon. The reality behind Emma's concern sinks in.

My friend didn't believe in me.

My mother didn't believe in me.

Worse, they thought I was possibly crazy, holed up with an old man on a dilapidated holiday-themed property.

"I know it's in bad shape and I know it's a huge undertaking," I spit out. "But Liam promised his late wife he'd get the park off the ground, and I want to help him. Plus, I need to take a chance, take a risk with something."

Emma sighs. "This again?"

I pull at one of my curls. "He wasn't wrong."

The "he," of course, is Cole. In the aftermath of catching him cheating, he'd made clear that a big part of what was wrong with us (meaning me) was that we (meaning me) never took risks. Complacent, he'd said. A wallflower in my own life. And that phrase – complacent wallflower – is stuck in my mind like one of those sticky labels on glass. No matter how hard I try, no matter how I pick at the edges of the phrase, its sticky residue is impossible to get off.

"You do take risks," Emma protests, just as she had when I'd first told her what Cole said. "You went to New York. You were living out your dream of being a set designer."

"*Cole* was in New York. I followed. And I used his connections for jobs. I never tried to get anything on my own." I pause. "And it wasn't just the job part. I lost myself." This epiphany – how much of myself I'd allowed to be absorbed by Cole – had been painful.

My parents divorced when I was six. My father all but disappeared, and my mother has had a series of boyfriends. For most of my life, I'd watched her morph into someone else every time she dated a new man. She'd adopt his hobbies and interests, suddenly becoming an avid gourmet cook or a Giants fan or supremely interested in genealogy. Her latest BOM (boyfriend of the month, the term my brother and I coined for it) is Jim, a fisherman. Mom's taking to sending me snippets from the blog she now follows: Fun with Fish. Her texts are almost always fish-inspired recipes.

I'd sworn to myself I'd never be like her in that regard. Then I accompanied Cole to poetry readings and avant-garde art displays so often, I'd forgotten I didn't like either of those things. Nor did I like port wine. Or brandy. Or rushing back to the apartment to get the reusable grocery sack because, of course, I wouldn't be one of *those people*, the environmentally unconscious. Even if it was only *one time*.

Thing is, after the spectacular crash and burn of our relationship, I couldn't remember much I did like aside from the obvious. Chocolate. And my niece, Betsy. I seemed, too, to recall that I liked bright colors more than the muted tones (read black, gray, and more black) that Cole preferred. But I couldn't remember how I spent my days pre-Cole. What did I *like* to do anyway?

Emma meets my eyes with a sympathetic look. She sets the stem of the candy cane gently on the ground. "I get it. I get why you'd want to take a risk. But –" She stops, and I can tell she's trying to find the most diplomatic way to finish her sentence. "Is there a plan? And what's in all this for you?"

I sweep snow off a bench. I tap the space next to me; Emma sits.

"Liam knows how much is involved in a project like this," I say. "He doesn't have the skills to do it on his own, but his daughter is well connected. Liam wants to do enough planning to convince her that Christmastown is a good investment. She can help him find the people he needs."

A squirrel skitters across the path and into a hole at the base of the building in front of us. Emma stares at the hole a long moment before speaking. "But what's in it for you? I mean, this is a lot of work. And, if you're here, you're not out there, getting experience."

"There's a lot in this for me if it works. *This* is the ultimate set design." I gesture around the space with my arms. "Theatre sets get used and broken down, never to be seen again. But here, I'm getting to reimagine Christmas. I get to create something permanent and lasting with my art. Something that will, hopefully, be part of the childhood memories for countless kids. It's a great resume builder."

She nods, eyes fixed on the hole in the building framework.

"If it makes you feel better, I'm still putting my resume in for design jobs. Just in case." I don't tell her that the jobs I've applied for are way above my pay grade.

"That's good." But it doesn't look like she thinks it's good. I know she can't see beyond the mess.

"Close your eyes."

"Why?"

I roll my eyes. "Just close your eyes." She does. "Now," I start, "imagine a beautiful lake with a flowing fountain in its center." I pause to let her get a vision of the lake in her mind. "Picture yourself walking around a red brick path with giant pine trees on the outside. You're in a thick winter coat and snow gently falls around you. Can you picture it?"

"Yes."

"The pine trees are illuminated with thousands of Christmas lights which reflect on to the lake water, dots of color on its surface. You reach a majestic gazebo, outlined in white lights, and step inside. In front of the gazebo, there's a festive street of Swiss chalet themed buildings edged in snow. Wreaths hang across the road, suspended by strings of white lights. There's a toy shop, a bakeshop, and a Christmas-themed restaurant. There are carts of balloons and glow sticks and mugs of steaming hot chocolate on both sides of the street. Children's laughter, Christmas carols, and the swoosh of rides fill the air. You inhale the fresh scent of pine."

Emma inhales; I smile.

"Can you feel it now?"

"I can." She opens her eyes and, as if on cue, a second squirrel goes barreling into the building across from us. "I just don't know how you get from this to that."

I smile. "Me neither. But," I say, standing, "if Liam's right about his daughter, we shouldn't have to worry about it."

I hold out a hand, grab Emma's gloved one, and pull her to her feet. "*Now* do you want to see the plans?"

She pushes at my shoulder. "Yes."

We walk in silence, our boots making prints on the slush-covered path.

"Hey," Emma says suddenly, "promise me something?"

I glance at her. "Promise you something?"

"Yeah. That, even if you throw yourself into Christmastown,

you'll leave yourself open to date again. I'd hate it if Cole ruined you for love."

"Cole did not ruin me for love," I quip. "But I'm not dating anyone."

She stops. "Why not?"

"I need to be on my own right now. Besides, there are no eligible guys around here." I wave my arms around the desolate area as if to prove my point.

"Well, it's an easy promise then. If an eligible guy comes to Christmastown, you'll go out with him. But since that won't happen…" She lets the thought trail off.

"Fine."

She pulls off her glove and wiggles her fingers. "Pinky swear?"

"Pinky swear to go out with the fictitious eligible guy? Okay." Emma pulls off her glove and we interlock our pinkies in the same manner we had as preschoolers.

"Now you have to do it, Andi."

"Of course," I say with mock seriousness. "I mean, we pinky swore."

I'm not worried. The chance that an eligible guy would suddenly show up at the doorstep of Christmastown?

Practically zip.

Zip would be an understatement.

CHAPTER 3

M *att*

I bounce the green superball with one hand, review a basic contract with the other. The dual movement would distract most people but for me and my ADHD brain, activity helps me focus. Bounce. Read. Bounce. Read. Bounce. Read.

My entire bottom desk drawer at the esteemed law offices of Quinn Gifford is filled with fidget toys. Squishy balls. Spinners. A Jacob's ladder.

Kimmy, the associate who started the same week as I did, pokes her head in. She eyes the ball. "Nice rhythm."

I close my fist over it and lean back. "Thanks." I throw the ball in the air and catch it. I hold it in between my thumb and index finger. "Want to try?" I lift my eyebrows and do my best to make it seem like a salacious invitation.

Kimmy, happily engaged and completely and utterly uninterested in me, takes the question in stride. "Tempting, but no." She edges in, half shuts my door, and whispers, "have you seen Bridget this morning? She looks like she could kill someone."

I open my eyes wide in mock surprise. "Are you scared? Want a Rubik's cube?" I pull open my drawer and produce one. "Stop, and yes." She retrieves the cube from my open palm. "I used to be able to solve these, you know." I gesture to the toy, an invitation. She stamps a high heel with an emphatic click. "I don't have time to do it now. I've got the White deposition. Look out for Bridget." Cube in hand, she moves into the hall, stealth-like, as if Bridget might be hidden behind a desk or a wall, ready to attack with a pile of unwanted work or a red mark-up pen.

Bridget Quinn is the senior and founding partner of Quinn Gifford, one of Philadelphia's largest law firms. Kimmy and I have both worked as lawyers in the business department for two years. Kimmy, because she's a genius, and me, because I am about as well connected as you can get. My mom, a descendant of the founder of the Philadelphia staple, Yumcakes, and my dad, CEO of SmartTech Appliances, a revolutionary company which completely disrupted the appliance repair space.

I was a disaster in law school, and I certainly wasn't Quinn Gifford material. I got the job through furtive phone calls and favor swaps to which I was not privy. Sometimes, I wondered what Bridget got out of the deal? A lifetime supply of Yumcakes? A line of tech-savvy appliances for family and friends?

Notwithstanding the Herculean efforts it took me to get into the firm, I didn't love the job.

Scratch that.

I hated the job.

Lawyering didn't suit my personality. The paperwork, the arguing, the sitting still at a desk for what felt like an eternity. I'd been thinking about a change.

I bounce the green superball again. My computer dings with an email message. I flip it on, check the mail. Bridget Quinn.

I drop the ball. It rolls with halfhearted momentum to the wall.

I click on the message. *Matt, can you stop by my office?*

I stare at the words. Stop by her office?

Since I've been here, Bridget Quinn has never asked to see me. Not once. Having received the YumCakes or line of appliances or whatever her end of the barter was for taking on a clearly subpar associate, she'd seemed done. Our relationship could best be characterized by indifferent nods. I'd thought she'd forgotten my name.

Now she wanted to see me.

Kimmy's words whir in my mind: "she looks like she could kill someone."

Me? Had I done something wrong?

I bend down, grab the superball, and shove it in my pocket. I twist it between my thumb and forefinger, make my way to Bridget's corner office. I peek in and spy her behind a massive and immaculate desk. She's sixtyish with short and still-blonde hair in a cropped style. Her face is angular, eyes sky blue. She wears the same expression I've seen in the hallway, polite and refined on the surface, calculating underneath.

I knock on the open door. "You wanted to see me?"

"Matt. Please come in." She holds up a thick glass; ice cubes rattle with the movement. "May I get you some water?"

I step across the office and sit in a plush chair across from her desk. "No thanks. I'm good."

She folds her hands and directs her gaze at me. I feel as if I've been transported back to the junior high principal's office and my mind jams with possible reasons I'm here. Was it the pranks? Had she gotten wind that I was responsible for the rubber rat in the break kitchen? Or that I wrapped everything in the new intern's office with wrapping paper?

I keep my eyes neutral and say nothing.

"So," she says finally, "you must be wondering why I wanted to meet."

"Yes." I practically exhale the word.

"It's about my father, Liam."

She takes a sip of water and I rack my brain trying to remember if I'd ever met Bridget's father. Or even heard her mention him. Maybe he was a friend of my parents?

"You haven't met my dad," she says, seeming to read my mind. "But I do think you could help me with a somewhat delicate matter."

I nod. I have no idea what kind of *delicate matter* I could help with, and I almost wish the meeting had been about the pranks. *That* I could deal with. Apologize for the jokes, promise not to do it again. But this? I have no idea where Bridget is going.

"Dad's always fancied himself an entrepreneur," she continues. "He's a dreamer." She glances out the window before returning her gaze to me. "Throughout my childhood, he's always involved himself in far-fetched schemes. When I was eight, he launched a business selling personalized cat toys. When that failed, he purchased dozens of gumball machines with a plan to install them at unspecified locales. The machines sat in our garage, end to end, for over a year."

I visualize a sea of gumball machines.

"He even bought chickens to rent out in some type of farm-test business experiment. He called it 'Cluck for a Buck.'"

I stifle a laugh; Bridget shakes her head. "I know. But these are the types of enterprises my father has been involved with." She picks up her water glass and takes another sip.

"Several years ago, my parents acquired this crazy rundown property in the middle of Pennsylvania for a song. Christmastown." She moves her hands like an underscore as she says the word.

"Christmastown?" I sit up straighter. "I've never heard of it."

"Exactly. It's been shut down for at least a decade. My

parents wanted to renovate the property but, like it is with dreamers sometimes, they had no plan, no means of raising the capital needed for such a venture."

I shift in my seat.

"My mother died two years ago. Dad's been depressed, and he refuses to move. He has this sentimental attachment to the land, to the idea of Christmastown." She twists a single bangle on her wrist. "I don't want to force him to move, but the property's rambling, the area's remote, and Dad's nearing ninety. The whole scenario is a recipe for disaster. So, I hired a caregiver, Andi, to live on the property a few weeks ago and, surprisingly, Dad's okay with it. He seems to enjoy the company."

She shifts her gaze outside, and I try to work out what any of this has to do with me.

"The problem is, Matt," Bridget continues "that this Andi person has reinvigorated Dad's fantastical imagination about a resurgence of Christmastown. I'm afraid he's on the precipice of making some unwise and irreversible financial decisions."

"Oh."

"I'd like you to work out of our Scranton office for a few weeks. Christmastown's about twenty minutes from there. I'll tell Dad and Andi that you'll need access to the property to do inventory for an insurance-related audit but, really, I'd like you to get a feel for their mental state. If I need to, I'd like to get a court to grant me a conservatorship, so I can make sure Dad is always taken care of." She smiles and holds out her hands like an invitation. "You, Matt, would be my eyes and ears."

I digest the assignment: go to Scranton under the guise of an audit but, instead, act as some kind of rogue spy.

I didn't hate the idea.

Bridget tilts her head, continues with details. "You wouldn't have much to do in the Scranton office. The Christmastown audit would be your primary responsibility." She smiles. "Are you interested?"

I recently broke up with Whitney Collins, daughter of my mother's best friend. A *very* unpopular decision. I hate my job. And I live in a brownstone with my uber-successful sister. I love Steph, but she drives me crazy.

A few weeks in Scranton would be a perfect break.

I squish the superball in my pocket.

"When do I start?"

CHAPTER 4

A*ndi*

The auditor is late.

I start the dishwasher, check the time. 12:10 p.m. Ten minutes late. This would not normally bother me. At all. I'm consistently late myself, and the tardiness of others typically makes me feel better. But Bridget, the woman Liam and I need to impress, had sent this man, and I don't want to mess anything up, let alone the time. Maybe I'd written it down wrong? Or worse, maybe he was wandering around the property without me. Something, after Emma's visit, I did not want. I needed to show him the sketches of the finished property first. That way, auditor man would have the final product in his mind when he saw the neglected buildings and rundown rides.

Liam's cat strides across the floor. Claus – yes, named for Santa Claus – is a massive cat, almost the size of a small dog. He's black with white markings and spends most days lying in sunny patches around the house. He barely tolerates me. "Where is this guy, Claus?" I ask in his direction. He ignores me and pads to the corner of the room, tail in the air.

Anxiety swirls in my gut. I know the audit guy's opinion shouldn't matter. He's only making a list of everything for insurance purposes. But I fear the guy – the bespectacled, persnickety audit man I've conjured in my mind– will give Bridget a report on the condition of everything without understanding its potential. Not what the property is, but what it could be.

"So, he's a no show." Liam appears in the kitchen in jeans and sweatshirt with a cartoon chicken on it. The caption: *Chickens. The Pet that Poops Your Breakfast.*

I gesture to the sweatshirt. "I thought you were taking this seriously. Remember, this guy is doing an insurance-related audit for *Bridget*. We need him to like Christmastown."

Liam straightens. "Everyone loves this shirt," he insists. "It always breaks the ice."

I widen my eyes.

"Fine. I'll change."

He returns in a blue sweater. The fabric hugs a noticeable potbelly; the color accentuates his eyes. Liam, with his full head of white hair and round, ruddy cheeks, looks much younger than eighty-seven. He holds out his arms. "Better?"

"Better."

He looks in my direction, seems to register me for the first time that morning. "You look nice."

"Thanks."

I wasn't sure of the protocol, so I'd forgone my normal sweats/t-shirt combo and put on real pants with a zipper and a green sweater. It felt good to look nice. Even if it was only for Bridget's finicky auditor guy.

Liam takes a seat at the table and swipes an apple from the bowl. He bites into it, the crunch sounding loud in the silence. I check my phone (again) and the clock (again). Where in the heck was this guy?

"He's coming," Liam calls.

I look past Liam's extended finger and see a man walking toward the house.

Not the man I expected.

This man is not bespectacled or pudgy. He doesn't have a pinched face or a dour expression. He doesn't have a notebook or a calculator but, instead, is holding a bouquet of bright flowers. For me? I don't know. Nor can I dwell on the question because all my brain power is being used to reconcile what I'd expected to see from the beautiful and stylish man walking toward the house. He's in jeans and black jacket, unzipped, a gray sweater underneath. He's tall. Six feet at least. Light brown hair is swept back from a face with bits of new stubble.

I stare at him. This couldn't be the auditor.

Liam moves to the foyer and opens the door.

"Hey, you must be Liam. I'm Matt."

Matt. His voice is deep and sexy and amiable. I imagine he has a firm handshake and a big, easy smile.

I vaguely hear Liam talking. My feet root to the kitchen floor. I'd prepared for a stodgy old guy, an official folio in his hand. Matt, with his firm jaw and subtle stubble, brought flowers instead. The difference between what I'd expected and the man in the foyer is such a surprise that my mind – and body – can't catch up.

I take a deep breath. I need to get on with it. Introduce myself, act like a rational, functioning human. I sidestep Claus, step toward the door, and ram smack into Liam.

"Oh, Liam, sorry." I step back. "Hey." I extend my hand in Matt's direction. "I'm Andi."

Matt's eyes, brown and as gorgeous as the rest of him, flash surprise. He grips my hand. "Matt. Nice to meet you." He lets go and nods to Claus. "Cool cat. Tomboy?"

"Big Tomboy," Liam says. "Found him behind a dumpster. Wee thing then."

Matt reaches to pet him.

"He's a little skittish," I volunteer. "He might not like it if you pet him."

Liam shoots me the look of a protective pet owner.

Matt scratches under the cat's chin. Claus stays perfectly still. When I'd tried that, I'd left the room with a half dozen scratch marks on my hand.

"Hey, big boy," Matt croons. Claus purrs.

Liam shoots me a triumphant look. He holds out the flowers. "Matt brought these."

Matt straightens. "I got them on a whim," he says quickly. "There was this woman selling them on the highway. No one was stopping."

He says this almost like an apology and I piece it together. Matt, the drop-dead gorgeous auditor from Bridget's office, kindly stopped on the side of the highway to buy flowers from an old woman. And now he's giving them to me.

"If you don't want them," Matt starts.

"No." I take the flowers from Liam. "They're beautiful. Thank you." I pull out a vase from under the sink.

"Well, I'll leave you two to it," Liam says.

I whip my head in his direction like this is unexpected. It's not. The plan was for me to show "the auditor" around. But now, with Matt being so, well, unexpectedly un-auditor like, I feel a little discombobulated. Liam might be better suited for the task. "Did you want to stay?"

"No. You've got it." He *winks* at me. I'm pretty sure Matt sees. Face pink, I busy myself with the arduous task of setting the flowers in the vase. It's ridiculously, painfully, silent.

Matt gestures to the floor, Claus still at his side. "I think you have a leak in your dishwasher."

My eyes dart to the floor in front of the dishwasher; water pools at its base. I practically pump my fist. Yes. My uncle owns an appliance repair shop in my hometown. I'd worked there several summers. Appliances are something I know.

I move to the dishwasher and assess all the reasons water might trickle out the bottom. "It might be a leak in the gasket." Matt flashes a smile with toothpaste commercial white teeth. "Nice diagnostic." He gestures to the dishwasher. "Should we see if you're right?"

I open the door, and we both feel around the rubber on the edge. I ignore the fact that his hands look super strong and super capable. And that he smells like cedar and pine.

"Can't feel any cracks on my side," I say.

"Me either."

We stare at the open machine. I scan through my repair knowledge. "It might be the float switch."

Matt's eyes widen. He looks at me as if I'd said something incredulous.

"What? You don't think that's it?"

"No, you're probably right. I'm just impressed."

I pull out the dish drawer, squat down, and reach back to where the switch should be. "My uncle owns an appliance store," I explain, feeling around for the switch. "I grew up around this stuff." I flick on the switch, stand, and close the door. "That was it, by the way." I nod toward the dishwasher. "How about you? How do you know appliance repair?"

"My Dad's in the appliance business too." He shifts his posture.

"Really? What does he do?"

Matt shrugs. "Retail." He looks around the room. "Should we get started?"

Right. I'd been so stunned by Matt's physical presence, I'd forgotten why he was here. Or who had sent him.

"Of course." I take a step toward the dining room. "I thought I'd show you some sketches of the final vision. We could take the tour after. Does that work?"

Matt throws me a million-dollar smile. "Works for me."

CHAPTER 5

*A*ndi

Matt stands in the dining room, staring at the dozen sketches I'd laid out on the table. "These are incredible." He touches one of a Gingerbread-man themed maze. "I would have loved this as a kid."

"Right?"

"And this." He points to the toy shop, the largest building and centerpiece of the property. In the sketch, it looks like a Swiss chalet with peaked roofs and triangular flags. "This looks exactly like I think the North Pole would."

"Me too!" I say as if having the same vision of the North Pole –one likely fueled by decades of commercialism – is an amazing coincidence. I internally scold myself. I am not on a date; Matt's here to audit the property. "Liam thought it could be a gift shop," I say seriously.

He angles his face toward me. "Nice. Tons of retail opportunity." He scans over the sketches. "This place is going to be awesome."

I force myself not to scream, "I know!" Matt's reaction was what I'd hoped Emma's would have been. Or my mom. It was validating that someone saw the same potential for Christmas-town as Liam and I did. It didn't hurt that he was ridiculously attractive.

"Hey. Can I walk around?"

I tilt my head. "Isn't that why you're here?"

"Right," he says, almost as if he'd forgotten.

We put on our coats, and I lead him to the main path.

Matt stops.

Crap. Did he see a problem already?

"Hey. What do you think about installing lampposts around the path with speakers? For Christmas music."

Oh.

Not a problem. An idea. And a good one.

"Great idea."

We continue from the lake to a path currently flanked by buildings in varied states of disarray. He shoves his hands in his coat pockets and walks with an easy gait, asking questions about different buildings as we pass. He doesn't take pictures or notes, the whole thing incredibly casual. This should put me at ease; I worry instead. Maybe the property's too far gone to matter?

"Wow." He stops abruptly.

I follow his gaze to Sleigh Slam, a winter-themed bumper car ride behind the building in front of us. Sleighs with thick black bumpers sit dormant around a circular track. "I loved bumper cars as a kid." He heads to the ride and hops over the railing in the kind of cool, fluid movement only certain guys - Matt Taylor being one, I guess - can pull off. He trails his hand along one the edge of one the sleighs. "You're going to keep this ride, right?"

"Of course."

"Good." He stares at the sleighs a moment longer before hopping back over the railing. "I love amusement parks," he volunteers. "I used to go to them with my dad a lot when I was younger. It was freeing, you know, being able to run around."

He looks at me, his eyes a mix of green and brown, and I nod though I don't fully understand what he means by *being able to run around*. But something had caught in his voice when he'd said it and it makes me think there's something more to the statement. I don't know him well enough to ask.

"Those work?" Matt points to the gondolas over us, the swinging ornaments that had swayed over Emma's head.

"I don't know." The question startles me. I'd never thought to see if the rides were operable. It seemed a down the road thing to do. "Is that a problem?"

"Of course not. But it would be cool, right?" He strides purposely toward the stairs to the gondola entry point.

I hurry after him. "Wait, Matt. I don't think it's a good idea. They might not be safe."

He reaches the stairs. "We'll never know unless we try, right?" He starts up, two stairs at a time.

"We should probably have them checked first," I call.

Matt stops and peeks through the slat of a stair. "Let's see."

I move fast up the stairs, my breath coming out in smoky puffs. Of all the scenarios I could have imagined for how today would unfold, me racing after the auditor guy, begging him not to start a ride featuring oversized Christmas ornaments, would never have crossed my mind.

Matt waits at the controls. When I reach the platform at the top, he winks. "Here goes nothing." He flips the switch. I hold my breath and the ride comes to life, the ornaments creaking and groaning into motion.

I watch the balls click along in disbelief. "It works."

Matt shoots me a triumphant look.

We stand still. The ornaments advance along the cable, gold and silver carriages suspended by steel hangers disguised as festive red bows. I glance at Matt and I'm seriously afraid he's going to suggest we ride one. "I don't think they're okay to ride yet," I say preemptively.

He flips the switch and the ornaments thump to a stop. He lifts his eyebrows and then moves as though he's going to get into a gondola.

I race across the platform, stand in front of the gondola, and throw my arms out wide. "No. This ride is unsafe."

Matt stops, his foot mid-air. "I'm not sure I'd use that line when you open the park." He places his foot back on the platform. A smile hugs the corners of his mouth.

I smile back, a little embarrassed. But I like the banter. Cole was *not* a teaser. I couldn't remember the last time I'd had a conversation like this.

"What?" I ask, my face a mask of innocence. "You don't think it's catchy?"

He scrunches his face like he's concentrating. "It depends on how you brand it. You'd have to have a park theme that goes with massively unsafe rides."

I stomp my foot. "I did not say the ride was massively unsafe."

"Right. Just unsafe. Very reassuring."

"What if we call it Polar Park Peril?" I move my hands like I'm underscoring the words.

"I like that," Matt says. "Polar Park Peril. Where your safety is always on thin ice."

An ugly snort laugh erupts from my body. I immediately cover my nose as though doing so would negate the sound that just came out of it. "Sorry. That's just funny." The snort comes out *again*.

"Safety is no laughing matter, Andi."

He looks at me with a deadpan expression. It seems like he's serious. I stop laughing. My eyes open wide. "Sorry –"

"I'm kidding. I'm kidding." He puts one of the strong, capable hands on my shoulder. "I'm sure everything will be perfectly safe by the time you open up." He looks at the gondola. "I wasn't going to ride it, you know. I was just teasing you." He moves back.

My face reddens. "Well, I didn't know. We just met each other."

He leans against the railing, his breath smoky. "We should get to know each other then. You could give me a tour of the town. And I could ask more about the park's safety protocols." He winks. "What do you say?"

What do I say? The hot bachelor I was sure would never show up at Christmastown is in front of me. But I came here to avoid dating. I need to find myself again and I'd planned to use every ounce of extra energy I had into reimagining an epic -- and very safe --holiday-themed amusement park.

So, of course, I know what I should say.

Instead, what comes out of my mouth is: "How about tonight?"

CHAPTER 6

M*att*

My car rattles down the drive of Christmas-town, bits of gravel flying under the weight of my tires.

What a surprise.

The venue. The girl. Neither one was what I'd expected.

The way Bridget had described it, I'd thought the park would be a couple of old buildings and some sad looking rides. And Andi? Okay. I'd expected Andi to be Andy – a guy. Um. *That* was clearly wrong. Long legs. Wild curls. Big blue eyes. The eyes. They would have gotten my attention on their own, but then there was the whole dishwasher thing. Andi fixing the dishwasher was attractive in a way that I'd never have associated with basic appliance repair. And the sketches of Christmas-town? Her talent was remarkable. Plus, the idea was unique. It's the only holiday-themed amusement park in the world. How could it not be cool?

I press the gas and visualize Andi's expression after I'd flipped the switch to that ride with the fat ornaments. Big smile, a little bit shocked. She was pretty. In a real way, not like the girls I was used to. No glued-on eyelashes, sprayed hair, or thick lipliner. Andi was all natural, like a wildflower in the woods. And she was funny.

"Turn left."

I follow the GPS commands toward my destination - wherever Quinn Gifford was putting me up for the next few weeks.

I think about how tonight will go. I shouldn't have asked Andi to show me around town. I don't want to keep up the auditor ruse, but I can't tell her the truth. How would that go? I'm not actually an auditor, I'm here to spy on you.

No.

I should cancel.

I will cancel.

I'll text Andi when I get wherever it is I'm staying.

I follow the GPS instructions through the University of Scranton campus and turn on to Taylor Street, a strip of narrow two-story homes with large porches.

"Your destination is on the left."

On my left is a residential home with peeling paint and what appears to be a structurally unstable front porch. *This* is my destination? I check the address, look back at the house. Yup. This is it.

I exit the car and grab my duffel. I start toward the house and realize I have no way to get in. I'd assumed there would be a realtor or concierge or someone to direct me, and I hadn't asked Bridget. I reach out to try the door as it swings open.

A tiny woman with stiff, gray hair steps on to the porch, a small brown and white dog in the crook of her arm. He's got steady black eyes, a pointed nose, and a decent amount of drool. The woman has on what could best be described as a housecoat and white, orthopedic shoes. She waves in my direction and the manners which have been ingrained in me since I was a child kick in like a superpower. Instead of asking why she and her dog were inside of my rental, I extend my hand. "Matt Taylor, nice to meet you."

She shakes my hand with her free one. "Matt. Wonderful. We've been expecting you." She gestures to the dog, and I wonder if he's part of the "we" or if there are more people inside. "I'm Ruth," she continues. "This is Rolo." She pushes the dog toward me.

I pet his head. "Hey, boy. Good to see you."

Ruth smiles widely. "Your room's all set. Number two. I'll show you."

Room?

I follow Ruth up narrow stairs covered in plush, mauve carpet. I search my mind for an explanation. Quinn Gifford is a multi-million-dollar law firm. Certainly, they can do better than a single room. Maybe the accommodations are part of my cover as the auditor?

Ruth stops at a bedroom door with a "2" stenciled in the center. She stands outside the closed door. "Laundry is in the basement. No wet clothes overnight. You have a kitchen cabinet and can use the third shelf in the refrigerator. I'll go over the appliances once you get settled." She pauses as though thinking through a mass of rules. "Watch anything on the television. Just know I watch Wheel of Fortune at seven. Usually with supper."

She reaches inside the pocket of her housecoat and produces a mint green crocheted key chain with a single key. "This is the house key." She thrusts it in my direction. "And this is your room." She pushes open the door.

I slip inside.

"Supper's at six-thirty. It's roast chicken and potatoes tonight."

"Great. Thanks."

A vision of the potential evening ahead materializes in my mind: me and Ruth watching Wheel of Fortune, TV trays of steaming roast chicken in front of us. I smile at her, still in the doorway, unsure of the protocol. "Thanks," I say again.

"You're welcome." She starts down the hall, Rolo tucked under her arm like a canine football.

I close the door and sit on a giant four-poster bed. A rocking chair with a scary looking doll sits in one corner; lace doilies cover every conceivable surface. It's about as big a contrast to my modern-but-made-to-look-old brownstone as you could get.

My phone buzzes. I pull it from my pocket and look at the screen. A text from Andi. *Pick me up at six?*

CHAPTER 7

M^{*att*} I weigh the roast chicken/Wheel of Fortune night with Ruth against the Scranton tour with Andi for all one second before I text back.

Sounds good.

The text message swishes, and I feel a twinge of guilt. I don't want to keep the auditor lie up. I'm not sure why, when I took the assignment from Bridget, that I'd thought I'd be okay with the untruthfulness. I guess I'd thought the project would seem more ridiculous or that Liam and Andi would be clearly off the rails. But neither of these things seem to be the case. Maybe tonight will be different. Maybe I'll see what Bridget meant.

I pull on a fresh pair of jeans and a navy sweater and head downstairs. The kitchen smells like Thanksgiving and I catch Ruth pulling a giant chicken from the oven with oversized orange mitts. She places it on the counter next to a bowl of fresh green beans and rolls that smell like a bakery.

"Ready?" she says. Her face lights up in a smile.

I feel like a jerk.

"Ruth, I'm sorry. I'm going out with a colleague, but if you have leftovers, I'd love a few. It all looks amazing."

"Thanks, dear. There'll be plenty of leftovers. I always make a lot. I'll put some on your fridge shelf." She smiles.

I think I like it here.

I arrive at Christmastown at six. Before I shut off the car, Andi's out the front door with a cute, rushed wave. She's wearing a cropped cream coat and tall brown boots. Her wild curls bounce; the tips skim the top of her shoulders. It's a good look, right at the intersection of cute and sexy. I look down, remind myself that I am "the auditor" and have no business acting like a date. Or thinking like one.

I hop out of the car and open the passenger door. "Hey."

Andi smiles and tips her head, curls shifting to one side. "How gallant."

"I like to get things started off on the right foot," I say as she steps inside. "In case I mess up later."

She laughs, a real one, and I like how her nose crunches up when she does it. "I doubt you'll mess up."

"We'll see."

I push the passenger door closed, slip in the car, and start the engine. I rattle down the drive and notice that Andi smells like flowers. Rose? Lilac? Whatever it is, I want a garden of it.

I flip on the radio. "So. Where does this tour start?"

"I was trying to think of something active."

I nod. "I like that. Active is good. But will I be *safe*? I mean, after this afternoon –"

I let the sentence trail off. Andi laughs.

"Yes. You'll be safe. Anyway, I thought we'd start with –" she pauses, seemingly for dramatic effect.

I bounce my hands on the steering wheel like a drumroll.

"An escape room," she finishes.

I swallow. Levity seeps out of me. No way did Andi just say we were going to an escape room. "Really?" I say, buying time.

"Yeah."

She says more but all I can think about is being trapped in a small space. *Confined.* Locked doors. Locked windows. No way out. My stomach knots.

I know why I'm like this. Six-year-old me was visiting my grandparents in their high-rise Orlando apartment building. Me being six, and hyperactive, and a bit of a prick, ran ahead of them in the hallway. I got on the elevator alone and decided to press every button. The elevator malfunctioned and got stuck. I remember it taking hours to fix; my grandparents said fifteen minutes. Either way, that was it. Matt the claustrophobic was born.

"Have you ever done an escape room?" she asks.

"This would be my first." I keep my voice neutral.

"I've done a couple. They're fun."

Fun. I'm sure they are fun for a person not terrified of enclosed, locked spaces. Crazy thing, Andi could have offered any number of high intensity activities that I would have been legitimately stoked about. But an escape room? I'd never been to one for a reason.

"Are you up for it?"

I could tell her. I didn't want to. What kind of first impression would that make? Plus, I *should* be able to do this. The elevator catastrophe was twenty years ago. And an escape room is not all that similar to an elevator. "Sounds great."

I follow Andi's driving instructions and try to forget the impending you're locked in a room until you smart your way out adventure. Andi shares details of her last escape room experience.

"It was Fantasy Island themed," she supplies.

I try to get into it. "Did Mr. Rourke make an appearance? Did you see a plane?"

"No. Not either."

"No plane? That's lame, Andi."

"Maybe this one will be better. The theme is haunted hotel."
I slide the car into a parking space in front of Big Time
Escapes and Andi and I enter the building. Hanging bubble
lights adorn the check-in area, a long, narrow desk sits across
one wall. A guy, twentyish, directs us to wait with our group or,
as he calls them, "the other hotel guests." The "guests" are an
older couple with matching white hairstyles, and a dad with a
little girl wearing an oversized pink bow. The girl is maybe
eight. I look at her. She's bouncing from foot to foot. The soles
of her sneakers light up pink.

Come on, Matt. Little kids are doing this.

We make small talk with our group and my nerves calm. The
game is pretend, and I'll be with five other people. Plus, I'm an
adult. It's an entirely different scenario than being stuck on an
elevator alone at six years old.

A kid in costume as a hotel bellhop materializes from a back
room and dims the lights. He starts a spiel about how the hotel
is haunted, how guests are not allowed to leave. He emphasizes
the confinement piece. Four times.

"The doors will be locked. You cannot leave."

"You and the other guests will be stuck."

"You will be at the mercy of the hotel, unable to leave the
premises."

"Now is your last chance to leave safely."

My pulse accelerates and I glance at Andi. Her face is difficult to make out in the dim light, but I can see enough to
know she's smiling. As is the white-haired couple. And the
dad. Only the pink-bowed girl seems grave, her expression so
serious it's almost as if she's receiving instructions to a nuclear
code.

"Are you okay?" Andi whispers.

"Yeah, fine. Why?"

"You're gripping my hand."

I look down. I don't know when or why I grabbed her hand

but mine is over hers, clutching it in a vise grip. I drop it like it's
on fire. "Are you okay?"

"All good." She wiggles her fingers.

The lights flip and the bellhop gestures toward a door to
the "hotel." Andi shoots me a quizzical look. "You're super
pale." She moves closer. "Is it too stuffy? Do you need to go
outside?"

Her eyes are wide with concern. I feel ridiculous. The hotel
is pretend. The bellhop is a kid.

The eight-year-old steps into the space, ponytail bouncing.

"I'm all set." I flash a smile.

"All right." Andi steps into the room. I follow, tentative, and
take in the space. It's plain and gray with numbered buttons in
rows on the wall.

The pretend room is an elevator.

* * *

"How long were you in there?" Andi asks after I finish telling
her my elevator story.

"It depends on who you ask. My grandparents say fifteen
minutes, but I'll tell you, it was hours, possibly a half a day."

I take a sip of beer. We're sitting in a Mexican restaurant
called La Casa at a hand-painted table. The restaurant is bright
with orange and yellow walls. Piñatas and white lights hang
from the ceiling. Plants in terra cotta pots are peppered
throughout the area. Mexican music plays softly in the background. A plate of loaded nachos sits between us on the table.

"You should have told me. I know how you are about feeling
safe." She smirks at me.

"Hey." I point a loaded nacho at her. "I would have perse-
vered. I'm sure it would have been fine."

"You're sure, huh? Because you definitely gave off vibes that
you were not fine."

"Oh?" I lean forward. "And what would those vibes have been?"

She looks up as if contemplating, a suppressed grin across her face. "Well, there was the pale skin. And the sweaty palms. And, of course, the vise grip." She holds up her hand. I slap my forehead. "That part was bad. Is your hand okay?" "It's fine." She flips her paper placemat to the other side. "In fact, I'll prove it." She pulls over the small canister of crayons on the table. "I'll draw something for you."

"For me?" I put my hand on my chest in feigned disbelief.

"For you. But it's a surprise." She takes the kiosk of condiments and places it in front of the mat. "Don't peek now."

"Never." I watch Andi draw. Her hair falls around her face like a frame. She bites her lip in concentration and, every so often she straightens, looks at the page from a distance, then starts again, crayons swiveling.

She glances up. "Hey. You're peeking."

"I'm looking at you, not the picture."

She points a crayon in my direction. "Well, cut it out before I decide to keep this one for myself."

I hold my hands out. "Enough said."

I watch her in secret and drink my beer.

After a few minutes, she taps my forearm. "Okay. I had to rush because someone couldn't stop looking, but here it is."

She flips over the paper. I laugh. It's a caricature of me stepping into one of those ornament gondolas. Over the top, in script, it reads, 'Polar Park Peril'.

"My eyes are huge." I bug out my own eyes in demonstration.

She taps on the picture. "Caricature artists exaggerate the first thing they notice about a person."

I lean back. "So, you noticed my eyes then?"

She blushes. It's adorable.

"Don't worry," I say quickly, "I noticed your eyes too."

Her cheeks get pinker; she's quiet a moment. "Well," she says, seemingly recovered, "from one person with noticeable eyes to another, this picture's for you." She pushes it across the table. "I signed it and everything." She points to a scrawled signature at bottom.

"Thank you." I set it on the side of the table. "Don't want food getting on my collector's item here."

Andi grins. "Good thinking. That drawing might be worth big bucks someday."

"I have no doubt."

The server arrives with our food, enchiladas for me, a quesadilla for Andi. She picks up a wedge. "So," she says, "tell me something about you?"

"About me? There's not a lot to tell."

"Well," Andi taps her fingers on the table, "here's what I know. You're claustrophobic, and you know about dishwasher repair." She pauses. "Oh. And you're impulsive."

I slap the table as though her correct assessment is an insult. "Impulsive?"

"Yes, impulsive. I'd call charging up the stairs and testing a ride that's been dormant for years a bit reckless, no?"

I laugh. "But cool, right?"

"So cool." She smiles again, bigger this time. "But, come on. I know there's more to you than that." She moves her fingers as if she's motioning me toward her. "Fess up. Tell me something about you that would surprise me."

"Surprise you?" I take a sip of beer.

"Come on, Matt." She holds up her margarita glass. "One surprise."

I look at her expectant face; I have to come up with something.

"Okay. How's this? I can juggle."

CHAPTER 8

M*att*

She lifts an eyebrow. "You can juggle?"

I hold a finger up and move my chair back. I grab the plastic salt and pepper shakers from the table, dump the crayons, and pick up the small canister they'd been in. I peek at Andi. "Are you ready?"

She waves at me. "Yes, please."

I throw the saltshaker up and hope for the best. I haven't juggled in years. I throw up the peppershaker and juggle both until I have a good rhythm. I reach for the crayon canister with my free hand and throw it. All three objects move in a steady, circular motion.

"Impressive."

"Thanks."

I keep going. Patrons at a nearby table stop eating and watch. A member of the wait staff pauses in front of our table, a tray of nachos perched in one hand.

I glance at Andi. She's smiling, a big toothy grin, her blue eyes light. She pushes her chair back. "This is quite the show."

"You asked for something that would surprise you."

"Well, you definitely delivered on that one." She smiles.

I keep going, the rhythm faster now.

A large man at the adjacent table angles his head in my direction. "Can you do more?"

"I used to juggle five," I answer, not breaking my rhythm.

"Five?" he questions.

"Five."

He sweeps the salt and pepper shakers from his own table and smacks them in front of me. It feels like a challenge.

Really?

I glance at him; he nods toward the shakers. It *is* a challenge. Jeez. I'm about to decline. But Andi's laughing. Hard. So hard that barely a sound escapes from her mouth. She's holding her sides. It's massively adorable.

Okay. I have to do this.

Challenge accepted, big guy.

I stop the movement; the shakers and canister tumble to the table. "Five it is."

I stand because there is no way I can juggle five objects sitting. I grab a saltshaker. Our server lunges forward and puts a sombrero on my head. All the patrons at the tables around us are watching and I feel somewhat ridiculous. But Andi's still laughing so I'll at least try.

I throw up one saltshaker, then a second. I add a pepper-shaker and juggle all three until I have the same, steady rhythm as before. I add the crayon canister. Four. I juggle four. I reach down and grab the second peppershaker. Five!

Saltshaker, saltshaker, peppershaker, crayon canister, peppershaker.

Saltshaker, saltshaker, peppershaker, crayon canister, peppershaker.

Saltshaker, saltshaker, peppershaker, crayon canister, peppershaker.

The objects whirl around, an endless, rhythmic circle.

Patrons, even the big guy, clap. I glance at Andi. Too long. My rhythm breaks and the objects tumble down with a clatter. The crayon canister rolls off the table to the floor. The patrons around us applaud. I bow, return the sombrero to the server, and swipe the canister off the floor. I sit across from Andi. "Did I surprise you?"

She smiles and waves her hand in a nonchalant manner. "Nah. Most of my dinner companions can juggle, you know." She winks. "But I did get a picture."

She flips her phone around and I see a picture of me in a giant sombrero surrounded by airborne objects. I look like an idiot. Andi flips the phone back. "Want me to send it to you?"

"I'm good. Seeing that picture once is enough for a lifetime."

She smiles. "Where'd you learn to do that, anyway?"

"I taught myself. I've got a good deal of energy."

She says nothing.

"I have ADHD," I volunteer.

I'm not sure why I say it. I almost never tell anyone about the diagnosis, not because I'm ashamed but because almost no one treats it seriously, at least not the people I've told. Most of them act like ADHD is about being distracted by squirrels or whatnot. They don't know how it feels to zone out in the middle of conversations, to lose focus in class, or to set out to complete a set of tasks only to find (hours later) that you've gotten sidetracked on step one. Almost worse are the people who think the whole issue can be resolved by popping a pill. But, for me, the pills altered my personality to the point where it was unrecognizable. I stopped taking them.

Andi fixes her gaze on me. I feel exposed, like I'd given her glimpse into myself that I wish I could take back.

"That must be hard," she says. "I'm sorry."

I exhale, stunned. It's not the response I expected. I wait for her to say more, but she doesn't. She leaves it at "sorry." A simple, empathetic response.

"Thanks."

She smiles. We eat dinner. Andi doesn't bring up the ADHD again. Instead, our conversation morphs into other topics. It feels like she accepts the diagnosis as no big deal, no need to follow up, no need to discuss. I like that.

The conversation is easy, and I learn all sorts of things about Andi that make me like her even more. Like:

She can fix all appliances, not only dishwashers.

She loves thrillers, the scarier the better.

She builds Legos with her five-year-old niece.

She's a chocolate addict and always has at least one bar in her purse.

She donates blood twice a year.

She's a sucker for HGTV.

She always makes going to the movies an experience, with full popcorn and candy and soda.

And she's obsessed with Christmas (duh).

By the time the check comes, I'm in huge trouble because I LIKE this girl. Not, I'd rather spend the night with Andi than watch Wheel of Fortune with Ruth kind of like. I feel a genuine connection with her. I sense she feels the same which, of course, makes me feel like shit because the whole premise of my being at Christmastown, of meeting her to begin with, is a lie. I'm at least glad that the auditor job didn't come up but then it does, on the way back to Christmastown.

"How do you like being an auditor?" she asks.

It's a benign question. One which, if I were actually an auditor, would be easy to answer. But I'm not. "It's okay." I say and immediately follow up with my own question. "How do you like working at Christmastown?"

She twists a lock of hair around her finger. "I don't actually work at Christmastown," she says. "I'm helping Liam generate ideas, you know. But I'd love to see him get it off the ground.

He's hoping his daughter will see the potential with the property. She a Philadelphia lawyer and has good connections."

I grip the steering wheel, hard.

"You don't know her, do you? Bridget Quinn? Her office sent you."

My mouth goes dry. I can't think of anything to say. I am the worst liar of all time, apparently. "I've heard of her," I say finally. Thankfully, the twisty tracks of Christmastown's Santa Coaster come into view. "There it is," I announce, too excited. I accelerate, fast, up the drive, and pull the car to a stop.

Do I know Bridget?

Man.

Do I.

I step out of the car and move to open the door, but Andi's out already, standing in a streak of moonlight, a gentle breeze blowing at her hair.

"Oh." She looks at the car door. "I forgot about the chivalry thing. Should I get back in?" She throws a teasing smile.

Normally, I would have said yes. I'd have made a joke and reopened the door in a ridiculous, over-the-top gesture. Instead, I stand frozen, my brain locked on how much I like her. Finally, I hold up my hands. "No need."

"All right," she says. "I'll remember next time."

Next time.

Right.

CHAPTER 9

ndi
Matt's car disappears down the driveway. I watch his taillights get smaller and smaller through the window.

Wow.

That, whatever it was – a date, a tour, a night out with a friend -- was fun. I'd forgotten, until the last two minutes of the car ride home, that I'd wanted to find out if he had any connection with Bridget, if he could help Liam convince her to help with the park. It didn't seem like he knew her. It didn't matter. I hadn't had that much fun since the Cole break-up and a long time before that even, things being sketchy at the end.

I go to my room, pull on pajamas, and scrub my face clean. I prop myself up with pillows on the bed and, feeling like I'm still in high school, I Facetime Emma. Her face appears in the rectangular screen. "Well?"

"It was fun." I keep my tone low-key, but I don't feel low-key. My face is flushed, my heart is thudding, and my mind keeps pulling up images of Matt.

"What did you do?"

I fill Emma in. I text her the picture of Matt juggling in the sombrero.

The message dings on her end. She pulls her face back. "He's hot, Andi. Like firefighter hot."

"Firefighter hot?" I question, but I know what she means. In a surprise trait for someone as practical as Emma, she adores romance novels. A lot of her favorites involve firefighters.

"You know what I mean. You're going to see him again, right?" She glances up from his picture and meets my eyes through the screen.

The question plummets me to reality. I have no idea if I'm going to see Matt again. I know I shouldn't care. Meeting Matt wasn't part of my plan anyway. "Probably not."

"What? Why?" Emma moves her face forward; it fills every bit of the screen.

"I don't know, okay? We didn't talk about it."

"Do you have his number?"

I roll my eyes. "I'm not calling him. I barely know him. I don't even know where he lives."

"You didn't Google him, did you?"

I shift on the bed. "You know I don't do that."

Before Cole, I went on a date with a guy who'd clearly Googled everything about me in advance. It was super creepy. Ever since, I'd stopped Googling people ahead of meeting them.

"Right," Emma says. "Well, I do." Her phone bobs along in her bedroom.

"Emma no," I call out. I can guess where she's headed.

As expected, she sits down in front of her computer. "Taylor right? Matt Taylor?"

She must lay her phone on the desk because my screen fills with a popcorn-textured white ceiling.

Click, click, click.

"Don't tell me anything," I say on principle.

Emma doesn't respond, and I feel strangely nervous, like I'm on the precipice of finding out top secret information.

"OH.MY.GOD."

She says it like this, with a beat between each word. I don't know if she's being dramatic or if she found out something. Something good? Terrible? I can't stand it.

"What did you find?" I rush out the question.

"I thought you didn't want to know," she teases and pulls the phone back so I can see her.

"I didn't until you sounded so surprised."

She turns her phone toward the computer so I can see her screen. "This is him, right?"

I stare at the screen. It *is*, in fact, him. Matt's brown/green eyes gaze at me like he's in the room. He's wearing a tuxedo and he looks, well, like a man that *should* be wearing a tuxedo. He's got the height, the broad shoulders, the five o-clock shadow. He's smiling too. It looks like someone just made him laugh.

"It's him?" Emma asks again.

"Yup."

"Hubba, hubba."

I don't respond and, a second later, Emma places the phone back on the desk. Her computer keys click. "Oh. Wow. Man."

"What?"

She pulls the phone back and looks in the screen. "You need to Google him yourself, okay? There's a lot here."

"Good stuff?" I prompt.

"I'd say so. Look him up and call me tomorrow. I'm going to bed."

She hangs up; I stare at the phone. Okay. Creepy or not, I *have* to Google him now. I type his name in the search bar. Images come up first. Matt in a tuxedo. Matt skiing. Matt on the beach. Matt at a gala, a full-figured blonde on his arm. Matt. Funny, handsome, juggling Matt.

His image is everywhere.

My heart beats more forcefully. I clink a link. What starts out as a quick search spawns into a forensic-level dive. The salient facts are clear. Matt does not work for an insurance company as I'd assumed. He's a Philadelphia lawyer and, I guess, doing the audit for Bridget. It's obvious he's wealthy too. There are dozens of photographs of him at black-tie events. And, notwithstanding his reaction to the escape room, he appears to be no stranger to adventurous activities. Tons of photographs of him on that front – bungee jumping, snowboarding, whitewater rafting. Of course, he looks impossibly gorgeous in all of them.

I impulsively click on an article about his family; their photograph fills the screen. His mother has the same angular face as Matt, his father, the same broad build. His sister, Steph, looks ultra-cool with a chic, short haircut. They look so perfect as a group, it's almost as if they'd been hired as family models.

I scan the article, one about a healthy eating initiative spawned by Matt's mother. I find out that her great grandparents had started Yumcakes and smile. Like just about everyone else on earth, I *love* Yumcakes. I keep going and see that Matt's Dad is founder and CEO of SmartTech Appliances.

I digest this.

Matt had told me his dad was in retail, not that he owned the company.

Everything I thought about this guy was wrong.

I collapse on the bed, angry for no rational reason. I was the one who'd made all the assumptions. And I was the one who didn't ask the right questions, who didn't Google him in advance. Matt didn't hide a single thing from me, far as I know. Still. I feel a little stupid now. I took this accomplished guy to an escape room, followed by dinner at a rundown bar. I'd drawn him a picture with crayons. Which meant that I took him to a restaurant *that had crayons*.

Yeah.

I feel dumb.

Worse, I'd let down my protective emotional gear – the one telling me to stay single and focused and get my life together as Andi Carter, the individual - and let myself think a whole slew of maybes when it came to Matt Taylor.

Maybe he liked me.

Maybe I would go out with him again.

Maybe my heart wouldn't get crushed.

No. No. And *definitely* no.

Matt Taylor was the kind of guy that broke girls' hearts. I'd thought that, sort of, when he was regular, insurance Matt. But online Matt was like the ultra-version of the guy from last night. Matt Taylor 2.0.

Not for me. Not right now. Not when I'm still finding the Andi that got lost with Cole. And I can't guarantee, with a guy like Matt, that I won't be right back there again, just like my mom, contorting myself to fit into someone else's life. Which is why, when Matt texts the next day with a request to do an inventory of Christmastown, whatever that entails, I pawn off the meeting to Liam.

CHAPTER 10

A*ndi*

The excuse I make is that I can't make the meeting with Matt because I have a doctor's appointment. Liam is genuinely concerned when I tell him this, so I add that it's a check-up and that I'm fine and not to worry. Anyway, once I'm in the car, I realize what should have been obvious when I'd made the plan.

I have nowhere to go.

I have no friends in the area, Emma's working, and though my mom is an hour away, I don't want to see her at this moment. Any initial niceties will likely morph into a serious talk about my future (and why it shouldn't involve Christmastown). Or worse, she'll say nothing at all about the venture and we'll end up talking about everything but Christmastown, the proverbial elephant in the room getting as big as, well, an elephant. I can't do that right now.

I drive to a group of outlet stores in Tannersville. The whole time, I think about Matt. How he looked and smelled and how his hand felt gripped around mine to start. But, also, about how strange it was that he didn't tell me about his background. I didn't even know he was a lawyer. It was good that he didn't feel a need to show off, but it seemed odd. Why would a lawyer do an audit anyway?

It shouldn't matter. It didn't matter. The last thing I needed right now was to think about Matt Taylor. In any capacity.

I arrive at the outlets, try to forget about Matt. I don't need anything, but I end up buying a bunch of stupid stuff on sale. I visit the same fragrance store, Scent it Up, twice. I push open the door for my third visit.

A girl with big hoop earrings and bright blue eyeliner tips her head in my direction. "Can I help you find something?" The way she says it makes it obvious that she's taken note of my prior visits.

I swipe a bottle of room spray from the nearest table and hold it up. "I wanted to pick up this." I glance at the label. Firefly Night. It's on sale for $6.99. Fine.

She rings me up, and after, I stand in the parking lot, the bottle of Firefly Night gripped in my hand. I've been gone for three hours and I'm pretty sure that, if I start now, Matt won't be there when I get back. I open the car door and, on a whim, spray the inside with Firefly Night.

I start back. Ten minutes in, the sky opens up and pours down rain. Thick drops pelt the windshield. Trucks cram the road. The scent of Firefly Night permeates the interior of my car. The scent is a combination of berries and flowers. It doesn't even smell good. I open the window, hoping to air out the space, but a wind gust pushes rain inside. Strips of water pelt my jacket and hair and I briefly debate which is worse: enduring the heavy scent of Firefly Night or being doused by gusts of rain. Water wins out; I close the window.

I drive, hands gripped to the steering wheel, my windshield wipers on high. I'm pretty certain Firefly Night has emanated inside my pores. My natural curls balloon; my make-up streaks during a poorly timed gas stop. When I finally pull into Liam's driveway, I feel gross. I peek at myself in the rearview mirror. I look gross too.

I exit my car and walk into one I didn't expect to be there. I step back.

No.

Matt's car.

He's still here.

I whip my head up and see him through the window. He's at the kitchen table with Liam. Even from the driveway, I can make out his biceps through the material of his shirt. Apparently, the stubble, the killer smile, and the surprise rich lifestyle hadn't been enough. He had to look like a guy who could bench press 200 pounds too.

He moves his hand. I avert my gaze from his biceps and realize he and Liam are playing chess.

Chess.

It strikes me as odd, and I'm reminded of the Yumcakes and the SmartTech and his job at biggest law firm in Philadelphia. Now he plays chess?

Who is this guy?

I walk toward the house. Half of me wishes I looked nicer. Or at least not gross. The other half is irritated he's still here.

I push open the front door, sturdy-handled shopping bags in each hand. I'd try to avoid the kitchen, but my headlights would have been visible through the window, and I don't want to look like I'm avoiding him. I walk into the room.

Matt's head shoots up as soon as I enter. "Andi! You're back."

He looks, and sounds, thrilled to see me. I'm thrown off. I'm not sure what I'd expected but it wasn't this. I push at my hair, hoping it doesn't look as bad as I know it does.

Liam twists around in his seat. "Glad you're home. First the doctor and now this terrible weather." He gestures to Matt with a chess piece. "Matt wanted to make sure you got back all right before he left."

Matt shrugs. "Well, I know how cavalier you can be about safety." His mouth curves, revealing a hint of a smile.

I meet his eyes. He looks like he's about to bust out laughing. "Well, I'm here now. Safe and sound." I set the bags on the floor.

Matt is *still* smiling with teeth that should be part of a good dental hygiene campaign. He glances in the direction of the bags, and it dawns on me how bad this must look. I blew off the inventory meeting and, as Liam said, I was supposed to be at a doctor's appointment. Instead, I'm surrounded by shopping bags which, I swear, have multiplied since I stepped inside.

I will myself not to care, which is hard because I do care, when Matt *winks* at me.

"I'll finish up this game with Liam," he says, eyeing the bags. "If you want to get yourself settled and all." A grin inches across his face for the second time.

He's trying to help me. I don't think Liam would care that I went shopping, but Matt doesn't know that. He's giving me time to hide the evidence.

I smile and pick up the bags, happy I'll be able to clean myself up more than anything else. "I'll be down in a sec."

I hurry upstairs, set the bags in my room, and eye myself in the mirror.

Ugh.

My hair is a mass of frizz, my skin super pale with make-up streaks. And I reek of Firefly Night.

I pull my hair into a ponytail and reapply my make-up. It's better. Not great.

I'm halfway down the stairs when Matt says something I can't make out. Liam erupts with laughter. I stop. It's a good sound, Liam's laugh. He'd become increasingly less depressed over the past months, but he rarely gave the full-bellied kind of chortle like the one I'd just heard.

I move to the last stair and wonder, briefly, what had been so funny. I don't want to interrupt to ask so, instead, I watch the two of them move pieces around the board. I spy an open bottle of Liam's imported Irish whiskey and two tumblers and I know right then that Liam is a Matt Taylor fan. He hardly ever offers his whiskey to guests. I learned that my first week here.

Matt takes a sip of whiskey, pushes his king on its side, and extends his hand. "Good game."

"Good game." Liam surveys the board. "I think that's it for chess tonight." He stands. I move into view.

Liam smiles and moves around me. "Good night Andi, Matt." His feet sound on the stairs, his bedroom door shuts.

Matt smiles. "Good hooky day? Seemed pretty successful, from what I could see."

My cheeks heat. "Ah. Got some stuff on sale."

"Love hooky days," Matt affirms. He takes a sip of his whiskey. "I was bummed you weren't here though."

"Really?"

Surprise flashes across Matt's face. "Yeah. I had fun last night." He pauses. "Didn't you?" His expression seems to convey genuine doubt.

"I had a great time."

He smiles. "Good. Hate to think I scared you off with my claustrophobia and the whole juggling act."

Scared me off? Was he insane? "We're good." I swipe Liam's empty tumbler off the table and carry it to the sink. "So, it's done? The inventory?"

He looks around the room. "There's always more to do."

"So, you'll be back?" I set the glass in the sink. "To finish out?"

The rational part of my brain is hoping he'll say: "Yup. That's it. See you never." And every other part which, I'm finding, takes

up a whole lot more space inside my head, hopes he'll say:
"there's *so* much to do. I'll be here indefinitely."

"I'd like to come by tomorrow, if that's okay," he says.

Yes! Take that rational brain.

"Tomorrow would be great."

CHAPTER 11

Matt

The next day, I arrive at the designated time and Liam lets me in. Andi's in the kitchen in front of the open dishwasher. She's got her hands inside the machine, a messy toolbox on the floor.

"What's this?"

She flips her head and smiles, crazy curls pulled back loosely from her face. She's got on jeans and a snug camo sweater. It's a good look.

"The machine ended up needing a new float switch after all," she explains. "Just about done with the new one."

She directs her attention to the machine, one hand twisting.

"Need help?"

"I'm good."

I spy Claus curled up on a kitchen chair and pet his massive square head. He opens one yellow eye. I scoop him up and stroke his back.

Andi shuts the dishwasher and directs her attention to me. "No way. He's letting you hold him?" She steps toward us. Claus growls. "He hates me."

I make a show of stroking Claus's head. "Don't feel bad. I just have a way with cats. It's like a superpower."

"A superpower?" she questions. "What? Like you're Catman?"

"Exactly."

"Do you have a theme song?"

"I do." I mimic the theme song from Batman but use the word Catman instead.

She laughs.

"I feel like you doubt that I'm a cat superhero." Claus, still in my arms, kneads his paws on my chest. His claws dig into my skin and, in the surprise of it, I drop him. He flips through the air, lands on his feet, and scurries out of the room.

Andi suppresses a grin. "Maybe you need to work on your skills a little."

I give a rueful smile. "Maybe a little." I swipe the composition notebook I'd brought to write down things for the pretend inventory. I felt ridiculous buying it, but I'd feel more ridiculous if I just walked around and talked to Andi. Even though that's what I want to do. I hold it up. "Ready?"

"Sure."

"I thought we'd start with the buildings. Maybe the toy shop first?"

"Great." We pull on coats and she moves purposely toward the building. We push inside to a space with yellowed windows and furniture piled high around the edges. Beams of light illuminate flying dust particles. Dirt and leaves are strewn about the floor.

Andi looks at me, expectant, so I flip open the notebook and feel around in the pockets of my coat and jeans. I don't have a pen.

I look up. Andi's gazing at me. "Need a pen, Catman?"

I shake my head. "And if I did?"

"I'd give you one." She unzips the small purse across her

shoulder and produces a pen and a chocolate bar. She hands me the pen and waves the candy. It's a Mounds. "Want half?"

"It's ten o' clock."

"And?" She pulls off the wrapper, shoves it in her pocket, and breaks the bar in two. She puts half on her palm and holds it out. "Don't tell me you've never had a Mounds before?"

"I have not."

"What? Mounds are the best." She takes a big bite and moves her hand with the bar half toward me.

I take it. "I'm more of KitKat guy but I'll try." I bite into the bar. Dark chocolate and coconut slide down my throat. "Good."

"Better than KitKats?"

"Not a chance. But I'll finish it." I pop the rest into my mouth and pull out my notebook. I write a list of everything I see. I have no idea if this is what an auditor taking inventory would do. I'm pretty sure it isn't.

After a few minutes, Andi moves into my line of vision. "Can I ask you something?"

"Sure." I move to a cabinet and open a drawer.

"I Googled you after our date."

I shift my gaze from the drawer to her. Panic slices through me. Does she know why I'm really here?

"You're a lawyer and your family owns SmartTech. Your Mom's the heir of Yumcakes." She shoves her hands in her jacket pockets. "Why didn't you tell me any of that stuff?"

I exhale. This question I could answer. "I liked that you seemed not to know."

"What do you mean?"

I shut the drawer and lean against the cabinet. "People assume all kinds of things about me based on my family. You didn't mention anything, so I figured you didn't know. And I liked that. I liked that you seemed not to have any preconceived notions."

This is an understatement. *Everyone* I'd ever gone out with knew about my background in advance. I'd always hated it.

A stream of bright light streaks in through a yellowed window and illuminates Andi's face. She leans against a table. "Okay. I get that. But you're a lawyer. Why are you doing the audit?"

I look at the floor. The answer, of course, is that I'm doing the audit to help prevent Liam from making a substantial investment in Christmastown.

It's not the answer I want to give.

"I'm low on the totem pole," I say instead. "And I'm not that good at being a lawyer. It's tedious and detail-oriented most of the time. Lots of sitting too." This part, at least, is true.

"Oh. The ADHD," she says, piecing it together. She twists a lock of hair with her index finger. "Do you mind me asking why you went into it?"

"Law?"

"Yeah. Seems like an unusual career choice, given what you've said."

She's right. Law was a terrible career choice for me. "It is," I acknowledge. "But it was the expectation in my family. Business or law. My sister, Steph, did business, so -" I let the sentence trail off.

"So you did law." Andi finishes the thought.

I shrug and reflect on how little I'd pushed back when my parents suggested law school. "I should have thought more about it," I say. "I've always been interested in computers. I'd love to learn how to program."

"You can, you know."

"I know." I have thought about going back to school, researched it in fact. But I never got momentum going long enough to do it. "I might."

I circle the room one more time, make a few additional marks in my notebook. "I'm good in here," I say and push open the door. We walk along a snowy path toward the carousel.

"This is my favorite ride." Andi taps on a reindeer as we pass. "There's something magical about a carousel. Almost everyone who has ever been to an amusement park has a memory of one."

As we walk, I conjure an image of me and Steph atop two ornate horses at an amusement park whose name I can't remember. We're both little enough that we're looped in by loose brown belts; our parents stand behind us. "You're right," I say. "One of my first amusement park memories is a carousel."

We reach Mrs. Claus's Bake Shop. The building has a sizable wraparound porch. Four weathered rocking chairs sit in a row in the front. Both the porch and the building were constructed to look as if made entirely out of cookies. Andi holds open a door shaped like a wafer. I step into a bright space with a counter across one wall, a slew of twisty stools in front of it. The floor is tiled in white; small sets of wrought iron tables are bunched up against the walls. I tap the counter. "This is in pretty good shape."

"This one's pretty good," she agrees.

I pull out my notebook. Andi's phone pings. She answers without looking; immediately steps outside. I hear her voice but not the words and I busy myself recording everything in the space. I wait a few minutes for her to return. When she doesn't, I step on the porch.

She's in a rocking chair, her phone face down on her leg. Her face holds a defeated expression.

"Everything okay?"

She shrugs. I sit in the chair next to her; neither of us speak. The energy is different. Not the teasing or laughing or mild flirting I was getting used to. It feels okay anyway. I can sit with Andi on this porch in silence for as long as she needs to process that phone call.

"That was my fiancé," she says.

I sit up straighter.

She shakes her head. "I mean, ex-fiancé. I haven't talked to him since we broke up."

"Oh."

"We broke up three months ago, before Christmas," she continues. "He called to see if I'd gotten the deposit from the hotel where we were supposed to have our reception." She rolls her eyes. "Cheats on me and has the nerve to call about a couple hundred dollars. Not to say he's sorry or find out if I'm okay but just, hey did you get that check in the mail?"

I can't get past the "cheats on me" part. "He cheated on you?" My fists ball; anger swooshes through me. The intensity of my emotion is over-the-top given I've only known Andi a few days. But the strong feelings are there nonetheless, and I feel like a stereotype of a guy, ready to avenge Andi's honor against this nameless, faceless, cheating ex-fiancé.

She shuts her eyes, opens them. "Yeah."

"What a dick."

She laughs and leans her head back on the rocker, angles her head toward me. "Thank you, Matt. That's very profound."

"I know. I mean, I am Catman."

"How could I forget?" She laughs again. "I have his two hundred dollars, you know. From the deposit."

"You do?" I sit up. "You're not giving it back, right?"

"No way."

"You should do something cool with it. Like buy a pair of fancy shoes or something."

She points to her old boots. "Fancy shoes?"

"Okay. What about a purse?"

She holds up a tiny sachel.

I open my mouth; she holds her hand out. "Let me stop you before you suggest I buy jewelry or the Barbie dreamhouse or something."

I laugh. "Or a dollhouse."

"Right."

"Fine. Maybe you could buy a toy tank."

"Or," she says, smiling, "I could save it for a special occasion which, in fact, I am doing." She stands. I follow her lead.

"What occasion?"

"Don't know yet. I'll know it when I see it."

I fall into step beside her, and we walk toward the next building. "One good thing about my break-up," she says, "is that it led me here. This has been good for me. I like Liam. And I like being here. And I've thrown myself into this project." She glances at me. "It's made me believe in myself again. If Liam and I can pull this off --"

She doesn't finish her sentence. She doesn't have to. I know how it ends. Andi needs Christmastown to become a reality.

And I've been charged with making sure that doesn't happen.

CHAPTER 12

M*att*
Two weeks after my conversation with Andi, I stand with Steph against the wall of a Philadelphia ballroom, a panda-shaped topiary beside her. Neither of us want to be here. But our mother is on the AnimalLIVE committee, she's de facto in charge of this gala. Missing it was not an option. We managed to find an out-of-the-way spot to stand, one that allows for a full view of the ballroom. The tables scattered throughout the space are dressed in green linens, each with a floral centerpiece shaped like a different animal. A live band plays a slow song, and a smattering of guests sway to the music.

"So," I say, "I need to convince Bridget that she should reconsider her stance on Christmastown."

Steph swirls her glass; ice rattles against the side. "Sorry. I still can't get over that it's called Christmastown. When are you done there anyway?"

"I finished yesterday." I tried to extend the time; Bridget insisted I come back.

Steph leans against the wall. She's got on a full-length

maroon dress with a slit up the side, her short, brown bob blown out straight. "You're done your job, but you still want to save Christmastown?" She angles her head toward me. "Are you sure you haven't escaped from a Hallmark movie?"

"Come on. I'm serious." I sound like the little brother I am. But Steph, insanely smart, a graduate of Wharton, and training to take over as the CFO for Yumcakes, knows things and people that I don't.

She moves and stares at my face.

I go hot under her gaze. "What?" I ask, the little brother tone still very much intact.

"Why do you care so much?" She averts her stare and takes a sip of her drink. "It's not like you have a personal stake in this park."

"I think it's a good idea. It's the only holiday-themed amusement park in the world."

"There's more to this."

"There's not."

"Come on, brother. I know you." She clinks her glass to my beer bottle. "Spill it."

"Fine," I say, "but first let me tell you why I think it's a good idea." I describe everything about Christmastown that makes it unique. I leave out how run down it is, how I'm pretty sure every building is infested with rodents, and how the lake is a muddy hole.

"Okay," she says, "it's different. That's good." She fiddles with a dangling earring. "What's the rest?"

"I like the people hoping to open it." I share a little about Liam and Andi, really skimming over the Andi part because Steph wouldn't take me seriously if she knew a pretty girl was involved. "The thing is," I continue, "Liam and Andi think Bridget is their key to getting the right people on board. They –" I pause; Steph fills in the rest

"They don't know why you're there," she concludes.

"Right. They think I'm doing an audit for Bridget. They think it's a good thing I'm there, that it shows Bridget is taking the park seriously." My heart dips as I say this out loud. "I want to give them a chance, you know. Use my contact with Bridget to help them."

"I still don't get why you care so much. You just met these people."

I know she has a point. But I don't feel like I just met Andi.

"I get that it seems crazy. Can you listen anyway?"

A waiter materializes with a tray of bacon-wrapped scallops. He dips the tray; Steph swipes two and hands me one. "Thank you," she tells him. A dismissal. She bites the scallop.

"Bridget is concerned that Liam will make a bad investment in Christmastown." I pause. "What I need to do is convince her that there are enough positives that she should at least look into the idea of reopening." I hand my scallop to Steph. "Are there people who do that? Who come in and see what's possible?"

She swallows. "Of course. What you need is someone to do a feasibility study."

"A feasibility study," I repeat, happy to be on the right track. "And who does those? Investors?"

"Anyone who thinks the park is a good idea will do one." She shakes her head as if anticipating my next question. "I don't know anyone, but Bridget should. The firm's huge." She waves at our mother, standing near the edge of the dance floor in leopard-themed dress. We start toward her. "From what you've told me, it sounds like the problem won't be a getting a person interested enough to do the study," Steph says, "it's convincing Bridget to find them."

"Stephanie," Mom commands as soon as we're in earshot. "I need you to talk to the Challendars at table 14. I told them you'd be around."

Steph salutes. "Aye aye, captain." She strides off.

Mom directs her attention to me. "And Matt," she says in the same manner she has all through my childhood, like I'm the biggest screw-up in the world, "you have a date." She points toward Whitney Collins, my ex-girlfriend. According to Steph, Whitney is still "wild" about me.

"She's not my date."

"Matt," Mom says, a warning in her tone.

I could argue; it's not worth it. It's one night. And I didn't bring a date which is entirely my fault. I could have asked Andi. I conjure an image of Andi, here, at the AnimalLIVE gala. *That would have been fun.*

"Matt," Mom repeats.

As irritating as her interference is, she has a massive amount of responsibility as chair of this event. I'm not going to add to it over something as petty as who I sit next to at dinner. "Fine, Mom. Happy to sit with Whitney but we are not dating."

I head toward the table before she can answer. Whitney's wearing a tight black gown with a massive amount of cleavage. Thick, straight sheens of blonde hair spill down her back. She's pretty. Okay, gorgeous. And a special events reporter for a local news station.

On paper, we're perfect together. We grew up in the same neighborhood, went to the same schools, and have enough in common to carry on decent conversations. But Whitney's shallow, fixated on her appearance more than anything else. And she talks nonstop, usually with wild physical gestures. Vigorous head nods. Gesticulating hand movements. Exaggerated shoulder shrugs. Worse, she says the last word of every sentence an octave higher than the rest which makes it seem like she's always asking a question. Not "the weather is nice," but "the weather is nice?" Half the time we dated, I felt like I had to duck for cover. The other half, I was trying to figure out if a question had been asked.

I reach the table. "Matt." Whitney stands and waves with

both arms. She hits a man passing. His drink spills down the front of his shirt.

Oof.

"Sorry!" Whitney grabs a napkin from the table and wipes at the liquid.

The man holds up his hands, his eyes fixed on the massive amount of cleavage on display. "It's fine," he says, touching her arm. "It's an old shirt."

She continues to dab.

"Can I get you something from the bar?" I say in his direction. "Replace your drink?"

He glances at me as if I've interrupted something. "I'm probably good for now," he says.

"Me too, Matt. Thanks." Whitney flashes a smile.

I weave through the guests toward the bar. Most are in some modest animal print attire, a few have outlandish accessories like wings or peacock feathers. I barely acknowledge anyone, instead consumed with thoughts of how to bring up the subject of getting a feasibility study for Christmastown.

I order another beer and, as I walk back to my table, try to put the dilemma out of my mind. Whitney's talking fixedly to the woman across from her, her head nodding wildly in some gesture of agreement.

I do not want to sit down.

Dane Foster, an acquaintance from prep school, meets my gaze and smiles. Crap. I might want to see Dane even less than I want to sit with Whitney. Dane majored in computer programming and has a job developing software. I'm generally jealous of his projects and, every time we speak, I end up hating my job even more intensely than before.

He taps me, hard, on the shoulder. "Matt, man. I haven't seen you in forever."

"It's been a while."

He throws back a glass of brown liquor, holds the empty

tumbler in his hand. He smells like whiskey, which reminds me of Liam, which reminds me of Andi. She's clear in my mind when I catch the tail end of his question. "Dating anyone?"

"Nah."

Dane nods toward Whitney.

"Still broken up. My mother sat us together."

"Nice." He smiles appreciatively and grabs a crab cake from a passing waiter. "So, how's the job? How's Quinn Gifford?" He pops the cake in his mouth.

I describe a few high-profile cases from the firm. Cases I have nothing to do with whatsoever. "How about you?" I ask because I have to, not because I want to know.

"I'm developing apps now." He puts his drink on a nearby table and pulls out his phone. "Check this out." He starts tapping and, in the next second, I'm looking at an app which Dane has described as "the next big fucking thing" in real estate. Three times. He pecks at keys. Images of houses and maps and prices flash across his screen in quick succession.

"Great interface," I say and it's true. It is a great interface. I'm super impressed and equally jealous.

He moves the phone so it's in my direct line of vision. "See this?" He points to a picture of a colonial house "Press it."

I don't move fast enough, apparently, because he repeats the command. "Come on. Press it."

I press. Boxes with labels replace the picture of the colonial house -- living room, family room, master bath, etc.

"Press one," Dane urges. "See what happens."

He says this as if what happens next would be a surprise. Like, I'd press the box with kitchen in it and, instead of a picture of a kitchen, confetti would shoot out the phone. Still, it's a cool concept; I want to see how it works. I punch the box with master bath written inside. A picture of the master bath appears on the phone's interface.

I tap his shoulder. "Cool, man."

He wiggles the phone. "Try again. Press another one."

I press patio and a picture of the patio appears. "Cool." I rap his shoulder. "Good to see you, man." I start toward my table and think of Andi's comment at La Casa: "You could still do that Matt." She'd been talking about me switching careers and, here I am, talking to a guy who has the career I want. I should at least ask him about it.

I turn back. "Hey Dane," I say. "If I ever decided to look into a career in programming, would you be able to help me figure out best steps?"

He smiles. "Sure. I actually teach a class for beginners at the community college." He reaches into his tux jacket and produces a card. "Call if you're interested."

"Thanks."

I tuck the card in my pocket and walk back toward my table. My phone vibrates. I slide it out of my pocket and peek. It's a text from Andi.

Call me when you can.

CHAPTER 13

M*att*   I don't think twice about it. I move to the rear of the ballroom and exit into the lobby of the hotel. I sit on a surprisingly squishy couch near the front desk and call Andi. I'm surrounded by leafy plants in expensive looking pots. A massive flat-screened television relays a news program on low volume. Music from my mother's event still plays, muted through the closed door.

"Hey!" Andi picks up right away.

She sounds happy; I smile on reflex. "Hey."

"Thanks for the Yumcakes."

The Yumcakes. I'd forgotten. Andi had told me how much she loved them, so I sent she and Liam a bunch of cases. "You're welcome. Living up to the hype?"

"I'm eating a peanut butter cake right now."

"Glad to hear it."

"Liam's having one of the coffee cakes," she adds. "We're watching Wheel of Fortune."

I picture this. The two of them sitting on the worn but cozy sofas in Liam's family room, an array of Yumcakes on the coffee table. Liam's likely in a shirt with a funny caption, Andi wrapped up in a blanket, fuzzy socks on her feet.

"Good episode?" Liam, like Ruth, loved Wheel of Fortune. I'd watched the show more times over the past two weeks than in my entire life.

"Always. You should put it on. Get some Yumcakes."

"Will do." The lobby's empty. I spy the television remote on the console and flip through channels.

"Wait," Andi says, "it's Saturday night. You're doing something fun, aren't you?"

I find the program and move back to the couch. "Not really."

"Come on."

I exhale. "Okay, if you must know, I'm at the AnimalLIVE gala for my mother and it is definitely not fun. I'm in the lobby and I just put on Wheel."

"Did you really?"

"Yes. Mildred just spun." The wheel stops on $2,000. A woman in a red shirt and sprayed black hair claps enthusiastically.

"Matt!" I like the way she says it. Like she wants to sound exasperated with me, but she really isn't. "How can you be watching television during a big event like that?"

"I like Wheel."

"Isn't it rude?"

That tone again, like she's smiling as she asks the question.

"Probably."

Liam, in the background, yells: "Twas the Night Before Christmas."

He's right and I laugh. "Now that's appropriate," I say.

"It is," Andi agrees.

We watch the final puzzle and the show ends. "What are you doing now?" I ask.

"I am paging through one of Liam's books. *The World's Stupidest Facts.*"

"Yeah? Tell me one." I lean back on the couch. This is my favorite conversation of the whole night.

"All right. How's this? EDM dance music repels mosquitos."

"What? Why would someone think to test that?"

She laughs. "I don't know. Maybe music's impact on mosquitos is a big field of scientific study we don't know about."

"Like using music is going to replace mosquito nets or something?"

"Exactly."

I smile. "Okay. Give me another."

"Oh. Wow." She snickers. "This is a good one. A pig's orgasm last thirty minutes."

"No."

"That's what it says."

"I don't believe you."

"I'll screenshot it."

A moment later a text comes through with a picture of the page from the book. I stare at the fact, written out exactly as Andi had just said. "Okay. Again, I have to ask, who is researching this?"

She gives the snort laugh. "Probably the same group researching mosquitos' reactions to EDM music."

I smile. "Okay. No more for today. I don't think I can take it."

"Okay, fair" she says, a tinge of laughter in the words. "I did have something to ask you anyway."

My heart dips. I hope the question isn't about audit. "Sure. Shoot."

"Would you want to come to a beef and beer next Friday? For Christmastown?"

I shift on the couch, relieved. "Of course. I'd love it."

"Great! I'll text you the details."

The ballroom door pushes open, Whitney in its frame. She looks like a woman on a mission. And one that has had a few cocktails. She strides toward me. "Matt. There you are!"

There's no way Andi didn't hear that.

She wiggles her hips. "I've been looking for you! I want to dance."

Or that.

"It sounds like you need to go," Andi says, a question in her words.

"Umm." Whitney's pulls at my hand. As much as I want to stay on the phone, it would be hard to gracefully extricate myself from the situation.

"I'll text you the details about the beef and beer." She clicks off and I stare at the phone like she's inside it. Whitney pushes at my shoulder. "Come on now, Matt."

I stand.

Only a few days to the beef and beer.

CHAPTER 14

Matt
The Friday of the beef and beer is, as it ends up, the day Bridget schedules our meeting to discuss my audit findings. She'd sent the invitation to me via my Outlook calendar: CTAF two p.m. I'd stared at the acronym a healthy amount of time before, finally, deciphering it's meaning. CTAF = Christmastown Audit Findings.

I'm nervous. I want to pull through for Andi and Liam more than I would if it were my own stake in the venture. I don't analyze this feeling because, if I do, I know I'll come to the correct conclusion. A small percentage of my interest in the project is based on promising investment opportunities for Christmastown and for Liam. The much larger percentage is based on my growing feelings for Andi.

I reach the door to Bridget's office, sweat pooling in my armpits. She looks up from her pristine desk. "Matt. Hello. Please come in."

I step inside.

"And shut the door behind you."

I pull the door closed. It feels ominous, this closed-door

meeting. It doesn't help that Bridget's dressed in all in black, like we're meeting to discuss funeral plans instead of those for a holiday-themed amusement park.

She leans forward. "I'll cut to the chase," she says, all business. "Have you found anything for me? Anything I could use to prevent my father from making an irreparable financial decision?"

"I have found some things." My voice is dry. I point to the refrigerator in the corner. "Okay if I get some water?"

"Of course."

I move to the fridge, grab two bottles of water. I hold one up in her direction.

"No. Thank you."

I place it back in the fridge, return to my seat, and take a long drink.

"You were saying," she prompts.

"Yes." I tell her about the potential I saw in Christmastown, about Liam and how he seems fine and capable and in his right mind. I mention the feasibility study, the possibility of getting an investor. None of it comes out the way I thought it would. My arguments are a babbling mess. I sound like a child trying to get a parent to buy a new toy.

When I'm done the inarticulate rant, I down more water. Bridget looks at me with an intense expression and I can't figure out if her unwavering stare is a good thing, like she's thinking seriously about what I said, or a bad one, like she thinks I'm nuts. The silence and her uncomfortable stare go on for so long that I open my mouth to say something more. She holds up a hand.

"Let me understand," she says in a way that I *know* is bad, "you've been in Scranton for two weeks with the singular objective of finding reasons I can use in court to stop my father from investing in this Christmastown venture. But, instead, you're suggesting *I* fund a feasibility study." She puts her hand across her chest which makes the "I" in her sentence seem more emphatic.

Additional sweat pools under my arms. I'm vaguely concerned it might seep through my suit jacket. I sit taller, do my best to sound confident. "In fairness, you didn't specify that I find reasons to halt Christmastown. You said I would be your eyes and ears. And I'm telling you -"

"Yes," she interrupts, "I'm aware of your thoughts. The park is," she refers to notes she made on her pad, things that I said during my ineffective monologue, "cool and fun and one-of-a-kind." She pauses long enough to make me feel dumb or, more accurately, dumber. Her eyes meet mine, unwavering. "These are not compelling reasons, Matt. Simply because something might seem *cool*" – she emphasizes the word – "does not mean my father should put his financial future at risk."

"But there's more to it. Liam promised his wife on her deathbed. Your mom. And it could be a gold mine, a once-in-a-lifetime opportunity." I lean forward. "It's at least worth looking into. Right?"

Bridget shakes her head. "It isn't. Trust me, my mother would not want my father to make any rash decisions, no matter what Dad may say or how convincing and jovial he may be."

"But how do you know if it's rash?" I shoot back. "You haven't even looked into it."

Irritation crosses her features. "I don't need to look into it. I grew up around Dad's schemes." She's quiet and, outside her picture window, a bird flies across a perfect blue sky. "I know I seem harsh," she says, her tone softer, "but I'm just looking out for him. I'm an only child. I'm the only one who can make these kinds of hard decisions." She rolls back in her chair. "Dad would hate being financially dependent if things went wrong with this. I have to help him help himself."

"But --" I start, but don't finish. I don't know where to go from here. Andi's sketches for the completed park click through my mind like a slideshow. I open my mouth to try to verbalize them when Bridget speaks again.

"Right now, a court will never award me a conservatorship over my father. I don't have enough evidence." She flashes a harsh look in my direction like it's my fault which, I suppose, it is. I didn't even try to look for the kinds of evidence Bridget might need.

"You know," Bridget says, sitting up straighter, "Dad hadn't mentioned reopening Christmastown or my mother's wishes since she died. This all started when that caretaker arrived."

My head jolts up.

"Andi." Bridget says, almost to herself. "She's the problem. She needs to go."

"No," I blurt. The word comes out too forcefully. "I mean that isn't the impression I got. That the caretaker, Andi, is spearheading Liam's interest." I pause and, when Bridget doesn't say anything immediately, I add a bold-faced lie. "She's almost *dis*interested."

"Really?" Bridget closes her eyes and taps her pen vigorously on the edge of the desk. Her eyes fly open, an expression on her face like wheels are literally turning inside of her head. If I wasn't so invested in the outcome, the whole scenario would seem comical. Bridget, like a movie villain, trying to stop the construction of an old man's dream for a holiday theme park.

"What is he doing?" she asks suddenly, her eyes on me, intense. "What is he doing right now?"

I shift; I don't follow her train of thought. "What do you mean?"

"Fundraising, permits, experts." She waves her hand around. "What is my father doing to make this park a reality?"

"Not much," I say honestly. I don't add that Liam and Andi are waiting on her, hoping she'll use her connections to get things going.

"Nothing?" She sounds incredulous; I'm defensive on Liam's behalf.

"He's having a beef and beer," I add in a small attempt to make his efforts seem more substantial.

"*A beef and beer?*" Bridget rolls her eyes. "Typical Dad. He's going to try to find funding for a multi-million-dollar venture by hosting a beef and beer."

The way she says it makes the idea seem preposterous. And I'd thought that too, when Andi mentioned it, that a beef and beer was not what Christmastown needed. But the way Bridget speaks about Liam, the way she's dismissed all of this out of hand, sits wrong in my gut.

She jabs her pen in my direction. "Okay. I have a new assignment. I want you stay in touch with Liam and Andi, work in the Scranton office on occasion. As long as nothing substantial is going on, nothing more than beef and beers –" she rolls her eyes – "there's no reason for me to move ahead and get the evidence I need for the conservatorship. Dad will never get to the point of investing real money and I don't have to be the heavy." A look of satisfaction flashes across her face.

"But what are you going to tell Liam?" I think about Liam and Andi waiting on Bridget's response. "He thinks you sent me for the audit. He's going to want to know what you think."

"I'll tell him I need more information. In fact, I'll tell him you're gathering information for a feasibility study."

"No," I say automatically. "I'm not comfortable lying anymore. And what happens later?" I add. "Gathering information can only go on for so long."

We're interrupted by Bridget's assistant, a wiry woman with horn-rimmed glasses. She strides in without words, hands Bridget a bunch of papers. Bridget signs them without looking. "He'll lose interest," she says and thrusts the papers back in the assistant's direction. "Give it a month or two."

"I'm still not comfortable."

Bridget looks at me a long moment. I brace myself, ready for a counterattack. Instead, she leans forward. "I understand."

Relief swells through my body but it's momentary. There's no way Bridget would give up so easily. "So, what happens now?"

"I'll send someone else."

"To Christmastown?"

"Yes, Matt, to Christmastown. I'm serious about saving my father from himself on this. I've lived this. I know how these things go." She glances back at her computer, a list of employees on the screen. "Ryan Gallo," she says triumphantly. "I'll send him."

Ryan Gallo? I hate Ryan Gallo. First-year associate, total prick. Slicked back hair, beady black eyes. The kind of guy that would do anything to advance. I visualize him slithering around Christmastown, soaking in the information I'd omitted sharing, including Andi's intense involvement. Andi would get fired and Ryan would get Bridget whatever she needed to gain conservatorship.

No.

Ryan Gallo cannot go.

I remain seated; Bridget looks at me. "Is something wrong?"

"I'm thinking," I say, not wanting to finish the sentence but not seeing a better option, "maybe I can go."

She raises an eyebrow.

"Don't tell them about the feasibility study," I say, knowing how much they will both get their hopes up if Bridget tells them that. "I can figure out what's going on without it."

"Are you sure?"

"Absolutely."

CHAPTER 15

A *ndi*

"MATT'S COMING TONIGHT, RIGHT?" Emma places a raffle basket on a pocked table.

"He's coming." I shift the baskets around, hoping a new configuration will make the room seem less sad. The space seemed fine when I booked it during the day but now, with the sun going down, the overhead lighting is dim. The walls, furniture, and rug -- all shades of dark brown or black -- add a shadowy vibe. The room smells like spilled beer and the floor, the portions that can be seen anyway, is a patchwork of unidentifiable stains.

"And?" Emma bumps my shoulder. She's not over the possibility that Matt and I may become more than friends.

"And we're friends. That's it."

"Why does that have to be it?" She grabs a mason jar out of a cardboard box and sets it in front of one of the baskets.

"Because he has a girlfriend." I hate how my voice catches on the word. It's not that I felt ready to date but I'd allowed a piece of my brain to consider it.

I pull out my phone and find the picture, the one I'd stalked on the internet the morning after Matt's admission he was at a the AnimalLIVE gala. I tip it toward Emma. I don't need to see it again; I've got both Matt and the girl, Whitney Collins, memorized:

Matt. Tall and striking in his tux, the affable smile on his face, a bit crooked, his arm around the girl's waist.

And Whitney. A supersized Barbie in an exquisite black sequined gown.

"Oh." Emma stares at the picture, eyes wide. I can guess what she's thinking: honey, you don't stand a chance. She's too nice to say that so instead asks, "how do you know that's his girlfriend?"

"I was talking to him on the phone, and she came out to get him. He said her name."

"And he left after she came out?"

"Um. Look at her. Yes, he left." I slide my phone from Emma's hand. "She's a news reporter."

"She's a *news* reporter?"

"Fluff stuff but still, she's on television. Some channel in Philadelphia." I pause. "There are other pictures of them online together too." Not proud that I stalked this.

Emma peers at me, her features empathetic.

My heart swells. "Look. It's fine. I wasn't ready to get back out there anyway. A few months ago, I was *engaged*. I told Matt that."

"What did he say?"

I smile. "He said he thought Cole sounded like a dick."

Emma pushes at my shoulder. "Ha! So it's not just me." She places a mason jar on the table. I place a ticket reel by the cash box.

"Andi!"

I whirl around. My mother stands with her latest boyfriend, Jim. Liam, in a green tartan kilt and dress shirt, is behind them.

"Surprise!" they say in unison, and I step back. My mother has on a Christmas tree sweater. Jim's in a sweatshirt with a trout in its center. Over the top of the trout, the shirt says "Missing Fishing."

I have no idea what they're doing here. I hadn't told them about the event. "Hey. Wow."

"I called the house and Liam told me about the beef and beer," Mom bursts.

"I thought you'd like the surprise," Liam says.

Mom's eyes cloud. "I felt terrible you hadn't thought to tell me about this." She pauses. "But I came dressed for the occasion." She presses a button on her sweater. The tree illuminates with tiny multi-colored lights; *Jingle Bells* sounds from the fabric. "Ta da."

I struggle to find words. *Jingle Bells* continues to ping out from Mom's sweater.

"Brian's coming," she continues. "And Chelsea and Betsy."

My brother's family. Three years older than me, Brian married his high school sweetheart. He and Chelsea have a four-year-old named Betsy, freckled and blonde and adorable.

"Wow. That's crazy." My brother and his family rarely venture out of their suburban New Jersey neighborhood.

"If Christmastown is something you want to see happen," Mom says, "we want to support you." She puts her hand on Jim's shoulder as if to include him in the "we."

"Yup, we sure do," he adds.

Before there can be more affirmation about how my mother – and Jim, apparently – are rooting for me, a lanky guy approaches our group. Liam claps him on the shoulder. "Aye everyone, this is Beckham."

Beckham steps forward. He's about my age and looks

straight out of a casting call for surfer dudes: t-shirt, jeans, leather slides with socks, and weathered skin. His hair's white blonde with a big bang that hangs over his left eye. When he opens his mouth, I almost expect him to say something like "gnarly" or "rad." Instead, he says, "hey."

"Beckham's my grand-nephew," Liam tells us. "He's going to be working on a construction project in the area." He looks at me. "He might do some work around the house too."

"Sure. Great."

I catch Emma's eye. "He's cute," she mouths, inclining her head toward Beckham. I look from my friend -- my super-practical friend, the one who schedules time to be spontaneous -- to Beckham the surfer dude and back. I don't see it. I smile anyway.

Guests filter in over the next hour. Liam's friends from the American Legion, some from golf. His barber, his bookie. Store clerks at his regular venues. Festive music, mostly Irish-themed per Liam, pipes through the speakers played by a teen DJ. Guests stack thick paper plates with beef, fries, and coleslaw. Raffle jars fill with tickets. A few people hit the small dance floor.

Small arms hug my legs. I whirl around and pick up Betsy. Her curly pigtails bounce with the movement. She's in a worn Cinderella costume and old sneakers.

Chelsea kisses my cheek and extricates Betsy from my arms. "Insisted on wearing the Cinderella dress again," she whispers. I smile. Betsy's love of her Cinderella dress is no secret. She's had it on three of the last four times I've seen her.

"You look beautiful," I say and kiss her cheek.

Brian sidles up, pushes horn-rimmed glasses up the bridge of his nose. "So Christmastown. An amusement park?" He scrunches up his face as if he can't fathom the concept. He probably can't. His idea of creative genius is signing his Christmas cards in red ink instead of black.

"Yup," I say. "It's geared for little kids." I bop Betsy's nose with my finger. "This one would love it."

Mom and Jim join us. And Emma. Also Beckham which I'm not totally clear on. We stand in a circle; Mom's expression like a Cheshire cat. "Emma told me you have a gentleman friend coming."

I roll my eyes in Emma's direction. "His name is Matt. He did an audit of Christmastown, he's a nice guy, and we're *friends*." I emphasize the word friends as strongly as I can, partly so Mom won't ask more. And partly to reaffirm the concept in my own mind.

"But that doesn't mean --" she starts.

Jim puts his hand on her shoulder. "Come on, Jill. If Andi says she's just friends with this Matt person, that's all it is. You shouldn't pester her."

Mom looks wounded and I stare at Jim, angry he's telling her what to do (even though, technically, he's taking my side). I half want to insist that Matt and I might be more than friends just to spite him.

Chelsea speaks, thankfully. "Who is *that*?"

Emma grips her arm. "That's him. That's Matt." She looks to me. "Right. That's him?"

I spin my head in the direction they're looking and, oh boy, it is him. He's wearing a flannel shirt open over a t-shirt and jeans. He looks taller and more good-looking than I remembered, almost like he spent the past week at some physique-enhancing spa instead of a law office.

"That's him." I say it casually, like I'm accustomed to having incredibly handsome male friends. Like my heart isn't pounding. Like I actually believe what I've been telling myself: I am *fine* in the friendship zone. No attraction on my end. At all.

Matt waves. I wave back. "Hey," I call, "come meet everyone."

I introduce him. He's perfect. Shaking hands, kissing cheeks. Making all that introductory conversation that's usually incred-

ibly awkward but with him, seems easy. Betsy, in the center of
our circle, lingers near him; he bends down. "No one told me
Cinderella was going to be here."

She gives the widest grin before acknowledging, gravely,
that she's not actually Cinderella.

"You had me fooled," he says, and she beams. Chelsea has no
chance of getting the worn Cinderella dress off her now.

Matt pulls out a wad of raffle tickets. "Bought these at the
front."

I eye the balled up mass of bright pink paper. "You didn't
have to get all of those."

He shrugs. "You told me you had a lot of good baskets." He
throws a smile in my direction. Still lopsided. Still perfect. "And
I heard they're expertly wrapped."

I grin. During more than one phone call this week, I'd
lamented to Matt about wrapping the raffle baskets. Even as an
artist, I couldn't get them to look right. Crooked bows,
scrunched up cellophane, collapsing pyramids of donated items.
The sad looking baskets were one reason I was glad for the dim
light.

"The baskets are beautiful," Mom chimes in. She points to
the back of the room. "And right back there."

I lead Matt to a table crammed with raffle baskets and
mason jars.

He picks up the basket donated by Lori Morris Hair Designs.
Shampoos, conditioners, a hair dryer, and a bunch of gels are
covered in cellophane, a gold bow on top. "This looks good. You
told me everything looked like it was covered in saran wrap."

"That one I did after a YouTube tutorial."

"Worth it." He flashes a grin and stuff a giant wad of tickets
in the nearest mason jar.

"You know you put all those in for the romance basket,
right?" I tap on the basket of romance novels. The one on top
features a bare-chested man who looks strikingly like Matt.

"I love romance novels," he says, a deadpan expression on his face. "The steamier the better."

"Good to know."

We walk the length of the table. Matt stops at every jar and stuffs a bunch of tickets inside. "Your mom and brother are here," he says, stopping at the automotive basket. "That's good, right?"

"I was shocked. I hadn't even told them about it. Liam did."

"And the guy? Jim?"

I wave at him. "Oh, the BOM. Don't worry about him. You probably won't see him again."

A quizzical look spans his features.

"BOM. Boyfriend of the Month. That's what me and Brian call it. Love my mom but she's not complete unless she attached to someone." I shake my head. "That sounds mean. Forget I said it."

"Doesn't sound mean but consider it forgotten anyway." He drops his final tickets into the last jar, one with over-the-top picnic supplies. "Your niece is adorable, by the way."

"Isn't she?"

Liam steps between us. He slings an arm around each of our shoulders, a slight scent of whiskey on his breath. "I've got good news." He pulls us so close, our heads touch. "I just got off the phone with Bridget."

He pauses.

"She's going to do a feasibility study for Christmastown to see if it's a good investment." He steps back and claps Matt on the shoulder. "And Matt here is going to help her."

CHAPTER 16

A *ndi*
"That's great news." I push Matt on the shoulder. "Why didn't you tell me?"

"I," he starts then stops. He stays silent so long that I start to think something is wrong.

"I wasn't sure she was going to do it," he finishes.

"Well," Liam says, "she is, and it calls for a celebration." He asks for three California Gold Rush shots from a passing worker.

The worker returns with three shot glasses of golden colored liquid. Liam passes them out. He holds his in the air. "To Bridget."

"To Bridget," I repeat, a toast I never thought I'd make. Matt seems to feel the same way. He looks ashen, actually.

We down the shots and I lean into Matt. "You okay?"

"I'm fine." His eyes stay on mine a beat too long. There's definitely something wrong.

Liam speaks before I can. "We should do the raffles."

I look to Matt. "Want to help? Pick the tickets?"

He shakes his head. "Nah."

I don't push it. Liam asks the DJ to stop the music. He takes the microphone.

"Hey all," he says, "quick interruption, I promise." He holds up a hand and there's a smattering of laughter. "I wanted to thank you all for coming, not just for me, but for my Colleen." He stops a moment. "Colleen and I, like many of you, did not have the easiest of times in life. But, every year, when Christmas rolled around, it was like a little pocket of joy, a reprieve from stresses and troubles. And when we found Christmastown, this little shut down park, we thought, this is it, our legacy. We can make a place in the world where the love embodied by Christmas lives each day. A place where families can visit and forget about their problems for a few hours." He stops, his expression wistful. "When she was almost gone, I promised Colleen I'd make Christmastown a reality. And, for the first time," he looks at me and Matt, "I think it's going to happen."

Mom claps with intensity and fervor well beyond what the moment calls for. She bumps Jim who, seeming to realize he should cheer, joins her chorus of shouts. Brian, Betsy on his shoulders, gives a fist pump. He nods at me. Approval.

I swallow a lump in my throat. For the first time since the Cole break-up, it feels like my life is clicking into place.

"And now," Liam's voice interrupts my thoughts, "time for the raffles." He hands the mic to me, and I smile. "First basket," I say, "is the football food basket, kindly donated by Route 31 South Grill and Deli." I grab the jar off the table and draw a ticket. "And the winner is Terri Grant."

An adorable blonde woman I presume to be Terri charges to the front of the room. She swipes the basket off the table and holds it high over her head.

I pick tickets for the movie basket and the pet lovers' basket and the Crayola basket. I move to the romance basket, pluck out a ticket, and look at the name. No way. A grin blooms across my face. "And the romance basket goes to Matt Taylor."

"Woo hoo, Matt," Emma calls out. "Spicy."

I hold up the basket, heavier than it might seem. I scan the room for Matt. He's not with my family, or at the bar. But it's dim so I call his name again. "Matt Taylor, winner of the romance basket." I wait a moment, set the basket down. "Well, I guess this one will have to wait."

I move on to the next several baskets, concerned when Matt doesn't reappear. When the drawing is over, overflowing baskets strewn about the room next to their winners, I look for him. I find him outside, propped up against the side of the building. It's dark and his body is illuminated by a streetlamp. He's smoking.

He glances in my direction and drops his cigarette. Immediately he stamps his foot on the yellow-red embers, hiding the evidence, almost like I'm a teacher who'd caught him in a high school bathroom. "I don't normally smoke. I mean," he looks me in the face, "it's something I do once in a while."

I shrug, not sure what to say because it seems that, if he's smoking and he doesn't normally, there's a reason for it. Maybe because it's a Friday after a long week of work. Or maybe he's celebrating. Or maybe there's something wrong. "Yeah," I say noncommittally. "You won the romance basket, by the way."

"Cool." He blows air, his breath smoky from the cold. "I think I'll read that one on top first, the one with the guy with the firefighter helmet on."

"*Firelust?*" I tip my head. "One of the classics. I'm surprised you didn't read it in high school. You know. *To Kill a Mockingbird. The Old Man and the Sea. Firelust.*"

He nods. "Right. I think my class wasn't that advanced." He leans against the brick wall. "But at least I can read it now."

"At least."

A car passes on the street. A group of patrons push out the door and spill out on to the sidewalk. It's cold. I pull my jacket tight and lean back against the brick wall next to Matt. He rolls his head to the side, his face is inches from mine, the bits of stubble clear on his cheeks and jaw. He smells like cigarettes.

"If you don't mind me asking, how much do you think you made tonight?"

I try to estimate the winnings. "Two, three thousand?" I wave my hand dismissively. I know two or three thousand doesn't sound like much, a ridiculously little sum in fact. "It's a first step," I add. "And now that Bridget is going to do the study, we're in better shape."

He lets out a long breath, almost like he's exhaling smoke without a cigarette.

"Don't you think? Having Bridget on board should help, right?"

He pushes off the wall and faces me. "Have you ever considered having a different kind of event?"

It's not an answer to my question; I consider it anyway. "Like what kind of event?"

"Something bigger. Something that would attract more donors or investors." He waves in my direction. "That was a great event, don't get me wrong. I mean I won a basket full of romance books." He smiles and spreads his hands out as if to demonstrate the expansiveness of his winnings. "But something on a larger scale might increase interest."

I shove my hands in my pockets. "You're thinking of the kinds of events you go to."

He looks me square in the eyes before casting his gaze downward. "Sort of. I mean –"

He lets his statement trail off and I can tell he doesn't want to offend me. I reach out and touch his arm. "I agree, Matt. A bigger event would be great. I've just never been to an event of that scale, let alone planned one."

I think about how long it took for me to put together this small event. Soliciting raffle donations, renting the place, figuring out food. Even getting the DJ took some time. "I think it would be good to wait until the study is over," I continue. "We might have some automatic interest and, maybe, not need the event at all."

"No."

Matt's word comes out forcefully; I take a step back.

"I mean," he continues, "we shouldn't, or rather you and Liam shouldn't, wait idly by for however long this study takes. It could be weeks or months." He bugs his eyes out as if he'd said decades or centuries. "Why wait? If you get interest in advance, it can only boost the study, prove this is a viable venture. And it could increase the competition, right, if there was more than one group interested?" He stops, suddenly, and looks at me. "You should do it."

I'm silent. The idea of planning an event of the scale he's talking about is daunting. I wouldn't know who to invite, what to serve, where to hold it. "I'm not saying it's a bad idea," I say carefully, "I would just have no idea how to plan something like that."

He looks around, everywhere but at me it seems, until he finally meets my eyes. "I'll help you."

CHAPTER 17

att

M Steph picks up a red and white container of fried rice and shovels a forkful in her mouth. She's sitting cross-legged on the couch in our shared brownstone, an array of Chinese food containers on the table in front of her. "So let me get this straight. Your boss, the head of the firm, Bridget Quinn, sent you to make sure there is no substantial fundraiser for Christmastown?"

I open my mouth; Steph holds up a hand.

"But, instead, you go down there and offer to spearhead your own big fundraising event?"

I pick up the box of sweet and sour chicken and shake it over my plate. "I didn't say I would spearhead it. I said I would help." I stab one of the pieces with my fork. "They'll never get what they need from events like beef and beers."

"Isn't that the point?"

"If you're Bridget it is. But she's wrong about this. Andi and Liam have a great vision. She won't give them a chance."

Steph lifts an eyebrow. "Do they know an amusement park, no matter how small or quaint or original, is a multi-million-dollar venture? I mean, if they're holding beef and beers, do they understand the magnitude of this?"

I don't know if either of them gets it, the magnitude of this venture. But they have a good concept. It should at least be explored. "They think Bridget is in their corner," I remind Steph.

She swipes the full container of cashew chicken off the table and points at me with her fork. "And since she's not, you're hoping to find the investors at your event."

"Right. I need an event that's going to attract investors that are in this kind of space. If I can get one or more legitimate people interested, Bridget will have to take the idea seriously." I pause. "I mean, she's all about Liam not spending his own money. If there are investors, he doesn't have to. It's a win-win."

"And what do you think Bridget is going to think about you having a big fundraiser?"

I stand and cross the room to the connected kitchen. I pull out another beer and a bottle of wine. I return, fill her glass, and sit. "I'm not going to tell her."

Steph whips her head up. "Are you kidding?"

"No."

"She'll find out. There's no way she won't find out."

I shake my head. "Bridget never goes to Christmastown. She thinks it's an eyesore." In my head, I hear her saying these exact words at our first meeting.

Steph shovels cashew chicken in her mouth. She has that look in her eye when she's analyzing something. I'd always imagined she had a slew of spreadsheets and charts in her head.

"I know I asked you this before, but why do you care about Christmastown so much? It sounds cool and I know you like Liam and Andi but, running an event of the scale you're talking about is a huge undertaking." She pauses and looks me in the eyes. "You're risking your job and committing a massive amount of time and you don't even have a real interest in this venture. Why?"

It's a good question, one that I'd thought about. I know Steph won't fully understand my reasoning. She's the golden child, the one who forged her own path without connections or struggles or the kind of stupidity that framed my daily existence as a kid. Helping get Christmastown off the ground, even in a marginal way, would be an accomplishment, something unrelated to my uber successful parents or sister. A small achievement like this wouldn't mean anything to Steph, but it would to me.

And yeah. I'll say it. I want to help Andi. I want to see her face light up in a smile like it did the first time I switched on that Sky Ornament Ride, like it did when she was surrounded by her family at the beef and beer. I want her to achieve her vision and, frankly, stick it to her ex.

I don't give these details to Steph. "I want to help," I say vaguely. "And Christmastown's not the only thing I have going."

"Is that right?" She tips her head. "Do you finally have an actual girlfriend instead of this fictitious one?"

I roll my eyes. "No. Andi and I are still friends." I pause. "She just had a bad break-up. She wants to be on her own."

"Can't argue with independence." She pulls her legs in and sits cross-legged on the couch. "So, what is it then? What's the other thing you have going?"

"I'm taking a computer programming class." I sip my beer. "You'll never guess who my professor is."

She swirls her fork around. "I don't know," she says after a moment. "I can't think of anyone."

"Dane Foster."

She leans forward, catches the box of cashew chicken before it tumbles to the floor. "No."

"Yup."

"Is he pompous?"

"Yup."

"How's the class?"

"I'm paying my dues, that's for sure." This might be an understatement. In addition to the class, I've spent several nights at the bar with Dane. He has multiple apps, all interactive, and I've been shown every part of every single one. "But it's worth it," I add. "I've got some app ideas that may tie into Christmastown." I pop the last two sweet and sour chicken pieces from my plate into my mouth.

She holds up her wine glass. "Well cheers to you."

I clink my beer to her glass.

It's nice to know she's on my side. Steph might not get the Christmastown thing, most people wouldn't, but at the end of the day, she's in my corner. And I'm probably going to need her.

"You should call John Evans. He does fundraisers."

"Your ex-boyfriend, John Evans?"

She shrugs. "He's over it. So am I." She sips her wine. "Last year, he ran a hugely successful fund raiser for Farm-to-Table, a group that brings affordable organic produce to underserved communities. I didn't go, but everyone who did raved about it." She sets her glass on the table. "Do you have his number?"

Steph and John had dated for four years; I'd liked him. He was an interesting guy, originally from England, his language peppered with British phrases like "brilliant" and "knackered" and "loo."

"I'm sure I have his contact somewhere."

Steph rolls her eyes. "Somewhere? For you, that means balled up on some post-it and stuffed in your desk or wadded into a jeans pocket. That number has probably been through the dryer a hundred times." She swipes her phone off the side table and punches at it. A moment later, John's contact appears on my phone.

"Thanks." I stare at the contact. "Night, Steph." I leave the room before I get into it, her assessment of my organizational skills. She's not wrong. I always think I'll remember where things are, or I intend to organize a big pile of stuff later. But then I forget or lose track of time and, well, my sister accuses me of leaving a wadded-up paper with a phone number in my pocket for over a year.

I call John the next day. The first thing he says is "Mate! I haven't heard from you in donkey's years," which makes me laugh. I tell him about Christmastown, and my idea to hold an event to, hopefully, gain the interest of some investors.

"Ace of a concept, man," he comments when I'm done. "Make sure any event you have is as original as that idea. You need something bloody unique. When we did the Farm-to-Table event, we held it at a farm. The guests fed the animals, hand-picked the food they ate. They loved the interactive nature of it, you know. It's different. Anyone can throw a gala. No one remembers it the next week."

I thought through the galas I'd been to; they all ran together. The clothes, the food, the people. Even the speeches sounded somewhat the same.

"Good advice."

He follows up with other advice on planning and on maximizing donations. I make notes on my computer so they can't be lost or stuffed in my desk. When he's done, I thank him for his time, hang up, and text Andi: *Good for a committee meeting for the Christmastown event on Saturday?*

She answers back immediately. *Absolutely.*

CHAPTER 18

Matt

The committee meeting is not going as planned.

First, I was late. Traffic on the turnpike. Not my fault but, still, I should have known. When I finally got here, they were all around the dining room table: Andi, Liam, Emma, and Beckham. Oh. And Ruth.

Yeah.

I'd re-rented room two. When I told Ruth about the event, she'd asked to join in.

I said yes, of course. Ruth was harmless and she loved Christmas (she told me this ad nauseum). But she'd come to the meeting with all sorts of Christmas-themed desserts.

It's been distracting.

Right now, Liam is in the kitchen to get milk to go with the cookies. Beckham's deep into a giant piece of chocolate cake. Emma's inspecting Ruth's tiramisu, marveling at how even the layers are. And Andi's eating cookies. A bit of powdery sugar clings to her lips. She's got on a light blue sweater, the same color as her eyes. Her hair is down, her cheeks tinged with pink.

That same natural look she always has. The one I can't get enough of.

Liam returns with the pitcher of milk. He pours everyone a glass like he's refilling beers.

"So maybe we should think about the event," I say. The fact that *I'm* the one keeping us on track says a lot.

"Wait." Liam holds out a hand. "Beckham. Pass over that cake, would you?"

Beckham slides the cake across the table and Liam cuts himself a slice.

"I think we need a longer knife for this tiramisu." Emma hops up, presumably to retrieve the knife.

"Dude, you've got to try the cake." Beckham points at it with his fork.

I ignore the suggestion; Emma returns with the knife for the tiramisu and carves out a piece.

"Any thoughts on the event?" I try. It's my plan to help, not lead. It's one thing to omit to tell Bridget about a Christmas-town fundraiser; it's another to quarterback it.

Liam stabs his cake. "We should have a party. Like the beef and beer, but fancy, at the Scranton Hilton or something. We could get a live band." He sits back a moment. "I've got a friend with a band. Old guys but good music. Call themselves *The Culchies.*"

"Good idea," I say, not meaning it. At all. "But maybe we could do something a little more unique. Something here." I point outside. "That way, investors see the real thing."

I glance at Andi. Her eyes are wide. "But it's a mess," she says. "I love it, but it's nowhere near ready for an event." She twists a lock of hair in her finger. It springs back to a curl when she lets go. "Maybe we should wait for Bridget's study?"

It's a statement. She says it like a question. The words sound timid and I wonder if that's what she meant when she'd told me about how she'd acted around Cole. I'd normally want to agree with her, to boost her confidence the way she deserves, but I can't, obviously, not with this.

"No," I say. "Waiting for the study will take too long. If we get interest in advance, it will only help." No one speaks; I continue. "We don't have to refurbish everything. Only a building or two. If the venue's unique, we'll get people here."

"You think?" Andi tips her head, curls shifting to one side.

"I do. What buildings and rides give the most impact?" I ask quickly, trying to get the topic off waiting for Bridget's study because of the obvious fact that there *is no study*.

"The carousel is in good shape," Liam offers. "Works too."

A quick image of Andi and me walking by that ride materializes. Her favorite one, she'd said. "That's perfect. And sits in between the cookie and toy shops. If we fix up those two buildings, that's all we'd need to do."

"Beckham can do that." Liam looks at his nephew. "Right?"

Beckham's face lights up like he's been given a task to save the world. "Yeah. Sure. And I can get some guys to help."

"Perfect. Thanks." Everyone's looking at me. "Any other thoughts?"

It's silent for a beat.

"You guys should totally get the Santas to come," Beckham says.

"Who are the Santas?" I ask, thinking it's a musical group.

"From Santa camp." Beckham says this in a way that presumes we all know Santa camps are a thing.

"What's a Santa camp?" Andi asks.

"Not *a* Santa camp," Beckham corrects, "*the* Santa camp."

Andi picks up her glass. "What's *the* Santa camp?"

"It's where the mall Santas go to get trained," Beckham explains.

Emma widens her eyes. "Mall Santas get *trained*?"

"Not regular mall Santas. Camp is where the real Santas go.

The ones that want the big gigs, like Macy's in New York. It's a big deal. High-end Santas can pull in $500 per hour."

What? How had I never heard of this? It was like Beckham had revealed some underground society of Christmas cheer. I try to visualize it. I can't.

"How do you know all this?" Andi asks.

"Friends of my parents own the camp. I worked there as a cook a few summers. And let me tell you, those guys can eat."

I laugh. We all do.

"What do they even do there?" I ask.

Beckham leans back in his chair, swipes a pen off the table. "They take classes. Beard care, what to do with crying kids, how to take a good picture." He fiddles with the pen cap. "Oh. And the best one, The Art of the Ho."

"The Art of the Ho." I shake my head. "How many Santas go the camp?"

"Dozens. Maybe a hundred."

"A hundred Santas?" I visualize them all over the property. This is it, John Evans's *bloody unique concept.* "We have to get them. Investors would eat up the idea of a Santa-themed event at a place called Christmastown."

"But if they earn $500 per hour, how can we afford them?" Emma asks.

Killjoy. My first sentiment. She's right. My second.

"Not all of them earn that – only the top ones and that's only at Christmas," Beckham explains. "Those guys are always looking for work off-season. There's a cult of them, a bunch of buddies. They're always looking for an excuse to get together. Plus," he adds, gesturing outside, "this place will be big for their industry. A lot of them will want to get in from the ground up. I'll call my parents' friends. See what I can do." He pauses. "What should I tell them the event is called?"

I look around.

Ruth claps her hands together. "How about Cocktails at Christmastown?"

I nod, impressed. "Pretty good."

"What about Holiday Hoopla?" Emma suggests.

"Festive fiesta," says Andi. "We could get Casa to cater. And hire their juggler."

She winks.

"Maybe we should bring Santa into the name." Liam twirls around his milk glass. "Since that's what we're planning on."

"Good idea." I think of possible names. Santa Party. Santa Soiree. Santa Social. Santa Shindig. Santa Spree. Santa Celebration.

No.

To all of them.

We need a catchy name. One that will make people think twice. One that reflects the type of interactive unique event we're planning.

"How about," I say, "The Santa Games?"

CHAPTER 19

A *ndi*

The day after the committee meeting, Liam's heater stops working. Liam makes plans to stay with his buddy, Sal, until the repairperson can come. I've met Sal. Although in his nineties, it's clear Sal still sees himself as a ladies' man. He stands too close when we talk and smells of heavy aftershave. It's not *that* cold; I offer to stay at the house with Claus.

I was wrong.

It's cold. Somewhat okay during the day; extraordinarily cold at night. The boxy portable heater I bought does nothing to make the place warmer. In fact, I'm pretty sure all it does is blow cold air around. Two days in and I'm done. Claus seems equally unhappy. He's not even up to hissing when I cross his path.

The heating repair company calls.

FOUR more days.

I pick up my cell phone to call my mom (and Jim) -- I know she'll let me and Claus stay with them -- when Matt rings.

"I'm inside of a glacier," I say instead of hello.

"Really? You're getting pretty good reception then."

I laugh and give the heating status.

"Andi, just come here."

He says it naturally like, of course, I would come and stay with him. Like we're the kind of friends that do that sort of thing – put each other up during extreme weather emergencies.

My thoughts scramble. I'd rather stay with Matt than in Liam's icebox house. And, as much as I'd look forward to a long discussion with Jim about the best fishing spots, I'd rather go to Philadelphia than mom's.

BUT.

It's a big but.

BUT I'm sure to run into Whitney, the Barbie-girlfriend. And, even though Matt and I are just friends, I'm not sure how I feel about that.

"I've got the cat," I tell him.

He coughs. "You have *the cat*? How did that happen? Doesn't he hate you?"

I smile. "Listen Catman, just because I don't have a good rapport with Claus doesn't mean I'm going to leave him alone inside an igloo."

He snorts. "That's big of you Andi."

"I'm a kind person."

"Bring him with you."

"No," I say automatically. "I can go to my mom's."

"But you don't like the boyfriend, right? Jim?"

I hesitate. It's not that I don't like Jim. I just never try to get to know the BOMs because they don't stick around for long.

"Come on," Matt urges. "It'll be fun. And we can brainstorm about the event."

* * *

I ARRIVE at Matt's Philadelphia brownstone that afternoon, Claus in a carrier in the back of the car. Getting him inside of it had been a challenge and I've got a slew of scratches on my hands and wrists to prove it.

The home is three stories and narrow, a giant bay window on the second floor. It sits buttressed between identical houses, all with a trio of cement stairs and thick, wooden doors. It's four o'clock, still freezing despite a bright sun. Icy patches shine on the sidewalk.

From the interior of my car, I stare at the house. Doubts worm their way through my psyche. I've only known Matt a short time. And I don't know Steph at all. Plus, I'm here *with a cat*. Who does that? Who shows up at a virtual stranger's house to stay for a few days with a cat? Clearly the cold at Liam's impacted my judgment.

Matt doesn't know I'm here. I could go home right now and make up a reason why I couldn't make it.

Yes.

No.

My indecisive brain is locked. Matt makes the decision for me by swinging open the front door and bounding down the cement stairs. He looks a little bit like a puppy might, excessively excited to see me. His reaction puts me at ease, and I turn off the car and step out. "Hey."

"Hey. You made it."

"Barely." I show him the scratches.

"Man, that bites."

"You mean he bites," I say and pull open the passenger door. Claus, who has been startlingly quiet the whole ride here, starts to loudly meow.

Matt peers over my shoulder. "Hey, Claus."

I look back at him. "I swear, if he stops meowing."

Matt pulls the carrier out. The meowing stops. "I think he just wanted to be out of the car."

"No. He just likes you. Fine, I'll admit it," I say in a mock frustrated tone, "you have a way with cats." I grab my duffel and the bag of Claus's litter supplies. I follow Matt into the house and down a narrow hallway to an eclectic sitting room. An ornate fireplace that looks to be hundreds of years old centers the room, a plush leather couch laden with pillows in front of it. Two overstuffed chairs buttress a round table in the bay window. Framed photos, books, and knickknacks sit inside built-in shelves. Artfully arranged mirrors and paintings adorn the walls. The space has a sophisticated ambiance, but it's homey too.

Matt puts the carrier on the floor and opens the door. Claus stays still inside of it. Matt pets his head, then stands. "Want something to drink? Water, wine?"

"Water's good."

"Go ahead and sit down." He gestures to the couches. "I'll get the water."

"Sure." I sit on the couch and glance at the framed photos on the shelves and tables. Some of Steph, some of Matt, some of their family. There's one of his family and another. Whitney's in that one. Her hair is half up and she's got on a silver jumpsuit that, if I wore it, would make me look like I was in a bad space movie. I marvel for a moment on how exactly symmetrical her face is, like her nose, eyes, and mouth were all measured to be exactly in sync.

I avert my gaze and stare at a smattering of black and white paintings on the wall, all by the same artist, D. Stanek. They have interesting lines and shading and I stand up to get a closer look.

"Love D. Stanek," Matt says, behind me.

I turn in his direction. "They're interesting paintings. I love this whole room."

Matt hands me a glass of water. "Mostly Steph. She's into all the decor stuff."

The front door creaks open. "Ah," Matt says, "there she is now."

Footsteps sound in the hallway. Nervous flutters beat in my chest. Steph had been an intimidating presence in my mind since I'd first seen the pictures of her online. She has an impressive job, an impressive life. And Matt clearly adores her. I have no idea what she thinks of me. I don't even know if she knows I'm here.

She turns into the room dressed in olive-colored jeans, a white blouse, and a clunky gold necklace with giant stones. Her boots have three-inch heels. In contrast, I'm wearing old jeans and plain blue sweater, no jewelry. I look like I tried to find the most boring and uninspired garments ever made. It doesn't help that I'm wearing faux fur lined slip-on shoes, the footwear choice of the very, very cold.

"You must be Andi." Steph advances toward me and gives me a half-hug. "Did you have an okay trip?"

"Yeah. Thanks."

"Where's the cat?" She looks around the space.

"Still in the carrier." I point to the carrier on the floor. Claus has retreated inside. Steph bends down and peers inside. I have this horrid feeling that Claus will leap out and scratch her face.

"He can be mean," I call out at the same time she reaches in and pulls out a completely docile Claus.

I look to Matt. "Catwoman," I mouth, and he laughs.

Still holding Claus, Steph looks to me then steps toward Matt. "Did you give Andi tap water?" He opens his mouth; Steph continues. "Why didn't you get her the wine? I got new pinot. And did you even ask her if she wanted to sit down?"

"I offered the wine," Matt says, sounding exactly like a little brother. "She wanted water. And, yes, I did ask if she wanted to sit down."

"At least give her Evian." She looks to me. "Sorry for my brother. He's a neanderthal. Please sit, and I'll get you some real water." She thrusts Claus into Matt's arms and extricates the water glass from my hand. She shoots Matt a look. "This isn't even cold." She sweeps out of the room.

A smirk creeps on to my face. I look at Matt.

"Well, that's Steph." Using Claus as a prop, he gestures to the couch I'd gotten up from. "You've got to sit now. I'll get in trouble if you don't."

"Of course." I sit. Steph re-enters the room and hands me a bottle of water so cold it feels like it had been stored inside a glacier.

"So," she says, turning to Matt, "you've got to sub in for quizzo tonight."

He sets Claus on the floor. "No. Not again."

Steph fingers her necklace. "Come on, *Les Quizzerables* is going to be there. We got a shot to beat them."

"No. Those people are way too into trivia. Besides, Andi's here." He gestures to me. "We're going to talk about the Christmastown event."

Steph waves her hand dismissively. "You'll have plenty of time for that. And Andi can play." She looks at me and smiles before turning back to Matt. "Please. Potsie and Baker will be there."

Matt bugs his eyes out. "Potsie and Baker are on your trivia team?"

"People like quizzo, Matt."

He looks legitimately dumbfounded, and I wonder, briefly who Potsie and Baker are.

Steph supplies the answer. "Potsie and Baker are Matt's college friends. Potsie made a mint investing in some company called Closers; Baker's heavy into animal rights. Whatever you do, *do not* talk to him about hunting."

I nod. "No hunting talk. Noted."

Steph continues. "Anyway. If you want dirt on Matt, they're the ones you'll want to talk to." She winks in my direction. The small gesture makes me feel a part of the warm dynamic in the room.

Matt looks uncharacteristically flustered. "Come on, Steph. I'm sure Andi –"

Before he can finish the sentiment, Steph turns to me. "Would you want to play a quick game of quizzo and meet Matt's college buddies? It's super fun and relaxed."

Matt snorts; Steph shoots him a look.

"The bar is just around the corner," she continues. "You'll have plenty of time to talk about Christmastown." She tips her head. "You in?"

I glance at Matt. He holds his hands up. "Up to you. I'm game if you are." He lifts his eyebrows. "But, be warned, there is nothing remotely relaxing about Tuesday Trivia at Finnegan's."

CHAPTER 20

A *ndi*

HOURS LATER, Matt and I sit in heavy chairs around a pocked rectangular table with members of Steph's trivia team, *The Quizzly Bears*. The space is dim. An old-fashioned bar made of thick, dark wood lines one side, a mirror behind it. We have on hats constructed to look like snarling bear heads, with faux fur and white teeth. Other teams have similar gimmicks. Members from *Quizzly Business* are wearing Tom Cruise-inspired black sunglasses.

Matt sits between me and Potsie. Baker, the only one *not* in a bear hat (disrespectful of the animals, apparently) sits across from him. The two of them make good-natured jokes about Matt all night. They make fun of him for knowing answers, for not knowing answers, for his beer choice, and for how poorly he'd apparently done at Lafayette College, their *alma mater*. They joke about his college obsession with McDonald's cheeseburgers and call him Grimace. They make fun of his clothes and his hair and a time when he threw up on a child's ride at a theme park. But the joking is clearly in jest, and I can tell how much his friends like him. The easy banter between buddies serves as a portal into Matt's world. I lap it up.

Potsie pushes a half-eaten appetizer tray to the edge of the table. He holds up a pitcher of beer. "Refill?"

Matt shakes his head.

Potsie shoots him a look. "Lightweight."

Matt pushes his chair back. "Oh, here we go."

Potsie looks to me. "Matt can't hold his liquor."

"What about the time –" Baker starts.

"Wait." Steph bangs the table; pencils and plates rattle with the movement. "They're going to announce the winner." She gestures to the bar. Sure enough, the trivia MC is headed toward the microphone, a sheet of paper in his hand.

I stare at my drink. I can't look at Steph without laughing. Even though we all, save Baker, have the bear hats on, hers seems especially silly. Online Steph, the one I'd conjured in my mind, would never sit in a rundown bar wearing a hat made to look like a bear head.

I like the real Steph much better than the person I thought she'd be. I'd expected her to be serious and intimidating; she'd been the opposite. I'm especially touched by her relationship with Matt. Like his friends, she teased him all night, but I can tell she's fiercely protective.

I would not want to get on her wrong side.

The MC steps up to the small microphone. "All right," he says, "time to announce tonight's winners. We got some free drink vouchers on the line." He holds up a stack of blue papers shaped like tickets and waves them over his head. Patrons, including everyone at our table, catcall and applaud. The MC picks up the sheet, shakes it with a dramatic gesture, and scans the contents. "Third place," he starts, "*Quizzly Busi-*

ness." A riot of cheers from the sunglasses-themed table.

"Second place –"

Silence envelopes our table because, of course, whoever didn't get second, got first. I'm personally nervous even though I'd provided no trivia help other than '80s sitcoms. My mother had been obsessed with them.

Steph puts two crossed fingers up in the air. The atmosphere is tense, like there's something way more serious at stake than free drink vouchers. Matt leans over to me. "Told you," he says in my ear.

"*Les Quizzerables.*"

Our table erupts into cheers that drown out the MC's voice announcing *Quizzly Bears* as the winner. Postie and Baker fist bump. Steph gives me and Matt high fives. The MC comes over, claps Matt on the back, and hands him the vouchers.

Matt stands and spreads out the tickets like a fan. "All right all. I'll get the celebratory drinks." He starts toward the bar.

"Don't bring back that crappy beer you drink," Potsie calls after him. Matt waves him off.

He walks, no saunters, toward the bar. I admire how good he looks in his jeans because, friend or no friend, it's hard not to notice. Then I see her at the bar. Whitney. Smiling at his front the same way I'm smiling at his rear side.

My heart slows. I knew I'd run into her if I came to Philadelphia. And I know Matt and I are just friends. It wouldn't be good for me to date someone so soon after the Cole debacle anyway. That is the opposite of what I need.

I *know* all this.

But a piece of me was having fun with imaginary what ifs. Wildly unlikely what ifs like what if Matt wanted to date me too?

Whitney plants a kiss on his cheek for so long there's an outline of her lipstick after. Matt wipes at it with his thumb but it's still there, like a brand. She's wearing black skinny jeans and a blouse with so many buttons undone, the top of her bra is visible (black and lacy from what I can tell). Her hair's pulled into a ponytail that looks more sophisticated than athletic.

She playfully pulls the bear hat off Matt's head and pops it on her own. It actually looks good on her, like she's about to do a television piece on the wilderness.

I'm staring. I shouldn't be. But it's like watching two perfect humans interact, and I can't look away.

A hand grips my shoulder. I jerk around and register Steph. My face heats. There's no way she didn't just see me staring at Matt and Whitney. "Hey," I say lamely.

"That woman," she tips her glass toward Whitney, "she loves my brother."

"Yeah," I say, doing my best to sound unfazed and like the feelings of jealousy I have, but shouldn't have, are not zinging in my chest. "Why's that?" I don't know why I ask the question. I know the answer. Matt's gorgeous and fun but, deeper than that, he's a quality person. One that's kind and humble and genuine. One that's easy to talk to, easy to confide in. Any girl would love him.

Steph interrupts my internal Mattfest. "Who knows?" she says with a shrug like she can't possibly fathom it. "Little brother can be pretty charming when he wants to be."

"Charming, yeah." Don't I know it.

She leans forward. "He's putting himself out there with this Christmastown venture, you know," she whispers.

"I know," I say and try to figure out if she means this as a positive for Matt or a warning to me, but before I can think much about it, she speaks again.

"You and Liam are serious, right? About the venture?"

"Yes, of course."

"I thought so," she says and shifts her gaze in Matt's direction. "I look out for him. He's," she stops and swings her head back to me, "he's a good person. Sometimes puts his heart before his head, you know."

"Yeah," I say, half wishing she had said he was a terrible person. Steph loving Matt so much makes me care that much more about him.

Matt walks toward the table with a tray of drinks, Whitney on his heels with two more. Even in spiked turquoise pumps, the kind most women couldn't walk two steps in, she looks like she's gliding. She's almost as tall as Matt.

Matt gives out beer to his friends and a martini to Steph. He calls Steph "mama bear" and his friends "the jerks." When he gets to me, he says, "and for Andi, the beautiful artist, a margarita." He places a sugar-rimmed glass in front of me. It's watermelon flavored, same as I'd had at Casa.

"Thank you." I'm not surprised by the gesture. It's that kind of thoughtfulness, Matt remembering how I like my margaritas, that makes him so likable.

He sits down; Whitney pulls up a chair next to his. I'm not introduced, not formally, and finally I wave at her and say, "I'm Andi."

"Whitney." She extends a hand with perfectly manicured fingernails. I shake it.

Conversations start around me, but I don't know the people or the places and end up sitting silent, like the worst wet blanket on earth. Whitney touches Matt's body an excessive amount, pushing at his shoulder, slapping his knee, even ruffling his hair once. Of course, it's fine. Fine. I just get tired of looking at it.

Matt tries to include me – of course he does because he's *nice* – but it's awkward because he has to catch me up on so much of the background of all the stories and we end up yelling "what?" across the table at each other.

I'm relieved when he suggests we leave. He doesn't invite Whitney to come; I'm glad. The public Matt-Whitney show is bad; I can't imagine how it would play out in the privacy of his house. Not something I need to see right now.

Matt doesn't say goodbye to her, not expressly, which strikes me as odd. I wonder, briefly, if they'd had an argument. I hope it's not about me staying over. I open my mouth to say something - maybe he should to offer to drive her home - but Matt speaks first.

"I think we should go to Jake and Joe's for breakfast tomorrow."

CHAPTER 21

M*att*

Bundled in sweaters and coats, Andi and I walk to Jake and Joe's the next morning. I pull open the thick oak door; Andi slips inside.

Jake, the cook and one of the owners, calls from a massive griddle in front of a long stretch of counter. "Hey, Matt. Sit anywhere." He gestures to the smattering of tables, all black and old, each adorned with a metal napkin holder and a laminated menu that hasn't changed since the place opened.

Bacon-infused steam rises from the griddle surface. When I'm alone, I sit at the counter, chatting with Jake and Joe, getting more refills on my coffee than could possibly be helpful. But today I want Andi to myself, so I pick a table toward the back. Andi slides into a seat and plucks the menu from the silver stand. She sets it in front of her; wild curls fall around her face. "What's good?"

"Depends on what you like."

"Everything." She smiles. "Everything breakfast," she clarifies.

"Well. If you like pancakes at all, the ones here are an experience. They're massive." I point at Jake. He's flipping a pancake the size of a dinner plate with two spatulas.

Andi does a double-take. "That is the biggest pancake I have ever seen."

"I know. They're crazy."

"Well, I'm in." She slaps her hand down.

"Impressive. I'll get one too."

When the server arrives, we order the exact same thing: THE pancake, a large orange juice, coffee. Not exactly a big coincidence given they are likely the most popular breakfast foods on the planet. Still. Another point in the column of compatibility.

Andi glances around the space. "What are all these photographs?"

"Obscure sports," I tell her. "Joe is one of the owners and his wife, Maureen, is a photographer. She covers them for a magazine." I look around, take in the pictures I'm used to seeing through Andi's eyes. Under each photograph is a framed explanation of the sport. Some are obvious by their name like Ice Yachting and Underwater Rugby. Others, like Gaffelhangen, a competition to see who can hang by their arms on a pitchfork the longest, are a little harder to believe. I see Andi's eyes stop at the Gaffelhangen photo, two boys at sunset gripping inverted pitchforks lodged between the strips of old monkey bars. I nod toward the photo. "You think you could do that?"

"Could I hang on a pitchfork? Sure. You?"

"Of course."

"What about that?" She points to a photo of Flaming Puck Unicycle Hockey. "That looks fun."

I glance at the picture, then back at Andi. "Chasing around a flaming puck on a unicycle looks fun?"

"You're surprised?"

I sit back and look like I'm thinking, hard, about her question. "No," I say, "now that I think about it, you have all the qualities of a Flaming Puck Unicycle Hockey enthusiast."

She tips her head. "And those would be?"

"A risk taker. Maybe a little off."

She swats my forearm. "A little off?"

"You do live in an amusement park."

She smirks. "Fair." Her eyes scan the photos. "How about you? Which of these sports would you try?"

I point to a photograph of two giant boats shaped like dragons. "I've done dragon boating."

"Hmmm." She stares at the picture. "Looks like crew. Not that impressive."

"It's not like crew," I insist, teasing. "There are two rows of seats, and we use oars, not paddles. Plus, the boat looks like a dragon. It's a completely different concept."

"The object is to row down a river the fastest as a team. Sounds pretty identical to crew." A smile hints at the corners of her mouth. She leans back. "But good for you. Not everyone can be a risk-taking Flaming Puck Unicycle Hockey player."

I laugh. "Well, I expect to be invited to your next meet. Or is it match?"

"It's a game, Matt," she says, her expression deadpan.

Jake personally delivers our pancakes, each of which, as promised, are close to a foot in diameter. "I put on some extra powdered sugar." He moves toward his griddle, his back to Andi, and winks. The gesture makes me realize that, despite having eaten here at least weekly for years, I've never brought a girl other than Steph. It wasn't intentional. I'd just never thought any girl I was dating – or friends with – would be into Jake and Joe's. But it hadn't once occurred to me that Andi wouldn't like the place. In fact, when she'd accepted my invitation to stay, one of the first things I thought is how much I wanted to take her here.

She slices off an impressive piece of pancake, swirls it in syrup, and pops it in her mouth.

"So," I ask, "any thoughts on the event?"

"We'll have it in six weeks?"

"Yeah." I stab the pancake with my fork.

"And you're sure that's enough time?"

It's not enough time. Not by any stretch of the imagination. Events like this are typically planned months in advance, some over a year. But the longer I keep the secret, the greater chance Bridget will find out about the event and shut it down. We need to move fast. "It's enough time," I lie and stuff the pancake in my mouth.

"Okay. Here's my thought." She pauses. "Don't laugh."

I swallow and point my fork at her. "Why would I laugh?"

"I don't know, it might sound dumb. Anyway. What about a scavenger hunt, one for kids, one for adults? The kid hunt could lead to activities for the kids run by Beckham's Santas, and the adult hunt could lead to different presentations about the park, sketches of the new attractions. It's a game. Get it? The Santa Games."

"Wow." The word blows out of me without context. A scavenger hunt is exactly the kind of "bloody unique" concept Steph's friend John Evans had been talking about.

Andi swipes her juice glass off the table. "Is that a nice wow or a wow wow?"

"It's a wow wow. I love it. It's interactive. It's fun. And it gets potential investors all over the property." I pause. "In fact, wow wow wow."

She lifts an eyebrow. "Only three wows?"

"Okay. Wow to the tenth."

She twirls a lock of hair. "Not sure what that comes to in numerical terms, but I'll take it."

She smiles and we ping more ideas back and forth. A Santa class. A craft station. Food carts. There'd be no talks or speeches; instead, investors and their families would view the property at their leisure, like a fair. The more we talk, the faster the ideas come. Andi pulls a notebook out of her purse and furiously scribbles, her pen swirling around on the page. Done writing, she looks up at me. A beam of light from the window illuminates her face and highlights the blue of her eyes, the bits of blonde streaks in her hair. I stare without meaning to, surprised by the romantic jolt. I've done an effective job of staying in the friend zone since Andi had told me about the Cole break-up. Even when she was in the brownstone in fuzzy pajamas with cat acrobats on them (silly but attractive). And when she'd been wearing the bear hat during quizzo (adorable). And every time I caught her, unsuccessfully, trying to win over Claus (also adorable).

Okay.

Maybe my thoughts have, on occasion, strayed away from friendship, but this moment, looking at Andi in the sunlight at Jake and Joes, feels more substantial. We'd spent the night together which isn't like spending *the night* together but, still, I know how she looks without make-up (beautiful), how she takes her coffee (with a dash of milk, no sugar), and if she drinks wine before bed (yes, one half glass, white). I've seen her look uncomfortable, like she did at Finnegans last night, and when she looks exactly herself, right now. I've learned that she's not fussy about pets or dishes in the sink and that she only ever wears bright red toenail polish because, "if you're going to go to that effort, you've got to go big." She plays Words with Friends with her brother, four games at a time, and decorates online fish tanks with her niece. She's *not* a morning person.

So, yeah, when the beam of sunlight hits her face, I see a different Andi than the one from before, one with more layers peeled back.

And I like every one of them.

"What?" Andi moves her head out of the sunlight.

The moment isn't broken entirely but I'm pulled out of my thoughts enough to speak.

"Nothing." I wave and look down at our plates. Neither of us has finished, but we've both made a pretty good dent. "Impressive showing for a newbie."

"Not done yet." She takes a forkful and pops it in her mouth. "Okay. Now I'm done."

I pay the bill, say goodbye to Jake and Joe, and we spill out on to the sidewalk. "What did you think?"

"Perfect. It's the kind of homey, different place that I love." We fall into step together. The sun is bright despite the cold and our breath comes out in smoky wisps as we walk. We sidestep a man cleaning up after his dog. She angles her head toward me. "I'm surprised you like it though."

I put my hand over my chest like I've been horribly insulted. "Why?"

She tucks her hands into her coat pockets. "I figured you'd go someplace more upscale."

I glance at her. "What gave you that impression?"

"Hmm," she says, teasing. "Maybe the black-tie galas or the skiing in Vail or the European vacations."

I nod. "Fine but, so you know, I don't need something fancy to have a good time."

She stops and squints in my direction. "Is that right?"

"Of course. I can have a good time on any budget."

Andi tucks a lock of hair behind her ear, a hint of a smile on her lips.

"*Any* budget," I say. "Come on. Give me one."

She leans against the brick of a storefront. "Give you what?"

"A budget. I'll plan a night for us. I'll show you. I, Matt Taylor, can plan an epic night without spending a lot."

The hint of a smile gets broader. "Epic? Okay. Stakes raised. You're on. Sixty bucks."

"Sixty bucks? I can do *loads* with sixty bucks. Easy." I stop, think about all we need to do to get The Santa Games off the ground. "But we should wait until after the event. It'll be like a celebration."

"The Sixty Dollar Soiree," she says, her hand underscoring the air. "You're on." She thrusts her hand forward then pulls it back. "Wait. What do I get if you can't do it?"

I cross my arms across my chest and smile at her. "Andi, Andi, Andi. There's no way I'm going to let that happen."

"But if it does?"

"I owe you sixty bucks."

She offers her hand. "Deal."

CHAPTER 22

ndi

A It's April, two weeks to the May event. It's a warm evening, the kind that promises summer. Beckham and his buddies, all of whom look like they should be skiing or surfing or both, sit in cheap folding chairs around a makeshift bonfire. They've been working diligently on refurbishing the toy store and the bake shop. The past few nights, they've stayed to blow off steam afterward. I make my way to the party.

Laughter, conversation, and the steady beat of country music fills the air. Big-bulbed colored lights on the surrounding evergreens illuminate the space. Liam stands behind a flaming grill, a spatula poised his hand. A thick aroma of hot dogs and burgers waft from the flames. He looks energetic and younger, almost like he stepped into a time warp and came out a decade earlier.

My phone pings, and I glance at a text from Matt. It's a photograph of a dozen people sitting on a body of water inside giant cut-out pumpkins with oars and the caption, West Coast Giant Pumpkin Regatta. Matt's text reads: *Just another version of crew?*

I laugh and respond, my fingers flying over the keys. *Yes! Row to the finish line first. Same objective. Same sport.*

He sends a laughing emoji and writes. *See you tonight.*

Matt's coming to check on the progress. We've seen each other a few times since Philadelphia. And we've continued the near nightly phone calls and the occasional distance "Wheel" watching. I look forward to these slices of Matt like dessert. It's not healthy and I know I should try to adjust my attitude. Not take every call. Not immediately answer every text. Not think about him ALL.THE.TIME. But I can't do it. My emotions are like a river current, carrying me along like a stray leaf on the water's surface, and I know, I *know*, I'm heading for the falls. Still, I can't wait until he gets here.

I approach the group. "Hey Andi," Beckham says, pointing at me with a hot dog, "some guy was looking for you."

"Matt?"

"No. Said he knew you from New York." He looks around. "Wait. He's back there. Talking to Em." He shifts his hot dog and points it in the direction of the carousel.

I shift my glance from Beckham to the space behind carousel. I can make out Emma in the fading light, arms motioning. I can't see the guy and take a few steps forward.

Oh.

I stop, shocked. My breath catches.

Emma's talking to Cole.

I creep closer and crouch behind one of the carousel reindeer.

Emma's tone is angry. "Go home, Fabio."

Cole shakes his head at the nickname, one I know he hates. "I need to talk to her."

"You lost that chance."

Memories flood my mind. Me, standing behind that pungent sausage truck, watching Cole kiss another woman. Cole's unkind words, and the remnants of feeling, for months, like the boring, uninspired wallflower he said I was. I remember how it felt when I slid the engagement ring off my finger. I'd left it on his bathroom sink in front of a glop of toothpaste.

"It's a good opportunity, Emma." He sounds pretentious. His feet root to the ground. "I'm not leaving." He crosses his arms.

"Why don't you text her, if you're so sure she'll talk to you."

"She blocked my number."

"Exactly."

The argument goes on; I can't focus on it. Cole is here. When we'd first broken up, I'd replayed how I would respond if I saw him again. In my dreams, I'd said something different each time, but it was always on point, always about how I'd been wronged. And I had been wronged. What Cole did was shitty and unforgivable and cowardly. I know that. I'm just less angry about it now.

I step from behind a painted reindeer. "Cole?"

He turns his head and the long black hair I'd once found so sexy whips with the movement.

"Andi. I've been looking for you." Though the phrase is innocuous, his tone is pretentious. Had he always sounded that way?

"I told him you're busy," Emma retorts, hands on her hips.

I flash Emma a smile. "It's okay."

She takes a step toward me like a guard.

"I can talk to Cole, Em," I add.

"All right," she says slowly. "But I'll be right over there." She points to the bonfire. "We *all* will." She emphasizes the word all as if Beckham and his group of surfer dudes would chase Cole off the property. Actually, they might.

Emma's feet crunch against fallen leaves and, when she's sufficiently far away, I take in Cole. He looks the same. Same hair. Same black-brown eyes. Same build, wiry and strong. He's got on his theatre wear – black t-shirt, black jeans. I expect to feel something. Longing. Anger. Nostalgia. Instead, it's surreal. Like Cole isn't standing in the shadow of Christ-mastown.

"This is interesting." He gestures his hands around. I can't tell if the remark is meant to be sarcastic. This is the kind of place Cole might have made fun of as "commercial" or "basic." But there's enough uniqueness that he might be sincere.

"How," he starts, and I thrust my hand out. I know where he's going. How did I end up here? What am I doing? What are my plans? I'm not about to tell him any of it.

I ignore the clear question in his remark. I'm not about to give an explanation or start spewing off any dreams I might have about this place. "What are you doing here?"

He looks down. "I have an opportunity for you. For us."

"For *us*?" I take a step backward.

He waves his hands. "Not us us," he clarifies and I'm not sure the quickness of his response makes things better. "It's an opportunity for you as a set designer." He goes on to explain the offer starting with a friend of a friend who had seen my designs for my last show, *Something Gained*. He loved them, apparently. There's another acquaintance and a relative involved before Cole gets to the punchline: I've been invited to submit set designs for a new play, *A Walk in the Park*. On The West End.

In London.

My mouth drops open. Anything I've ever done is minus-cule, even *Something Gained* was off-Broadway. Off-off-Broadway actually.

"They're looking for someone fresh," Cole says by way of explanation.

I sit on the edge of the carousel. Cole moves next to me in a way that's too familiar. I inch away, and he must get the picture because he moves an equivalent distance in the other direction. We stare at each other a moment. I wonder if he has any regrets that things ended.

There's raucous laughter from the bonfire and I glance back before returning my gaze to Cole. "What's in it for you?"

"For me?"

"You said it was an us opportunity." I pick up a stick and twirl it in between my fingers. "Where's the you part?"

"Oh. Right." He cast his eyes downward. "They might need help with theatre management."

"But," I start, because Cole already is a theatre manager.

"The West Riding is under new management," he says quickly.

Oh. It clicks into place. Cole needs a job. The opportunity is not an us opportunity. It's a me opportunity. That Cole wants to capitalize on. The irony is not lost on me. Cole is hoping to get a job on my coattails. *Following* me. It's the kind of scenario I might have dreamed up months ago, the big "ah-ha" moment where I prove Cole all wrong. Only I don't want to anymore. More importantly, I don't need to. It doesn't matter. I don't care what Cole is doing or what he thinks of me. I'm not even sure I want the job.

"Can I forward you the information?" he asks. He stands up and brushes debris off his jeans. He looks comically miffed by the dirt.

I stand. "It can't hurt to look." I do my best to sound non-committal.

"It's a great opportunity, Andi."

The way he says it makes it seem like I'm the same old Andi, always a follower, never taking a chance. Anger flashes through me. I'm *not* that girl. "It's my opportunity, Cole," I say firmly. "I'll decide if it's right for me."

He doesn't move. In his black clothes, he looks like a shadow, the image accentuated by the bright backdrop of the colorfully lit evergreens. "I'm sorry how things ended," he says finally.

I'm not sure how to take this. Other than to ask for his

deposit money back, he hasn't spoken to me in months. Now that he needs me for something, he's sorry.

I don't need his apology.

"Thanks for coming by Cole." I look directly in his eyes. "I'll let you know if I decide to put in a design for *A Walk in the Park.*"

I turn on my heel and walk away from him.

CHAPTER 23

M*att* I find Andi on the platform of the Sky Ornament Ride. She's sitting against the railing, knees pulled to her chest, her face illuminated by a bright moon. She's got on an oversized University of Scranton sweatshirt, an index finger wrapped around her hair.

I sit across from her. "Hey."

"Hey." She unwraps her finger and her curl bounces back, a shiny coil.

I set down the small cooler I'd brought and sit across from her. Emma told me Cole had been here. "I heard you had a visitor."

She pulls her sweatshirt over her hands. "Yeah. Quite a surprise."

"I can imagine." I want to ask more. I want to know why he was here. If he said anything to hurt her. Or if he wants her back. But none of it seems appropriate for me to ask. I pop open the cooler and wait for her to supply the details she's comfortable with.

"He didn't want to get back together," she says.

The words come out matter of fact, not edged with emotion. Relief swells through me. I'm glad Andi doesn't seem hurt and, well, if she's over Cole –

I don't go there.

I can't let myself go there.

This whole friend thing is delicate. I can't mess it up with a misunderstanding. I pull two beers from the cooler and hand her one.

Andi grips it. "He had information about a job opportunity."

"A good one?"

"Pretty good. It's not an actual job. Just an invitation to apply for one."

I take a swig of beer, set the bottle next to me. "And will you?"

She hesitates. I hope she's not going to turn this opportunity down over Christmastown when there's no guarantee of an investor. I can't let that happen. "You should apply," I say decisively.

She points at me with her beer bottle. "You don't even know what I'm applying for." There's a trace of amusement in her voice. "What if the opportunity is being a wild animal trainer?"

"Or the newest member of the US Extreme Ironing Team?"

"Right. Or maybe I'm applying to be a tightrope walker, you know, like one of those people who walks across the Grand Canyon on a wire."

I whistle. "Whoa. That would be hard to watch."

She leans forward and slaps my leg. "Well imagine doing it! You've been cavalier with your advice here, Matt. You could be encouraging me to apply for virtually anything."

"True. Sorry." I swipe my beer from the platform. "What is it then? This job?"

"It's an invitation to apply to do a set design for a new production."

I slap my beer down. "That's fantastic."

"It's in London."

Oh.

I force my face into a smile. "Even more impressive."

She smiles, pride evident in her features. "Apparently, some friend of a friend of someone liked the designs for the last play I did."

"I have no doubt." I clink my bottle against the neck of hers. "Congratulations."

"Thanks."

I want to ask if she thinks she'll get the job, if she plans to take it if she does. But then, of course she would. And she should. I know that. I just don't want her to. I force the thought from my mind and look toward the renovated area. "Things are looking good."

She follows my gaze. Flickering lights from the firepits cast light on the carousel and nearly completed toy and bake shops. Amazingly, they look identical to those in Andi's sketches.

"Sometimes I can't believe it's happening," she says. "It like a storybook scene come to life."

"It looks like a storybook scene. You should be proud, Andi. This was all you and Liam, your vision."

She takes a sip of beer. "No. If it weren't for you, all we'd have is a bunch of rundown buildings and a couple thousand bucks from the beef and beer. This –" she angles her bottle toward the illuminated space "—is as much because of me and Liam as it is because of you. You're the one who got everyone fired up. You're the one who thought of The Santa Games. This is something you should be proud of too, Matt. You're the captain of this ship."

"Thanks," I manage but my stomach drops. I'm still worried about Bridget, about the lie – okay lies – and about my current role as the worst double-agent of all time. I can usually push it out of my head, believe that it will all work out in the end. But hearing Andi call me out as "the captain of this ship" is disconcerting.

She bumps my foot with hers. "Earth to Matt."

I blink. "Sorry. Lost in thought there for a moment."

"Well, I have some fun gossip," she says, "if you're ready."

I sit up, liking the change of topic. "Fun gossip. Okay."

"Liam's dating someone."

I process the statement. Liam's dating someone? "Who?"

"You'll never guess." She purses her lips; her eyes are smiling. She looks like she might burst.

"Well," I say after a moment, "are you going to tell me?"

She tilts her head. "Mmm. What's in it for me?"

I smile and gesture to her now empty beer bottle. "I already gave you that drink."

She holds up the bottle. "One drink. For this juicy intel? I don't think so."

"Okay." I put my fingers on my chin like I'm thinking, hard, about an offer. "What if I promised you a juggling act?"

"But I've already seen you juggle."

"It could be a private juggling act."

"A private juggling act? That does sound promising."

"With refreshments," I add. "And more beer."

She smiles and her whole face lights up. "Philly cheesesteaks."

"If that's what it takes."

"Okay," she says after a moment. "Done." She schooches across the platform on her rear-end and holds out her hand.

I shake it and, without meaning to, I inhale her scent. I forget about Liam's new girlfriend until Andi says the name.

"It's Ruth."

My mouth drops open. "Ruth?"

"Yup. It's adorable. She brings him pies and gobs of those Yuletide cookies. They cook a lot together. He's gained five pounds at least. And he's teaching her to play chess."

I lean back. "Ruth and Liam. That's so cool." I think about Ruth, how happy she would be to have someone to spoil besides her sporadic tenants and Rolo. "Does she bring her little dog around?"

"Rolo? All the time. Claus hates him. Maybe even more than he hates me."

"I doubt that Andi."

She waves off the comment.

"Has Ruth crocheted anything for you yet?" I ask.

To date, Ruth has given me a crocheted toilet paper cover holder (Steph was *not* amused when I put it in our bathroom), a set of four crocheted coasters, and a something she called a "scrubby duster."

Andi rolls her eyes with a smile. "She's making a prototype for a crocheted Santa-face keychain to sell at the park."

We both laugh. She moves so we are sitting side by side, our backs against the wooden railings. Her outstretched legs touch mine. She turns her head and looks at me.

The moment feels intimate.

Then she screams.

CHAPTER 24

M*att*

"Oh my God!"

Andi jumps up and I see the licks of red and orange.

Christmastown is on fire.

"Shit!"

I leap to my feet and bolt down the wooden stairs, two three at a time. I sprint toward the rising flames, Andi's panicked breaths behind me. Thick smoke permeates the air. Sickening cracks of tree branches succumbing to flames sound over upbeat country music.

No.

No. No. No. No. No.

This could not be happening.

I reach the fire, breathless. Andi's not behind me anymore. I see her outline, running on the outskirts. I call out, but my voice is lost in the din of Beckham's friends. She disappears in a haze of smoke, her figure obscured by flames and people and chaos. Someone shoots water from a hose by Liam's house, the water stream ludicrously far from the flames.

My heart plummets and I swipe a water bottle out of a nearby cooler. I wrench off the cap and uselessly throw the contents on the flames. Guys, half-obscured by the smoke and haze, run with a cooler full of water and dump it. There's a momentary hiss on a small part of the flame's edge before the rest of it flames higher, like a punishment for insolence.

Liam appears out of nowhere with a kitchen fire extinguisher. He holds it, tight, gnarly fingers gripped around the release lever. A violent spray of chemicals shoots out; Liam falls backward. I sprint forward, grab the extinguisher, aim the nozzle at the moving edge of the flames. I cough; my eyes tear up from smoke.

I'm horrified. Helpless. The flames are, thank God, a distance from Liam's house. But the main buildings for Christmastown, the renovated ones, are an ember away from igniting.

Sirens wail. I whip my head toward the sound. A giant fire engine hurtles up the drive, lights flashing. A police car follows, and an ambulance, the driveway a sea of blue and red flashing lights.

The firetruck pulls to a stop and a man in a flame retardant firefighter coat sprints toward the fire, arms gesticulating. "Everyone back! Everyone back!" Men and women in hard hats and fire gear leap off the truck, grab at its hose, and pull it toward the flames.

Dumbstruck, I stay in place with Liam's extinguisher, uselessly spraying the edge of the fire. A firefighter puts her hand across my chest. "Stand back, sir." She extricates the extinguisher from my hand, and I stumble backward. A jet of water spray from the fire engine hose flies toward the flames; liquid shoots out in a heavy, forceful stream. A team fights to hold the hose in place, a giant, writhing snake of liquid.

I move further back behind the buildings. I stand with Beckham's shocked crew, all of us covered with grime and sweat.

Smoke billows; the fire burns with awful snaps and cracks of wood and branches. Country music still blares.

I look for Andi through the haze. I see her, near Liam's house. Her eyes are wide, streaks of sooty tears on her cheeks. I run toward her. "Oh, God, Andi, I'm sorry." I put my arms around her shoulders and squeeze, my face close to her ear. "I don't think anyone is hurt," I say and pray to God it's true. It feels like the fire is my fault. If I hadn't insisted on this event, none of this would be happening.

"This is so awful." Andi says the words without looking at me, her eyes fixed on the firefighters holding the still-writhing hose.

We stand, watching, like the nightmare is unfolding in a movie or an immersive experience at an amusement park.

But it's real.

I scan the area for anyone that looks hurt. Medics stand with their ambulance; I can't see what they're doing. Emma's arms are wrapped around Beckham, her face illuminated by ambulance headlights. I catch the edge of Liam's form behind the toy store and let out a breath at the sight of him. He looks fine but who knows? How much smoke did he inhale? Did any of us?

A second ambulance speeds up the drive. Eventually, both Andi and I are examined by an EMT. A police officer asks questions of two guys behind me. The dissipating smoke and dying embers and varied uniformed personnel make the space look like what it is: a major accident scene. My mind swims with what-ifs: What if someone got hurt? What if the flames had gotten out of control? What if Liam had lost his home? The attorney in me worries about a lawsuit.

Andi falls into my chest, and I wrap my arms around her. Her heart pounds; her hair smells like smoke. It's unreal. Less than an hour ago, we were talking about Ruth and Liam on the platform of the Sky Ornament Ride.

Less than an hour ago, I thought I might kiss her.

She exhales, her breath on my chest. I hug her close, put my mouth near her ear. "It'll be okay," I whisper.

I can only hope it's true.

CHAPTER 25

M *att*

I call into work Monday and let my assistant know that I'll be working in the Scranton office. There's too much going on post-fire. No one who'd been present seems to have any injuries other than the handful of first-degree burns treated on site. Still, Liam's old and I'm afraid there might be some aftermath of the smoke inhalation. And I don't want Andi to be sick either.

I'm at Christmastown now, eating a late lunch with Liam and Andi. It's silent, our mutual attention on the two fire inspectors patrolling the site in heavy boots. One takes pictures; the other puts ash and dirt in vials.

"I guess they're trying to figure out the cause of the fire," I say.

"It was the bonfire," Liam says. "I could tell them that."

Andi gets up, retrieves a pitcher from the refrigerator and pours all of us more tea. It's awkward. None of us have brought up The Santa Games even though the event is supposed to take place in two weeks. We could still hold it. None of the buildings were severely impacted. Still, it's like the water and chemicals that doused the fire simultaneously put out our momentum for the project. Kind of like the old adage: it's all fun and games until someone's property is almost burned to a crisp.

Day two post-fire, I sit at my desk at the Scranton office of Quinn Gifford. I can't find too much to do, it's not like any of my files or cases are here. I need to either go back to Philadelphia (which I don't want to do for obvious reasons) or hold the The Santa Games (which I also don't want to do due to the unmistakable cosmic warning of having a *fire* at the venue).

I pull open the top drawer of my desk and my only fidget toy here, a yellow squish ball filled with a gel-like liquid, rolls to the side. I clutch it in my fist.

"Ms. Quinn. I wasn't expecting you!" The receptionist's voice rings out, her tone a combination of alarm and surprise.

I sit up straight, like a kid who'd been caught daydreaming in class. Bridget is *here*. I grip the squish ball, hard. It bursts inside my hand. I drop the remnants under my desk and brush the gross liquid from inside of it on my pants. Crap.

"Yes," Bridget responds, her voice honey-smooth, "this is an impromptu visit." She pauses, and I picture her lips pressed together in a half smile. "Does Matt Taylor happen to be in?"

I don't listen for the receptionist's response. Instead, I immaturely think about how I can escape before she walks down the hall. There's no way. My window is four floors up and there's only one door. Which swings open, Bridget in its frame.

I'm not sure what I was expecting. That she'd have steam coming out of her ears, or lasers shooting from her eyes, or that she'd look bigger and tougher than the undeniably petite older woman in the doorway. She looks unintimidating too, dressed in a fitted beige suit. It's almost like she's breezed into town for an early spring wedding.

She edges into the office with a smile. Maybe this isn't what I think it is. Maybe the "impromptu visit" has nothing to do with the fire. I let out a breath.

She shuts the door; the smile fades. "May I have a word?" She reaches into the oversized tan bag slung over her shoulder and produces a newspaper. She spreads Sunday's edition of *The Scranton Times* across my desk, smooths wrinkles in the paper with manicured fingers. The headline: *Fire at Christmastown.* Under it is a half-page black and white photograph of Liam struggling with the fire extinguisher, flames inches from his sneakered feet. Mrs. Claus's Bake Shop stands in the backdrop, and it looks as if Liam is singlehandedly preventing the fire from overtaking a building constructed out of cookies. And, just to make the photo more perfect, my face and body are clear in the background, my arms dormant, my mouth a wide "o". It must have been taken the moment before I'd stepped in.

Bridget taps on Liam's image. "My father was put in a position to put out a fire?" Her voice is cool, but anger pulsates under the words.

"No. No. I helped with that. We all did. And the fire department came."

"So, I understand." She sits, swipes the paper from the desk, and reads snippets from the article. "Unattended firepits." "A raucous party." "Inebriated individuals."

"Liam's grand-nephew, Beckham, was there with some friends. They had a bonfire. It got out of control."

"Yes. I'm familiar with Beckham." She says his name with distaste. "He's my second cousin. Not someone I'd put around an open flame, I'll say that."

She pauses. It's uncomfortable. I don't know if she's just upset about the fire or if she knows about the event. I tell myself it doesn't matter. I'm an adult. Liam is an adult – her father. If he wants to hold an investor event for *his* property, what Bridget thinks or wants shouldn't matter.

But I know it does.

Bridget can help.

And Liam wants her support.

Plus, she's Andi's employer, not Liam, so, again, I've put her job in jeopardy. I know Andi doesn't intend for the job to be long-term, but I don't want my lack of double agenting skills to alter her time frame.

I swallow hard and wait, hoping that this undercurrent of anger is, rightfully, about the fire. I'm about to assure her that Liam is all right when she flaps the paper with a flourish. "According to Beckham Quinn," she starts, "he and his work crew have been readying the property for a *huge*," she looks up at me for effect, "event for weeks. The aim of the showcase, coined The Santa Games, is intended to find investors for Christmastown." She sets the papers down and lifts an eyebrow.

I shift in my seat like a chastised schoolboy. I'm no stranger to stern talks from authority figures, but this moment is worse than all the dean-principal-RA-parent-manager talks combined.

"What, exactly, is going on?" She meets my eyes in a way that makes it impossible to avert her gaze.

"Liam's planning an event."

"Yes. An event for Christmastown. After you expressly told me nothing was planned. Numerous times."

It's not a question. It's a statement. One I can't deny.

"Liam would like to see if there is any interest in the venture," I manage.

Bridget's eyes widen and she sits on the chair across from me. Her polished facade breaks; worry stretches across her features. "Matt." She says my name like a long breath. "I've told you, in great detail, about my concerns with my father and the ideas he gets in his head." She leans forward. "I've lived through his schemes. Many times. And while it might seem cruel that I've been working against him, I swear it's for his own good."

She leans back. The light from the window catches her eyes and all the humanness I don't normally attribute to Bridget Quinn reflects back. She doesn't look cold and calculated. She looks like a daughter legitimately worried about her dad.

"How far are you along in all this?" she asks finally.

"For the event?" I clarify.

"Yes."

"There's still a lot to do," I say honestly. "But I've got some investors interested in attending. The venue, Christmastown, is clearly the big draw and that's all ready."

Bridget leans back and crosses her arms. She shuts her eyes, clearly thinking. "Okay." Her eyes fly open. "Proceed with the event. In fact, email me the information. I'll see who I can line up. If Dad wants to see if this can work, let him. I suspect no one is going to want to put substantial money into a theme park in the middle of Pennsylvania which is only relevant one month a year."

"But –" I open my mouth to explain the ideas Liam has to make it more of a year-round destination, then shut it. I'm getting what I want; no reason to ruin things.

"And don't think," she continues, "that me temporarily supporting this event means I'm okay with you lying. I trusted you, Matt."

She meets my eyes; guilt oozes through my body.

She stands and smooths out her skirt. "We'll see how things go." I don't know if she means with me or with the event or both. "I'll see you at The Santa Games."

CHAPTER 26

ndi

In the morning, Matt tumbles down the stairs at Liam's house. His hair is adorably rumpled; he's got on the white t-shirt he sleeps in. I've learned this because he's practically lived here the past week. He started out mainly at Ruth's, but as the event edged closer, he started staying at Christmastown later and later until Liam finally told him to "knock off" in one of the guest rooms. As luck would have it, he picked the room next to mine. The way the beds are set up, we're next to each other, side by side, separated by a few inches of wall.

Nightly, I conjure all kinds of images of Matt. Some are sweet. Matt's sleeping face on the down pillow, his giant foot stuck out at the comforter's bottom. Other images are, well, less sweet, and I have to remind myself that he has a very real girlfriend and that I've made a very real promise to myself. Me first. No getting lost in someone else. Which is why, whenever my mind strays to what I've now termed as Mattmode, I work on the set design for *A Walk in the Park*.

"Hey," Matt says, and reaches behind me to the coffee pot. I open the cabinet and hand him two mugs. One for his coffee and the other filled with the sugar packets Liam takes whenever he eats out. "It's part of the price of the meal," he told me when I questioned him.

I know what Matt will do next. He'll pour a bit of milk in his coffee while standing in front of the open fridge. He'll shut the fridge door and dump the contents of exactly two sugar packets into his coffee. He won't mix it. After, he'll place two slices of bread in the toaster, set it to dark, and slather the done pieces with peanut butter and honey. He's a morning person, a fact which surprised me, but he's aware I'm not and he's done a pretty good job of waiting to start any conversation until after nine a.m.

Today I don't need to wait. "I've got something exciting to show you."

He rubs his hands together and smirks with mock salaciousness. "Really now?"

I wave at him. "Oh, stop." I walk over to a big box on the kitchen table. I pluck a tri-fold map from the top, and wave it in Matt's direction.

"They came?" He sets his coffee down and takes the paper from my extended hand. He unfolds it. His mouth curls into a big smile. "Andi, this is unbelievable."

I step behind him. "I think it turned out pretty well."

"Pretty well? This is awesome. It looks like a real park map."

We both stare at the unfolded map I'd designed. I'd drawn cartoon images of all the attractions where they would ultimately sit. Each had a corresponding number, a list of their names in a column on the right. I'd made the scene snowy (of course) and drawn warmly dressed parents and children on little brick paths. Fireworks shoot out over the lake, lit up Christmas trees everywhere. I drew a bride and groom in the gazebo, part of a future wedding package. I'd even included Claus, his black cat face peeking out from a bumper sleigh.

I point to a man on the stairs of the Sky Ornament Ride, tall with broad shoulders and rumpled hair. "That's you," I tell Matt.

"Me?" He puts his hand over his heart. "You'll never let me live that down."

I smile. "Why would I?"

"Where are you in all this?" he says, looking over the map.

"Running everything behind the scenes, of course."

He gives me a teasing eyeroll. "Of course." He glances at the map again. "In all seriousness, this is impressive." He looks at me. "I think it will make a difference on Saturday."

"Thanks," I manage, a lump in my throat. I'd wanted to show Matt the map from the instant I'd finished the design. His reaction was exactly as I'd hoped it would be and, as much as I don't want to, I bask in the glow of his attention.

"I have a surprise for you too," he says.

"Really?" I lift my eyebrows and try my best to duplicate his pretend-salacious tone.

"You are so bad at that." He laughs. "Promise me you'll never try to pick someone up using that ridiculous tone."

I stamp my foot. "It's not that bad."

"Oh, but it is. Trust me." He points a finger at me. "You don't need a gimmick anyway. Not when you've got blue eyes like that."

I feel pink in my cheeks and can't seem to make my mouth work to respond. I'm used to Matt teasing me, not complimenting me, and I don't know what to say.

"My surprise," Matt says, not seeming to realize he just made my heart stutter, "takes place outside." He holds out a hand. "I know you're not a morning person so, once you're fully awake and dressed, I'll show it to you."

"Okay." I inch past him, my body touching his as I pass. I look back. "I'm intrigued so I'm inclined to get dressed quickly, just so you're warned."

"Noted."

In my room, I pull on a blue shirt, one I know is the same color as my eyes. *I know.* But, if my friend thinks I have nice eyes, what's wrong with showing them off? I throw on jeans, ball my hair into an unruly ponytail, and meet Matt downstairs.

He pushes open the front door and waits for me to pass through, a bit of politeness I still find attractive. As soon as we step out, I'm excited. Red and green tents dot the property. I know from setting them up, that each houses two easels: one for a sketch of depicting the vision for the space, the second for a foam poster with the business-investor information Matt gathered from research and colleagues. Two of Beckham's Santas will be assigned to each tent – one to play interactive holiday-themed games, and a second to make sure each guest has everything they might possibly need.

"So," Matt says, pulling out his phone with a flourish, "remember the computer programming class I'm taking?"

"Hmm. I'm not sure. Have you mentioned it?" I tilt my head, feigning confusion

Matt rolls his eyes. "Okay. Maybe I've complained about the class a few times. Anyway, my final project was an app." He pulls his phone from his pocket. "And I made one to go with your scavenger hunt idea for the kids."

I stare at him. "You didn't."

"I did." He presses a few buttons and hands the phone to me.

I inspect the screen. There are six circles. I press on the first, one with a Santa hat in the middle. The screen changes to eight Santa-themed items. I press on one; the app shows a camera.

"The idea," Matt says, "is for the kids to take pictures of what they find. If they get all the ones on a list, they can get one of Ruth's prizes." Matt put Ruth in charge of prizes, and she delivered. Glow sticks. Bubbles. And a plethora of crocheted items.

"This is awesome. All I was going to do is give out a list with checkmarks."

He shrugs. "We all can't be Catman, you know."

I push on his shoulder. "Humility being his greatest attribute."

"Clearly." He smiles. "It's a pretty basic app."

"It doesn't look basic."

"Once the park opens, we can make it more interactive. Maybe use your map." He taps me on the shoulder at the word map.

"So, a collaborative effort. I like that." And I do. I love the idea of collaborating with Matt. On Christmastown. On an app. On things that I won't let myself think about. "Let's try it," I say suddenly. "A race?"

I download the app on my phone, and we spend the next half-hour running around the property looking for the snow-themed items we'd set out yesterday. We both know where everything is, so the event becomes more of a sprint than a hunt. But I forget where the last item is. Matt must too because we both stop running, breathless, dormant phones in our hands.

"Are you looking for the snowman?" I call out to him.

"Maybe."

"I'm going to find it first."

Matt jogs toward the carousel. It looks shinier than normal, like the ride knows the importance of Saturday. He walks inside the tent top structure, examining the 3D Christmas ornaments affixed to the mirrored center pieces.

I pass by him with bold steps toward Mrs. Claus's Bake Shop. I swing open the door and temporarily forget the game. The redone interior is one of my favorite parts of Christmastown. It looks like an old-fashioned soda shop. A thick silver counter and twisty tools line one side. Behind the counter sit covered glass cases which, on Saturday, will house Ruth's Yuletide cookies. A few sets of white-washed wrought iron tables sit on woven red and green rugs. Mint green walls feature framed old-fashioned photos depicting varied images of Mrs. Claus.

My phone pings. I pull it up. It's a picture of the final snowman, peeking out from the exit gate of the carousel. A second ping. This one a selfie of Matt and the snowman, his face in a grin, one thumb stuck up. *Better luck next time A.*

I smile at the message. A. I like the familiarity of that nickname. And I like that Matt feels comfortable enough with me to use it. I can only hope it lasts past Saturday.

CHAPTER 27

M*att*

The day of the event, I wait for everyone in front of Liam's. We – the original Christmastown committee -- agreed to do a final walkthrough of the property as a group. And, though today is a culmination of all of our efforts, something we should all be proud of, I'm agitated.

Scratch that.

I'm nervous as all get out. I received two emails yesterday, investors I'd locked in, cancelling. There were others attending but, still, the last-minute cancellations seemed like a bad omen. Right after, Bridget texted to confirm, the timing so coincidental, I had a paranoid thought that she'd orchestrated the cancellations.

It rained overnight and the ground is still wet, giant muddy pools in spots. And my polo shirt - Emma had ordered red ones for all of us - is too small. The fabric stretches uncomfortably across my back and the word Christmastown, embroidered on the left side, pulls so much that it's almost distorted.

I'm not in the best mood.

Andi pushes open the door. She tumbles down the stairs, a

big smile on her face. Seeing Andi smile usually makes me feel better. But that's part of the reason I'm so nervous. I want this to go well for her more than I want it to go well for myself.

"Hey. Nice fit." She points to my shirt.

I make a muscle in jest. "Thought I'd show off the wares, you know."

"Good move."

My phone pings with a text. I pull it out. *Not sure I will make it today, Matt. Sorry. Andy.*

Crap. I'd told Andy, a friend of my parents, about the event last week. He was a long shot to do anything but still, another last-minute cancellation. It doesn't make me feel better. I shove my phone in my pocket and look up. Andi's inspecting my features. I force a smile.

Liam and Ruth join us in the front and, as if on cue, Emma pulls up in her car. She and Beckham spill out. We congregate in a circle. We've all got on the red shirts, like we're part of a festive athletic team. It feels like we should do a cheer. "Ready?" I say instead.

We walk along the property. Huge bouquets of red and green balloons adorn seemingly every unoccupied space, a monstrously large arch of them at the entrance. A caricature artist and a photo booth stand near the gazebo and, next to those, several tables are set up to for crafts: elf ornaments made from popsicle sticks, reindeer-themed candy pots. One giant table features "Santa Slime."

Two Santa bands (The Fruitcakes and The Jingle Ballers) are scheduled to play on the makeshift stage Beckham had constructed over the charred ground where the fire had blazed. Food trucks supplied by a friend of Steph's line one side of the lake, cartoonish drawings of personified fried Oreos and corn dogs on their sides.

Though it's day, the gazebo is fully lined in lights. Two giant red chairs sit inside, dozens of fake wrapped Christmas presents between them. Liam and Ruth have agreed to dress as Santa and Mrs. Claus and pose in the chairs for formal photos.

Despite my nerves, despite the cancellations, and despite last night's rain and the muddy aftermath, everything looks fantastic. It's the kind of day I wanted -- self-led and interactive. No long presentations. No forced fancy dinner. Guests would go at their own pace.

We stop at the entrance. A bus pulls up.

"The Santas are here," Beckham says though it's obvious. The sea of red suits are visible through partially darkened bus windows. "They're stoked," he continues. "I partied with them at their hotel last night. Those guys, man." He shakes his head is if recalling a mad cap event from the previous evening.

An image of a group of bearded, pot-bellied old men charging the streets of Scranton pops in head. I'd normally think partying Santa Clauses were fantastic; I'd likely have joined in the fray. But, given that they are the linchpin of the event, the idea of potentially hungover men is more alarming than amusing.

"Nothing too crazy, right?" I try to make the question sound light.

Beckham lets out a laugh. "Nope. All's good. Mikey and Jimbo – funny guys, one short and stocky, the other tall and thin –"

Before he can finish, the bus door squeaks open. The first Santa appears in a traditional red suit, boots and all. He's followed by more and they stream toward us like a sea of merry ants. We'd slated for fifteen, plus the band members, but the crowd of bearded, red suited men tumbling down the bus stairs far exceed that amount.

"I told you," Beckham whispers, "it's a FOMO thing. One's doing something cool, and they all want in."

I step toward the pack of bearded men. A few have on traditional gear; others wear festive shirts printed with crazy Christ-

mas-themed patterns. A bunch have on stripy socks. A few wear
vests. All don the signature red cap and, from what I can tell,
every single one has a real beard. It's almost like a prerequisite.

"Hey guys," I call. "Thanks for coming. If you follow me, we'll
get you your assignments."

I walk down the path to the toy shop, dozens of Santas
streaming behind me. I feel like the pied piper of Christmas
cheer. Over the next hour, Beckham and Andi check in forty-
one Santas and assign them to locations throughout the park.
There's such a surplus, Beckham designates his favorites, Mikey
and Jimbo, to be dancers. "Start moving when the Jingle Ballers
start singing," he directs. Then, almost as if he'd willed it by the
statement, live music sounds.

Four Santas stand on the stage, microphones in front of
each. One's beatboxing; the rest are singing an acapella version
of *God Rest Ye Merry Gentlemen.*

A gentle breeze ripples the tents and balloons. The smell of
hot dogs and funnel cakes and other fair food permeates the air.
Santas stand all over, like a live Where's Waldo picture.

Pride courses through me.

I'd organized this. I hadn't done it alone, of course, but I'd
taken charge. I'd done something on a large scale and, at least so
far, it had turned out better than I'd expected. I bask in my pride
for one minute before checking my watch. The numbers are big
and bold and clear. 1:10 p.m.

1:10?

I look again. It can't be right. It can't already be 1:10. Right?

Nope.

My watch is correct.

It's 1:10.

The event started ten minutes ago. And not a single investor
is here.

CHAPTER 28

M *att*

Ten minutes later, I stride toward the entrance. To greet people, I'd said, but really, there's no reason for me to be there. The park isn't that big and it's well-marked. But I don't want to stand with the committee. If investors come, great. If they don't, I don't want to be witness to the change in perception, when nervous excitement morphs into the horrible realization that no one is coming.

But someone has to come. Right? After numerous long – and painful -- meetings with potential investors, I'd gotten a decent number to commit. At least fifteen, less the three cancellations so twelve. Twelve solid yesses.

I stare at the parking lot, my mind fixed on willing a flesh-and-blood investor to show up. A man appears in my peripheral vision. Yes! I shoot my head in his direction. Oh. One of the Santas taking a leak.

Nice.

I don't turn toward the park. I don't want to see everything behind me. The festive space that had turned out way better in person than it had in my vision. The legions of Santas who had come, free of charge, to support the first ever Christmas themed park. Liam and Ruth in their make-up and costumes. And Andi. Seeing Andi right now would be the worst.

Bridget's Lexus pulls in.

I stand corrected.

Seeing Bridget right now would be the worst.

She steps out of the car and walks purposely in my direction, her face in a wide grin. Instead of the typical fitted suit and spiky, pointy-toed heels, she has on jeans and a green shirt. The casual clothes and uncharacteristic smile set me off balance.

She waves in my direction, the strange, foreign smile still on her face. I hold up my hand in acknowledgment. Then, in what must have been a punishment for past wrongs, Andi's mom and boyfriend appear behind her. In Santa hats. Jim's has a trout embroidered on it.

My stomach knots.

The three of them advance toward me and I smile by force of habit. Andi materializes by my side. She doesn't acknowledge the obvious.

"Matt. Andi," Bridget calls, "this is impressive. I can see how much you've done with the property already." She waves her hands around and smiles *again*. Who is this woman?

"Merry Christmas!" Andi's mom gushes.

"Merry Fishmas!" Jim adds and points to the trout on his Santa hat.

I force a smile and the three of them stand in a row like a trio of expectant, jolly day campers. I cannot make my mouth work and stand, stupidly mute, a fake smile plastered across my face.

"Welcome to Christmastown!" Andi's voice rings out next to me, smooth and enthusiastic. She holds out three maps. "Come this way. I'll show you around." She leads them down the path toward the park. I stare at their retreating backs, I don't know for how long. Eventually, I sit on a stump near the balloons, head in my hands. It's been close to an hour. I know I should get up and go talk to my committee. To all the Santas. To Bridget and Andi's mom.

I need to acknowledge the obvious.

No one is coming.

"Matt."

I jerk my head up, half expecting no one to be there, the word an auditory mirage fueled from desperation. But no. Roger Mills, a marketing guru and one of the first people I'd reached out to, stands with a woman I presume to be his wife and two red-headed little boys.

I shoot to my feet, pump his hand. "Hey. Good to see you, Roger. Welcome to Christmastown." I hold out the pile of maps.

"Sorry we're late." Roger takes a map and one for his wife. "There's a big jam on the turnpike. You'll have some other stragglers, I imagine."

Stragglers.

A jam on the turnpike.

More than a few.

I smile, a real one this time. "Good to know. Thanks." I point toward the toy shop. "Check in at the shop and we'll get you all set." Roger and his family head toward the structure. His boys run ahead in sneakered feet.

I shoot Andi a text. *First investor has arrived!*

Her response is immediate. *Woo hoo!!!*

I picture her smiling, the upward curve of her lips, the light in her eyes. I'm so relieved that I haven't let her down, it's startling. I try to convince myself that the feeling is a culmination of the stress and fatigue I'd felt all morning, all week, but, deep down, I know that's not true. I like Andi. Way more than I should.

More investors arrive. My mind veers from Andi and soon, The Santa Games is in motion. The carousel runs, half dozen tiny riders on the backs of moving reindeer. A handful of people stand in front of the stage. The Fruitcakes play a jazzy version of Jingle Bells. Groups walk with cotton candy, hot dogs, and other fair foods. I can't see inside all the tents from my vantage point, but the ones I can see are occupied. It's everything I'd hoped for.

"Matt!"

Andi sprints toward me, wild curls bouncing. I smile automatically. "This is going so well." She falls into step beside me.

"Yeah," I say, feeling lighter than I have all week. "This is pretty good."

"Even Bridget's having fun." Andi inclines her head toward the food trucks and craft tables.

I look toward the craft tables. Bridget stands with an oversized chocolate ice cream cone in one hand, a mason jar of Santa Slime in the other. She appears to be having a robust conversation with the Santa assigned to the table. "Bridget Quinn with a jar of Santa slime. Now there's something I thought I'd never see."

"Right? I overheard her talking to Liam and Ruth. She could not stop raving. I think she's on board."

Bridget on board? I let out a breath. "That's good news."

Two pre-pubescent boys dart in front of us, phones outstretched. "Maybe there's one by the balloons," one says, and they both take off.

Andi pushes at my shoulder. "They're playing your game."

"Looks like." I try to sound casual but pride flickers in my chest. I'd made an actual app. And saved these poor kids from the torture of sitting still.

Andi inclines her head toward the food trucks. "Should we eat?"

"Thought you'd never ask. I'm starving." We move toward a truck, a gleeful personified hot dog on a stick painted on its side. "You know," I say, "it's not a real carnival unless you eat at least one piece of food on a stick."

She angles her face toward me. "Is that so?"

"Absolutely. I mean, there's a variety of choices – cotton candy, popsicles, fruit kabobs. And of course," I gesture to the truck, "corn dogs. But you must eat at least one."

"One food on a stick. Good to know."

I order the food and, a few minutes later, we sit on a bench near the lake with corn dogs and sodas, a flimsy paper basket of cheese fries balanced between us.

Andi gives more specifics on what she'd overheard from Bridget's conversation with Liam. I share which investors I think are the most promising.

I pick out a particularly gooey fry and pop it in my mouth. Andi does the same. Excess cheese whiz dribbles down her chin. She looks around, I'm guessing for something to wipe it with.

I pull a napkin from the food bag. "I got you." I wipe the cheese with a gentle stroke, my face close to hers. I look directly in her eyes, for too long, I think. It feels intimate; I draw back. "All set."

"Thanks." She touches her cheek.

We eat in silence. One of the Santas creeps up behind us, a sprig of mistletoe in his hand.

No.

I already made things weird with the cheese-wiping gesture. I don't need this.

He waves the mistletoe. Neither of us speak.

Vigorous waves now.

"Come on," he encourages, "you young lovers know what this means."

"We're not –" I start but Andi's hands grip the sides of my face. She pulls me toward her.

Then she kisses me.

CHAPTER 29

A *ndi*

Matt doesn't kiss me back.

Oh.

Crap.

I'd intended to give him a platonic peck but once my lips were on his, it morphed into something more. Not a passionate kiss exactly, but not the innocent one I'd intended. I inch back on the bench. My face is hot. I'm *mortified.* "Sorry I –"

"No problem. There was mistletoe and a very insistent Santa Claus."

He moves back on the bench and stuffs the rest of his corn dog – almost half of it -- in his mouth. His face is pink; his eyes wide with surprise. He seems embarrassed for me, which, of course, makes things so much worse.

"I totally didn't mean that," I say with a dismissive wave that belies my pounding, racing heart. "At all. I mean you and me –" I shake my head, like the idea of us together is preposterous instead of one I think of every time I see him.

He holds up a hand. "It's okay."

"I -" I start again, still humiliated.

"Andi, it's alright," he says, a bit of frustration in his voice. "I know we're just friends."

Silence envelops the bench, the kind of that used to feel companionable. It feels awkward instead.

He pops a fry in his mouth and stands. "I should go check on stuff."

I don't want him to leave, not with things so awkward. "Is Whitney coming?" I ask, standing. After kissing him, I can at least acknowledge the existence of his girlfriend.

He shrugs. "I asked her. It's out of her reporting area. And not the right time of year to get special permission, apparently."

"Oh." I wonder why she wouldn't come anyway, but don't ask. It's not my business. And I already made things weird with the kiss.

He gestures to the park. "I should see how things are going."

"Right."

He grabs our trash and throws it in the nearest bin, a mundane task he manages to make look athletic. He angles his head back at me. "See you."

"Yeah. See you."

I watch him walk toward the nearest tent then, feeling stalkerish, stride in the opposite direction, my heart in my stomach. I spy Emma taking Santa pictures by the gazebo. The line is five deep. "Hey Em," I yell. "Do you need help?"

She turns from the two children she's posing. "Yes. The photo picks." She inclines her head to the area where we'd set up a computer monitor for guests to view their photos.

"I can do that."

I step to the monitor and help the first group. The task is easy, and the line remains long. I stay inside the gazebo, hiding behind busyness.

Mom and Jim line up for a photo. She grips my free hand. "This has been fantastic," she gushes.

Jim shakes my hand. He nods at the lake. "Think you'll stock that with fish?"

I say nothing and he bumps my shoulder. "Kidding! Though it might be good for the off-season, right?"

"It's a thought for sure," I say.

They get their photo taken, say goodbye, and walk toward the exit. It's dusk and the white lights that outline the toy store glimmer in the starting darkness. I turn and practically slam into Bridget. She's got one hand gripped around the mason jar of Santa Slime; the other holds a paper cone filled with cotton candy.

I can't wait to tell Matt.

Ugh.

Because there's the ill-timed, partially passionate, and wholly embarrassing kiss.

I'm mortified all over again. I direct my attention to Bridget. "Did you have a good time?"

"It's been wonderful," she says. "Impressive."

"Thank you." I want her to say more, and I force myself not to ask something ridiculous like "you're going to help us now, right?"

"No matter what happens, this event is something to be proud of," she says.

Notwithstanding the cotton candy and Santa Slime, her face is serious. My heart drops. What does she mean "no matter what happens?" Does she know something? Or is it a benign remark that the event alone is something to feel good about. Before I can conjure an appropriate clarifying question, Emma's voice rings out.

"Time for your photo, Ms. Quinn."

Bridget flashes a smile and moves into the gazebo. She sets down her slime jar and hands the cotton candy to a nearby Santa. She grips Liam in a bearlike embrace, her face over his shoulder. I can't be certain, but it looks like her eyes are welled.

When the final investor, one with a three-year-old that did not want to get off the carousel, leaves, Matt steps to the microphone used by the Santa bands. "Hey! We did it." Whooping cheers erupt. "Now it's time to celebrate. The food trucks are open, the band's going to play on. Congratulations!"

Matt steps back and The Jingle Ballers start to play. Santas emerge from all over the property. They pile thick paper plates with staggering amounts of food. Ruth passes out extra cookies and leftover glow stick packages. The colored bulbs on the tall pine trees surrounding the space are visible in the dark.

I sit on the edge of the carousel next to Emma and Beckham. Emma fashions the glow sticks into necklaces and headbands and all three of us adorn ourselves with both. A plate of sugar cookies with red and green sprinkles sits in front of us. The band plays Jingle Bell Rock. Santas are everywhere in unbuttoned coats and abandoned hats. Tall black boots pepper the property.

Matt joins us. I try to avoid him while simultaneously looking like I'm not avoiding him. I'm terrible at it. My heart beats hard and my face heats whenever he looks at me. I'd usually be teasing him; instead, I barely talk to him at all.

I'm relieved when the party dies down and I can hideout in my room. But, of course, Matt's makeshift bedroom is next to mine, and we walk together toward the house, both of us still tricked out in glow stick headbands and necklaces. He seems to feel as awkward as I do. Which is incredibly awkward. So, there's that.

"That went well," he says finally.

"Yeah."

He holds opens the door to Liam's.

I step inside. "Do you think there's investor interest?"

"I think so."

"Great."

We walk the rest of the way to our rooms in silence. I whip

open my bedroom door, give a quick look in his direction. "Good night." I step inside and shut the door so fast it's like I'm keeping out an invader. I collapse on the bed and pull off my glow stick headband.

I should feel ecstatic. Instead, it feels like I lost my best friend.

CHAPTER 30

A^{*ndi*} The morning after Kissgate, I make a decision.
Enough.

I will not be embarrassed by the kiss. And I'll drop my secret adoration. It's foolish. It's not going anywhere. And it's causing me to do stupid things.

I pull out my computer and bring up my set design for *A Walk in the Park*. Cole texted me twice about the London opportunity, but I'd been so consumed by The Santa Games, I'd put him off. Liam might get an investor for Christmastown; he might not. Either way, I need something else to focus on. Something that's mine. And something that doesn't, in any way, involve Matt Taylor.

The play takes place with scenes in each of the four seasons. I've already mocked up a circular prop design divided in four, one for each. I work on tweaks, my favorite part of design, my mind fully absorbed in the task.

I finally get hungry. I dress in super casual clothes (aka old sweats) and go downstairs. Matt's sitting with Liam, his duffel at his feet. A plate of soda bread sits on the table.

"Aye Andi," Liam says. "Bread?"

"Sure." I pick a piece from the plate and nod my head toward Matt's duffel. "You taking off?" I try to make it sound casual.

He stands. "Yeah. Work."

"Right." I pop the soda bread in my mouth and swallow. "You'll tell us if you hear something?"

"Yeah. Of course." He picks up the bag and slings it across his shoulder.

Liam stands and shakes Matt's hand. "Thanks for everything."

Matt puts his other hand over Liam's and looks him in the eye. "It was a pleasure."

He looks to me. My feet root on the floor and it appears I've lost the ability to know what's appropriate when it comes to Matt. A big hug seems in order but I'm not doing that, not after yesterday. A handshake seems too formal. Instead of either, I hold up my hand in a lackluster wave. He meets my eyes. "See you, Andi."

"See you."

The door shuts.

Not a minute after, Liam asks, "Did something happen between you two?"

I'm startled by the question "No. Why?"

"Seemed different. That's all."

I clear dishes. "I think we're tired."

Liam leaves it and after, I submit the set design template for *A Walk in the Park*. It's the best Matt elixir I can think of.

* * *

MATT FACETIMES THREE DAYS LATER. It's the longest we've gone without talking. I've told myself it's because we don't have as much to say now that The Santa Games is over, but it's clear my kiss put a kink in our friendship.

I accept the call. Matt's face fills the screen. He's smiling. "Good news."

"Good news?" I repeat and forget about feeling awkward.

"Is Liam around?"

"Of course. It's 7:10."

Matt laughs because he knows what I mean by that. 7:10 is prime Wheel time. "Ruth is here too."

I walk the phone into the family room. Ruth and Liam are next to each other on the couch, plates of cake on their laps.

I wiggle the phone. "Matt's got some news."

They exchange a look. I sit next to Liam on the couch and prop the phone up against a bowl on the coffee table.

"You've got an investor interested." Matt's face erupts into a smile. "Sawyer Hughes of Fun Overhaul wants you to come for a meeting in their New York office next week."

I gape at the phone. I don't remember who Sawyer Hughes is but the words "meeting" and "New York" and "next week" all ring loud in my mind. "Wow. That's awesome."

"I know." Matt explains that Fun Overhaul is a company which specializes in upgrading and reimagining venues.

When he's done, Liam asks the question I'm thinking: "Would you come with us to New York?"

"You should be there, Matt," I chime in, meaning it.

He pauses and I think he's going to turn Liam down, another ricochet of that stupid ill-timed kiss. Instead, he smiles. "Sure. I'd love that."

Liam returns to watching Wheel with Ruth. I move to the kitchen.

"I have a good picture for you," Matt says.

I slip into a kitchen chair, glad for the bit of normalcy in our relationship. My phone dings and I pull up the image. It's a photo of an airborne cat flying through a hoop. I smile. "What is that?"

"Cat Agility Training. It's a new kind of extreme sport."

My phone dings again and I pull up a second picture, this one of cat on a high ramp. "And the cats compete?"

"Yeah. One of the competitions is in Paris. You should train Claus."

I snort. "No. *You* should train Claus." I spy the cat curled up in the corner of the kitchen and angle the phone so Matt can see him. "He doesn't look too motivated right now, coach."

"He just needs a training regimen. I'll have him in tip-top shape in no time."

"Okay," I laugh.

"Maybe we can talk about his training in New York next week?"

It's more than a silly question. It's an invitation to have the kind of friendship we had before. And though a big piece of me intensely dislikes our *just friends* status, I jump on the opportunity. "You're on."

CHAPTER 31

M*att*
Liam, Andi, and I arrive for our meeting with Fun Overhaul. The offices are housed in one of Manhattan's largest skyscrapers and we stand in front of the building, distorted reflections of ourselves in the glass. I've got on my standard black suit and a blue tie. Liam refused to wear a suit, but he's got on khakis and the red Christmastown polo. He's cheeks are ruddy; his shirt pulls at a pot belly. He still looks like Santa Claus.

Andi is wearing a vibrant red dress that clings to every curve. Her hair, straightened, hangs down her back. Seeing her makes me kick myself (again) for not kissing her back at The Santa Games. I was surprised and then the moment was over and then she made sure that I knew the kiss was a mistake. Multiple times.

I push Andi and the kiss out of my mind. Liam pulls open the door and Andi and I follow him through. I give a final look around for Bridget who, to my surprise, declined Liam's invitation to attend. I half expect her to still show up. I don't know if her presence would be good or bad. She's been distant since The Santa Games.

Though it's on the twentieth floor, I take the stairs. I'm in good shape but still, twenty flights are a lot and I'm breathless when I reach the top. Andi and Liam stand in front of the door to the stairwell. "It's about time, Taylor," Andi says.

"Here now."

I follow them to the doorway to the office, Fun Overhaul on a gold nameplate in front. I pull open the door and immediately take a step back.

Whoa.

The entire back wall is covered with white Lego-like building bricks, Fun Overhaul spelled out in primary colors. There are no magazines or flyers but instead baskets of toys that mimic those in my desk at the office– scrunch balls and jacks and fidget spinners. A marble run runs across the wall next to the building brick one. Colorful, cushy couches surround a giant rectangular fish tank that serves as a table. I stare at the array of tropical fish and realize that the tank is a mini version of the waiting room, fish swimming over plastic replica couches, a brick wall in the background.

I'm floored.

Without thinking, I move to the marble wall, pluck a silver ball out of the basket, and set it on the top of the run. It rolls down levers, ramps, and spirals before *disappearing into the wall* and reappearing through a happy clown-face at the bottom. I pick up another marble, turn and hold it out to where Liam and Andi had been standing.

Except they're not there. Instead, they both stand in front of a desk shaped like a Rubik's cube, talking with a grim-faced woman who, from what I can tell, is the least fun thing in the room. I step next to them and pretend I hadn't been playing with toys. "All set?"

"All set."

"You have to wait," the grim woman tells us. Like that would be a problem. I *wanted* to wait in this room. And this from me, a man with the attention of a hummingbird. Liam sits in a chair, and I plop next to Andi on a cushy red couch. A giant blue button centers the side table next to me. I press it. Bubbles flow out of the tabletop. *Bubbles.* I look to Liam and Andi and mouth "watch." I press the button again and, again, bubbles fly out.

Liam stands and touches the button. Bubbles fly out for the third time. "Ruth would love that," he says.

"If this is what they do with a waiting room," Andi whispers, "imagine what –"

The door swings open, interrupting her words. Not that she had to finish the sentence. I know what she's thinking – if Fun Overhaul made a waiting room this epic, what would the company do with a venue like Christmastown? The stakes for this meeting had just risen ten thousandfold.

"Sawyer Hughes," the man says. He's tall with shocking blue eyes and longish sandy-blonde hair. He's wearing a black t-shirt, black jeans, and boots. He looks like he could be a rock star as easily as the CEO of a company. He waves a hand. "Follow me."

We follow him down a hall into a large conference room with giant windows that line one wall. The other walls feature framed before and after pictures of spaces the company had transformed. One group of photos depicts a rundown inner-city playground metamorphized into a fantastical jungle with oversized butterflies and caterpillars. Another pair features a corporate board room redesigned to look medieval, like a place King Arthur might have met with the Knights of the Round Table. My favorite is a children's hospital cafeteria made to look like outer space.

Sawyer stands at the head of a long glass table and holds his hands out in an expansive gesture. "Welcome to Fun Overhaul. Sit. Please."

We sit in plush chairs. Sawyer remains standing. "I like to start these meetings with a bit about our company. You get to know us, understand our philosophy. And I'll get to know you." He looks at each of us individually before continuing. "Good?"

"Perfect." I practically shout the word.

"The aim of Fun Overhaul is simple," Sawyer starts. "Our company takes ordinary spaces and transforms them in such a way that being in the space itself is an experience. Like our waiting room."

I think about the waiting room. The bubbles, the fish tank, the marble run. Waiting as an experience. That was a concept I could get behind.

Sawyer crosses the room and stops at the picture depicting the medieval corporate board room. "This is the corporate board room of Hang It Up, a company that makes nothing but padded, high-end clothing hangers." He taps on the photo. "Big money maker, huge. I mean, everyone's got hangers, right?" He leans on the conference table, his fingers pressed against the glass. "Do you know how hard it is to attract high level executives when all you make is hangers? I mean, what's the fun in that?" He pauses and taps on the picture a second time. "So, we came in and dramatically changed the look of the space. Which, of course, changed the feel of the space which, in turn, changed the culture." He looks from me to Andi. "Hang it Up is a hot place to work now. They even have a line of medieval hangers, if you can believe it." He winks.

I nod, riveted. Medieval hangers? Sawyer Hughes made *hangers* fun. I love this guy.

He moves and sits in the chair at the head of the table. "The caterpillar park on the back wall? It's been duplicated by thirty-five municipalities across the nation. The concept singlehandedly revolutionized the playground space. Fun Overhaul will reimagine anything – parking lots, waiting rooms, hospitals. This is what we do. We make the ordinary extraordinary. We inspire fun." He pauses. "Of course, with Christmastown, our approach would be different. A holiday-themed amusement park is inherently fun already. It's high concept so what we'd look to do is partner with you to revamp it. Reimagine it possibly." He makes his fingers into a steeple and looks toward the ceiling. "Any thoughts so far?"

Foolishly, my only thought is, "when can you start?"

Andi speaks out. "What do you mean, reimagine? We laid out our plans at The Santa Games."

Sawyer leans back in his chair, fingers still in the steeple position. "With something like a theme park, we'd strategize to maximize the profitability of the space."

"And by that you mean?"

"We'll revamp to make sure we all get the most from our investment."

"And this would be a partnership," Liam asks, "Fun Overhaul and Christmastown?"

"Partnership, buy out. It's all on the table."

Liam's eyes go wide. "I don't want to sell."

"No sale necessary." Sawyer sits up. The chair reverberates with the sudden movement. "Look. I don't like to beat around the bush. And I don't play games." He stops a moment. "Well, I do play games, just not with my business dealings."

I laugh. Too hard.

"Bottom line. I'd love to partner with you. I love your vision, appreciate the research." He nods at each of us. "But I like to put my own spin on things." He waves his finger. "How about I put together a holiday-themed concept, complete with my own market research, and present it to you in a few weeks." He runs his hands through his hair. "If you're not interested, no problem. If you are, we'll get a contract together."

We agree on a date. Liam and Andi ask a few more questions. I don't need to.

I've found my guy.

CHAPTER 32

M*att*

I bound down the stairs after the meeting, loosening my tie as I go. Excitement pounds in my chest. Andi and Liam wait for me at the bottom of the stairwell, their faces unreadable.

I try to restrain my enthusiasm. This isn't my decision. But honestly, why wouldn't they want to work with Fun Overhaul?

"Recap over lunch?" Andi asks.

"Sounds good."

Liam agrees and we spill out on to the busy sidewalk and push through the crowds toward a restaurant aptly called New York Deli. We order subs, grab drinks, and squish into a booth with a window view, Andi and Liam on one side, me on the other. People pass by outside in a steady stream. Inside, it's loud.

Liam sweeps the napkin canister to the side of the table. "I don't want to sell."

Andi puts her hand on top of his. "You don't have to sell."

"I want to see it through. I promised Colleen. And we've come this far."

Andi removes her hand and cups her drink. "I want to see it through, too."

My head pings from Andi to Liam. Neither seem particularly excited. After the waiting room and the before and after pictures and Sawyer, I'd thought we'd all want to sign. This opportunity with Fun Overhaul is exactly what I was hoping would come out of The Santa Games. "Sawyer said all options are the on the table," I note. "There's no reason to think you have to sell."

Andi sets down her sub. "He also said he wanted to reimagine things."

"He said *maybe* reimagine things."

"But he couldn't explain what he meant by that, right?" She fingers a potato chip.

Liam takes a swig of root beer, sets the bottle down. "Andi has worked hard on the concepts. We don't want someone to change things up. We want someone to invest in what we've got."

Irritation pings in my chest. What are they saying? Sawyer Hughes is the kind of leader who makes clothing hangers cool, who turns run down playgrounds into works of art. His waiting room has a wall-sized marble run. Working with him would be the opportunity of a lifetime. "I don't think he's planning to change things up. I think just he wants to make the most of the venue."

Neither respond. We eat in silence. Conversations from other tables fill in the space, their noise amplifying the quiet.

"We should be celebrating," I say finally. I look from Andi to Liam. "We have an investor. That's what we set out to do, right?"

Liam balls up his napkin. "I want to make sure it's the right investor."

My irritation morphs into anger. Six weeks ago, he and Andi hosted a beef and beer. They had no chance of attracting any investor, let alone one like Sawyer Hughes. I played double-agent, risked my job. And for what? For them to tear down a legitimate opportunity because they're afraid of a little change?

Andi looks at me. "We're not saying no. At least I'm not." She looks to Liam. "It's just some of the things he said are a bit concerning."

"It seems like he's only focused on money," Liam adds.

I tear at a napkin, surprised by the intensity of my feelings given I have no actual stake in what happens. "Are you going to listen to his presentation?" I ask neutrally.

Liam meets my eyes. "It would be stupid not to."

"I know I want to hear him out," Andi adds.

"All right. Good." I take a bite of my sub, but I can't shake my irritation. Even with Andi, which is a first. I can't remember a single other time when being in her presence didn't make me just plain happy.

Liam pulls apart a chip bag. It pops with the effort. "How about those bubbles in the waiting room? Craic. Right?" He stuffs a bunch of chips in his mouth.

I smile, but the moment is lost. It's clear we're not on the same page.

Back in the hotel lobby, Liam announces he's turning in for the night. I open my mouth with the intention of saying the same, but Andi juts her hand out and puts in on my forearm.

"Matt. Wait."

Liam ambles toward the elevators; it's just the two of us.

She meets my eyes. "I know I'm being cautious about Sawyer. It's just, it's just –"

She scrunches up her face and looks so flustered, my irritation wanes. Christmastown is important to her. Of course, she's being cautious.

"I just want it to be our vision. Not some reimagined version dreamed up by Sawyer Hughes." She holds out a hand. "Not that he isn't impressive. He's clearly good at what he does." She leans against the wall of the lobby. "I'm just proud of what we've come up with."

Hotel guests push past me, and I move to stand next to her against the wall. I understand what she means. Getting Sawyer Hughes interested was my accomplishment. But hers is the vision. She wants it to be respected.

I move my head to look at her. "I was probably being a little impulsive with my support." I say honestly. "Go figure."

She laughs. "Well, I like impulsive Matt. He's fun." She steps out from the wall, sweeps her hair across her shoulders. "And I would like to take impulsive Matt out on the town tonight. These are my haunts, remember?"

"Right. I forgot." It's true. I associate Andi so closely with Christmastown that I forgot she lived here, in the largest city on earth, for years.

"Let me put on some casual clothes." She gestures to the clingy red dress like it's a cumbersome business suit. "Meet in an hour?"

"Can't wait."

We meet in the lobby an hour later, Andi in form-fitting skinny jeans and black blouse, buttons undone at the top. She has on the same high heeled pumps she'd worn to the meeting, a stylish square purse on the crook of elbow. She gestures toward the door. "So, are you ready to see New York?"

CHAPTER 33

ndi

A I walk down the street, past all the people, Matt by my side. He seems more himself since our talk in the lobby. I'm glad. Our friendship had just recovered from the mistletoe incident.

He looks at me. "I must admit, I'm a little nervous. The last time you surprised me with an outing, I almost had a panic attack."

We weave around a group of tourists posing for a picture. I glance up at him. "Impulsive Matt nervous? That can't be."

"Tell me there's no confined spaces and we'll be good."

"No confined spaces." I smile. "And no elevators."

"Phew." He makes a show of moving his hand across his forehead.

He falls in step beside me. "Do you ever miss New York?"

"Sometimes. I loved the city when I first moved here, but it got old after a while."

"How so?"

"The crowds and the noise. The expense." I take a few paces

and think about Cole and how I'd allowed myself to get dwarfed by him. "Other things too."

Matt doesn't pry as to what I mean by "other things." He's good at reading me, never pushing for information I don't want to give.

"Hey," he says suddenly, "did you ever submit a design? For that play? *A Walk in the Park?*"

I thought he'd forgotten. With The Santa Games and the Sawyer Hughes meeting, I'd practically forgotten myself. "I did." I don't share that I'd worked on it almost non-stop while our friendship was in limbo.

"If you want the job, I hope you get it," he says.

If I want the job. I don't know that I do, but that's a topic for another day. One that will probably never come up. My chances of getting a set design job on the West End are minuscule.

We approach our venue. I start up the stairs to a brownstone.

"Friend's house?" Matt asks.

I angle my head toward him. "You'll see." I continue up the stairs and pull open the door. Matt walks through, I step inside behind him. "Welcome to Bar Centrale. New York's best kept secret."

I watch him take it in, the bar and restaurant hidden inside what had once been a residential home.

"It's a speakeasy," I tell him. "Or modeled after one, anyway."

"This place," he says, looking around with appreciation, "is fantastic."

I beam at his response. I knew he would love it. I do too. It's expensive, but I always came here after opening night with groups of friends, Cole too. Cole and I had a lot of nights here actually. Weird that I hadn't thought of that until now. I'd wanted to show Matt a place that had meaning for me in New York.

I check us in with the hostess, get a buzzer, and point to the bar. "Drinks first?"

Matt holds up his hands. "Your night but sounds good to me."

We move toward a black chrome bar. Liquor lines dark shelves which stand out against painted white brick. We crowd into the space. There's a television in the corner. My heart drops. Whitney Collins parades across the screen in a revealing sundress. I watch a moment. She's doing a piece on pop-up smoothie bars. I shouldn't care.

Matt glances up. He has to have seen her. She's there. On the screen. In a tiny sundress. But there's no reaction. Instead, he leans forward. "What do you want to drink? A Manhattan?"

"Sure." Maybe he's used to seeing her on television? I gesture toward the screen. "Is it weird?"

He looks at the television and back at me. "What? Seeing Whitney?"

I hate the way her name sounds on his lips. "Yeah."

"No. I mean, it was the first few times I saw her, but I got used to it. I don't pay attention to what she's doing. I almost forget, you know." He moves through the crowd toward the bar and returns a few minutes later with two Manhattans in thick glass tumblers.

"Is it touristy?" he asks. "To order a Manhattan in Manhattan?"

I barely comprehend the question. I'm bothered by his reaction to Whitney. He doesn't pay attention to what she's doing? It seems unMattlike. "Have you told her about the Fun Overhaul meeting yet?"

A quizzical look crosses his features. "Told who?"

"Whitney."

"Why would I tell Whitney about the meeting?"

Now I give a quizzical look. "Isn't she your girlfriend?"

Matt steps back. "Girlfriend? No. We dated briefly. But that was almost a year ago." He sips his drink. "Why did you think she was my girlfriend?"

I don't answer. There are the tons of images of the two of them together online, including the one from the AnimalLIVE gala. And the picture of their families together in his family room. Whitney pawed at him after the quizzo game. Steph said she loved him.

I can't tell any of these things to Matt.

"I'm not sure," I lie.

"Well, we're not dating. She's not my type." He holds up his glass. "Drink to that?"

I clink my glass to his. Stunned. I'm stunned. I'd lived with the narrative that Matt was dating Whitney almost from the day I'd met him. Is he *single*?

Matt peers at me. "You all right? Because I can go on a date with Whitney if it means that much to you."

I laugh, almost from relief. "No. No need."

The buzzer vibrates in my hand. I hold it up. "Our table's ready." We follow the server and, in the short distance from the bar to the table, I get a hold of myself. Matt might be single. He might not be. It doesn't mean he wants to be more than friends. And there's no reason to believe the dynamic between us will suddenly become awkward. Nothing has changed for him, after all. He's been single, or probably single, the whole time.

The server gestures to a table covered with thick white linens in the back. She hands us menus featuring the same entrées they had the last time I'd been here.

"Fancy." Matt holds up the menu. "Remember, I took you to Jake and Joes."

"Yes. The big pancake. Hard to forget."

He points at me. "Hey. I still owe you a date."

I tip my head. "A date?"

"Yeah. The challenge we made at Jake and Joe's, remember? You said I couldn't treat you to a good time on sixty bucks."

"Right." The memory of the bet comes flooding back. "The sixty-dollar soiree." It seems so long ago that I thought Matt would be too snobby to enjoy simple things. I'd been wrong. About a lot of things, apparently.

"As I recall," I say, "you promised me not just a good time but –" I make quotation marks with my hands – "an epic night."

Matt swipes his glass off the table. "And I'll make good on that." He holds up his glass and smiles. "Just you wait."

CHAPTER 34

Matt

Andi orders us fish tacos, a lobster quesadilla, and steamers. When she's done and the server walks away, I look at her. "Hey," I say, teasing, "bold of you to place my order."

"They're the best things on the menu. Trust me." She swats the air in my direction. "Plus, I'm paying."

"You're paying. How come?"

A smile inches across her face. "Remember the money I kept? From Cole's share of our wedding hotel deposit?"

I give her a conspiratorial look. "Really? For this?"

She shrugs. "It's a special occasion, right?"

I hold up my glass. "Nice. To you."

"To us," she says and clinks her glass to mine.

To us. I like the sound of that even though I know she doesn't mean it that way, like we're a couple. She'd been clear about that when she apologized for kissing me. My thoughts skirt to the kiss. I brush them off.

"Andi?" Two women charge our table. Andi puts her hands over her mouth, stands, and hugs each of them. "Oh my gosh.

Hey guys." She looks to me. "Kate, Lauren, this is my friend, Matt. Matt, these girls are Broadway's future stars."

"Future waitresses more like it," Lauren says with an eyeroll. Andi shakes her head. "No way. The future of Broadway. Right here."

"I'm impressed," I say.

They talk a moment at the edge of the table and our server asks if she wants us to set two more places. Andi looks to me. "I'm game."

After sitting, the three of them launch into a discussion of people and plays and rehearsals. Andi laughs. A lot. The full-bodied kind that makes me feel like I want to laugh just listening to it, even though I don't know what's funny. I love seeing her in this element and it strikes me how it might be lonely for her living with Liam in Scranton after having a life like this, in a city like New York.

Kate leans in Andi's direction. "So what have you been doing? I haven't seen you since-"

She lets the statement trail off, but the end is obvious. Kate hasn't seen Andi since she and Cole broke up.

Uncertainty crosses Andi's features.

"Andi works as the creative designer for an amusement park," I supply. "That's why we're here in New York. We had a meeting with an investor earlier."

"An amusement park?" Lauren says, incredulous. "That's crazy interesting."

Andi fields a plethora of questions about Christmastown and her design ideas. Cole is not brought up again. When there's a break in the conversation, Andi mouths "thank you." I give her a discreet thumbs up.

We finish dinner. The bill comes and Andi slides cash into the leather portfolio. She winks at me as she does it. My body feels warm under her gaze which might be from the several Manhattans. But I'm pretty sure it's because of her.

I take her hand because – Manhattans – and we step outside the restaurant.

It's raining.

Not drops or drizzles. Major rain. Sheets. We stand under the overhang of the restaurant, Andi's hand still in mine.

"I didn't bring an umbrella," she says. "Did you?"

"I didn't even know it was going to rain." Sobered a bit, I let go of her hand and pull out my phone.

"You won't get an Uber," Andi says, reading my mind. "Not anytime soon. Let's walk." She takes a step forward. Rain pelts at her and she looks back. "Don't tell me you're too much of a pretty boy that you can't get a little wet?"

Pretty boy. Not the first time I'd been called that. I'd always hated it. But, on Andi's lips, the words sound cute. I step into the rain. "I can get wet."

We hurry down the steps and spill on to the sidewalk. One block in and we're already soaked. Across the street, I spy a man selling umbrellas. I run to his kiosk, hand him twenty bucks, and pull an umbrella from the bin. I return to Andi and open it in a gallant manner.

It's a children's bubble umbrella. Cartoon ladybugs crawl all over its sides.

"I'll exchange it."

Andi grabs the crooked red handle, her fingers brushing mine. "Don't you dare. I love this umbrella." She steps under the plastic. "Come on. Get in here with me."

I eye the small space, clearly designed to fit one child. "Is there room?"

She stamps her foot. "Yes. Come on. You're getting wet. Or wetter."

I stoop down and pop up under. I'm inches from Andi, her fist tight around the handle. We walk, our steps hard to navigate in the confined space. I step into the front of the umbrella. Once. Again. After the third time, Andi puts her hand on my shoulder. "You've got to remember I'm shorter than you, Mr. Six Feet."

I glance at her shoes, spikey heels at least two inches. "Not in those shoes, you're not. How are you walking in those anyway?"

"Not very well," she admits.

"Well, I'll slow down, given that someone didn't wear appropriate city footwear."

She rolls her eyes. "Thank you, Matt."

I smile. We walk a few blocks in companionable silence. Then Andi stops without warning; I slam into the front of the umbrella. I turn to tease her about the abrupt stop, but her eyes are fixed on a bridal shop.

"It's still here," she says without explanation.

Rain pelts the umbrella. She bends down and moves to stand under the white awning in front of the shop. I place the ladybug umbrella on the ground and step beside her. I don't say anything and, after a long moment, Andi gestures to the dress in the window. "I tried on that dress."

I look at the dress, think about Andi in it. "You must have looked gorgeous." I mean it. It's a perfect dress for her.

She pulls her phone out of her purse, punches at it, and tips the screen in my direction. I take the phone from her and stare at an image of Andi in the dress. I meet her eyes. "You're stunning."

She doesn't answer. Heavy rain pelts the awning and wind whips the plastic. I hold her phone, my eyes fixed on the picture.

"I sent that picture to Cole," she tells me and, over the next few minutes, shares the rest of the story. I can't believe it when she's done. A complacent wallflower? No wonder she's needed time to get over the break-up. I'm physically angry. "What a jerk."

She smiles but it's not the usual Andi smile. It's wrought with emotion.

I grab her hand. "Andi, let me tell you something."

She half smiles. "Okay. What?"

"If you had sent me that picture, do you know what I would have done?"

She shakes her head.

"First, I would have tossed up a prayer of gratitude that a woman like you – beautiful, smart, and wildly talented – would go for a guy like me." I pause. "And then I would have kissed you."

CHAPTER 35

A *ndi*

Matt looks at me with a tender expression. My knees feel weak. I'm soaking wet, the wedding dress I tried on for Cole on a mannequin behind me. My heart beats harder, my face flushes with anticipation. I've never felt so primed for a kiss in my life.

Matt doesn't move and a gust of wind blows down the sidewalk. It catches the ladybug umbrella and it's airborne, half flying, half tumbling down the street, toward pedestrians hurrying under hoods. Matt sprints after it. It stops and rolls toward the street. He grabs the handle and walks back toward me, his face peeking out behind plastic lady bugs.

"That was a close one." He glances at the dress in the window and shakes his head. "Cole is officially the stupidest man on earth."

I laugh, but the moment, the moment where I felt Matt was seconds away from kissing me, seems lost. I stand still, hoping to recapture it, but Matt stays rooted under the umbrella. He holds it toward me. A gesture, I guess, to get going.

I duck under and, from that moment forward, everything is textbook friendship. Matt talks about *the rain* on the way back. At the hotel, I take the elevator; he takes the stairs. We meet Liam for breakfast in the morning and walk as a trio the train station. We stand in front of the giant electric train schedule, bags at our feet, crowds bustling around us. When Matt's train arrives, he gives me a hug not all that different from the shoulder pat he gave Liam moments before. Matt couldn't a give clearer signal that he wanted to be "just friends" if he tattooed the words on his forehead.

He shuffles in the pocket of his duffel and his swoon-worthy statement from last night re-orchestrates itself in my mind. It's clear that Matt didn't mean *he* was going to kiss me. He meant he would kiss me *if he were Cole.* I'd misunderstood.

He extends a folded paper with the hotel insignia on top. "Your invitation."

I take the paper from his hand; my fingers brush against his skin. "My invitation?"

"To dinner, remember? The sixty-dollar date?"

"Right." Right. Okay. I hold up the paper and give my best *I'm okay just to be friends with you even though we're both single smile.* "Looking forward to it."

"Me too." He flashes that ridiculous, perfect smile and moves toward his train.

Our train is called. Liam and I squish into a small seat, luggage under our feet and bags on our laps. I flip open Matt's paper, still clutched in my hand. His scrawl, in crayon, fills the page:

Dearest Andi,

I request the honor of your presence at a formal date on Friday the 20th of June. Shall you accept this invitation, I shall collect you from your residence at 7:00 p.m. Please reply via text.

Sincerely, Matt Taylor

I re-read the words. Who does this? Who can make something romantic and gallant and funny at the same time? Using hotel stationery and crayons?

I pull out my phone and type a text. *Yes. And what do u mean by formal?*

His response is immediate: *I'm wearing a tux.*

Tux? He has to be kidding. Right? I type back: *Ha ha. What r u really wearing?*

A tux. He sends another text almost immediately. *Did not buy it. Not part of $60.*

I laugh at this; I can't help it. *OK. C U Friday.*

* * *

EMMA INSISTS on coming to help me get ready for the date. She arrives with an armful of dresses, a bag of high-heeled shoes, and a what looks like a small suitcase of make-up. Hair supplies too. Flattening irons. Curling irons. Mousse. "We have to tame the beast," she says and grips a piece of my wet hair.

I tilt my head. "Thanks?"

"Don't worry, you'll look gorgeous." She rubs her hands together. "And he'll look gorgeous."

"Stop."

She gestures for me to sit in the desk chair in my room at Liam's. "What do you mean stop? He likes you. And you like him." She pulls out a dryer with a wide-mouthed tube on the end and grabs the largest round brush I have ever seen. She re-parts my hair with a comb.

"I don't know if he likes me that way." I don't insist I don't like him that way. I've already told Emma everything, including the moment in front of the wedding dress shop.

She rolls her eyes. "Yeah. Platonic friends always go out on formal dates in tuxes and gowns."

I wave my hand. "It's a joke. We're probably bowling or something."

"I doubt it."

Over the next twenty minutes, Emma pulls at my hair with enough force it's like she's having an upper body workout. After, she flips open her suitcase of make-up and painstakingly applies powders and creams. Every minute or so she steps back, inspects my face, and grabs something else from the case.

"That bad, huh?"

"That good. Almost done." She dips a sponge-like Q-tip into eyeshadow. "Close your eyes."

I do. Emma wipes the sponge across my lids.

"Okay. Open them."

I open my eyes.

"Yes." Emma accompanies the word with a fist pump and grabs a hand mirror. She holds it in front of me.

I peer at my reflection. My hair is in loose curls around my face and my make-up, despite how long it took to apply, looks natural. It's just that my lips look a little pinker, my eyes a deeper shade of blue. Even my cheekbones look defined, something I'm pretty sure has never happened before.

Emma wiggles the mirror. "Well?"

"I love it."

She sets the mirror down and claps. "I know, right? You look gorgeous already." She swipes the dress off my bed. "Now for the dress." She holds it out. It's long and black and fitted with a slit up one side. I look at Emma. "You're sure it's not too much?"

"It's incredible."

"Is it slutty?"

"It's sexy."

I finger the material.

"Come on," Emma encourages. "You tried it earlier."

I take it from her hands. "You don't think he's going to think I'm trying too hard? Like, if he is thinking this is a joke date and I come down in a dress like this?" I set the dress on the bed.

Emma grabs it. "It's not a joke, Andi. He likes you. Why is that so hard to believe?"

I shrug. All this time I thought Matt had a girlfriend, a perfect match. The idea that he doesn't, that he might be interested in me as more than a friend, is hard to comprehend.

She thrusts the dress in my direction.

I swipe it from her hands. "Fine. I'll try."

I step inside the circle of material and pull the bodice over my shoulders. Emma inches up the zipper and the fabric tugs, tight, around my body. She steps back and swipes a pair of silver high heels from the bed and hands them to me. I slip them on. Emma squeals and twists me around so I can see myself in the mirror.

Okay.

Not bad.

The sweetheart neckline of the dress shows cleavage, but not so much that it's obnoxious. With the possible exception of standing in the wedding dress (which I am NOT going to think about right now), this is as beautiful as I've ever felt.

"You're stunning."

I smile.

"You know it." She waves her hand at me. "Come on now. Own it."

My face reddens. Emma parades across the floor with her hand on her hip, an imitation of someone "owning it," I guess.

"Please stop."

She moves in front of me and puts her hands on my shoulders. "You are an exquisite human being." She turns me around and marches me toward the door. "Now get out of here and get that guy."

CHAPTER 36

A*ndi*
I baby step out of the room and descend the stairs, gripping the banister like a piece of life support. I reach the bottom and step into the kitchen. Liam glances at me. "Aye, Andi, you look lovely."

"Thanks," I manage, but my face, still hot from Emma teasing me, heats up even more. I knew this would happen. If I'm self-conscious already, how will I feel once Matt arrives?

Illuminated headlights appear in the driveway.

"He's here." Liam gestures to the window. I peek out.

Matt emerges from his car in a tux, a single rose in one hand, a box in the other. He's strides toward the house. He knocks and Liam leaves to answer. I'm positive my face is bright red. What should be butterflies in my stomach feel like bats.

I open the door from the kitchen to the foyer and peek around, unseen. Matt steps inside. He sets the box and rose on the credenza, shakes Liam's hand. The photographs I'd seen of him dressed up online did nothing to prepare me for how perfect he looks in person. His hair is slicked back with gel in a way that accentuates his eyes. The stubble remains, trimmed down.

At the same time, he looks like the Matt I've come to know. The guy who watches Wheel of Fortune over Facetime and who sends me texts of ridiculous sports pictures. The one who talked me up to my friends, who juggled on our first night out. I think about him racing up the stairs of the Sky Ornament Ride at that first meeting and shut my eyes. When I open them, Matt is looking directly at me.

"Andi." His face erupts in a smile.

I inch into the foyer, heart still beating hard.

"You look incredible." He steps back.

I look down, desperate to abate the heart-racing, cheek-burning feeling ripping my guts. "Ah. This old thing?" I shrug. "You look pretty nice yourself."

He ignores my compliment. "Seriously, Andi. You're stunning." His eyes sweep down the length of me. "Unbelievably beautiful."

I want to say something flip like "don't sound so surprised" but the moment is too intense. Matt's staring at me, I'm staring at him, and Liam is gone. It's only the two of us.

Matt swipes the rose from the credenza and holds it out. "For you."

I take it from his outstretched hand; my fingers graze his. The flush from my face creeps into my chest. "Thanks."

"Of course. And I have something else." He picks up the box, opens it, and pulls out an insane necklace, one with dozens of tiny diamond-encrusted flowers. "May I?"

I touch my bare neck and stare at the necklace. The diamonds shimmer in the light. "Matt –" I start.

He holds up his hand. "It's Steph's. She lent it to me." He holds the necklace out a second time. "May I?"

"Of course."

He moves behind me, his breath on my neck, capable hands on my skin. "There."

He steps back. I turn to face him. I put my hand on the necklace, the diamonds press into my skin. "Thank you. It's beautiful." "It's perfect." He looks at me another moment. "Shall we?" He holds out his elbow. His elbow! It is, without comparison, the most romantic start to a date I'd ever had.

I link my elbow in his and expect we'd head to his car. This is probably where the night gets light. Where we leave to bowl or mini-golf or eat in some rundown diner. But, instead of going toward the driveway, Matt guides me toward the back door. He pushes it open. "So," he says, glancing down, "I had to be creative with the venue, given the budget and all."

"I'm intrigued." My mind might have flashed to where we could possibly be going, but all I can think about is Matt. How he's looking at me. How his breath feels on my neck. The sensation of walking beside him, my arm safe inside his.

"It's a short walk, but through the woods."

"The plot thickens."

He guides me over uneven terrain. We hit a muddy patch and my feet, bare in the heels, sink into a pile of mud. I pull up a foot. It's covered in mud splatters.

Matt's head shoots down.

"Oh no. Your feet. And your shoes. I'm sorry." He stares at the ground. "I didn't think about mud."

I wave in his direction. "Matt, it's fine. Emma brought me these shoes. She got them on sale for almost nothing. Really, a little mud is no problem."

He shakes his head, eyes still glued to my feet. "No." He looks up at me. "No. I will not have your feet covered in mud." He gives a sheepish smile. "This is supposed to be the most epic date ever, remember? I can't have your only memory be how I got your shoes and feet all muddy."

I gaze at him in the tux, his features illuminated by gentle moonlight. "I'm pretty sure that's not the main thing I'm going to remember."

"I'm not taking any chances. So, if you'll excuse me for this -" He bends down and places once hand behind my knees and the other behind my back. He lifts me like it's nothing. His perfect, stubbled face is inches from my own. "Sorry."

Sorry? A handsome man in a tuxedo carrying me? I could not have designed a more sensual start to the date had I stayed up all night reading romance novels.

"Hey," he says, his voice soft, his mouth close to my ear. "Our venue is around the corner. Would you be willing to close your eyes? So, it'll be a surprise?"

"Of course." As if everything about tonight had not been a surprise already.

I close my eyes and Matt takes a few steps forward. It feels surreal and I half think I'm about to wake up and find I'd imagined the whole thing.

Matt sets me on the ground, the earth hard under my feet. A gentle wind caresses my back.

"Okay," he says in my ear, "open them."

CHAPTER 37

M^{att} Andi's hands fly to her mouth. I keep my arms around her. I mean, who wouldn't with that dress? I view my handiwork. Awesome.

Tall trees in full bloom surround the clearing in the woods. I'd hung a dozen white lanterns on the branches of the tree that overlooks our table. I'd set a sheet on the ground, dozens of tealights along its edge. Ruth's card table, covered with a lace tablecloth, sits in the center with lit candles of varied heights, waxy white drips down their sides. Liam's crystal and fine china are set out in two formal place settings. Easy music from my iPhone fills the space. Cheap wine sits in an ice bucket on a long table; gas-heated chafers hold our food.

"Matt. This is unbelievable." She extricates herself from my arms and turns to looks at me. "I can't believe you did all this."

I smile. "Told you I could plan a good date for sixty bucks."

She looks around, puts her hand on Steph's necklace.

Steph, man, she'd been right. The formal clothes and dinner had been her idea. When she'd pulled out her necklace for the loan, I'd waved it off. "Andi doesn't seem like the kind of girl who likes jewelry," I'd said. Steph looked at me like I was the dumbest guy on earth. "Every girl likes jewelry, dumbass."

So, I'd brought the necklace along, kind of thinking I'd leave in the box. The whole idea of pulling out Steph's necklace had seemed kind of cheesy. But then Andi appeared in that incredible dress, her neck bare. And I had to see how it would look. When I'd put the necklace around her, I could barely it clasp it, my fingers all thumbs.

Worth it.

Andi looks up. "Okay. You win. This is incredible. Even if we left now, it has to top out as one of the best dates of all time. I'm in the middle of a fairytale."

"It turned out better than I thought it would."

She stares at one of the hanging lanterns. "I don't think any guy has ever gone to this much effort for me."

"If that's true, a whole slew of guys completely missed the boat."

She waves me off. "You say that to all your dates."

I catch her eye. "Andi, I don't." I pause a moment. "And, for what it's worth, I've never gone to this much effort for a girl before."

She blinks and looks at the ground. The atmosphere is emotionally charged. I can't tell if it's good or a bad on her part, so I pull the wine from the ice bucket and make a show of holding up the bottle. "Madam, our best under ten-dollar wine. May I?"

She smiles and grabs a crystal glass from the table. "Please."

I screw off the top, fill both our glasses with white wine and hand one to Andi. I hold up mine. "To Christmastown."

"To Christmastown."

We clink glasses. Andi takes a sip, holds up her glass again. "And to sixty-dollar dates."

"May we all have fun on any budget."

We clink our glasses again and I move to the chafers. "Let me present our food." I lift a bowl of greens and set it down. "We've got Caesar salad, extra croutons." I put my hand on the first chafer. "Fish tacos." I move to the second chafer. "Lobster quesadillas." I look at her. "A little light on the lobster for budgetary reasons." I move to the third chafer. "And steamers." I lift the cover to the final chafer. "And, in case none of these are good, my back-up." I wave my hand over a tray of chicken tenders and mac and cheese.

Andi steps to the long table and examines the food. She angles her face toward mine. "You did not make all my favorites from Bar Centrale."

"I may have had a little help."

"Liam and Ruth?"

"How did you know?"

"The two of them are always cooking. I swear, Liam's going to need new clothes soon."

I laugh. They did have a comfort level together in Ruth's kitchen, both crowded around recipes, mixing bowls and whisks and baking trays strewn about the avocado countertops.

"I made the cake myself though." I pull a cover off a cake plate and reveal a lopsided two-tiered cake, chocolate icing smeared all over the top and sides. "I think it will taste good," I offer.

She looks from me to the cake. "I can't wait."

"Well," I hold out my hand. "Dig in."

Andi gets a little bit of everything, including the chicken tenders, and sets her heaping plate on the table. I push in her chair. On a whim, I grab a bottle of ketchup I'd placed next to the tenders (I know this is how Andi likes them by now), stand over her shoulder, and, in the manner of a server with fresh-ground pepper, ask "ketchup for your tenders, ma'am?"

She glances up at me. "Of course. What kind of person doesn't have ketchup with their chicken tenders?"

"I can't imagine." I open the ketchup, hold it over her plate, and hit the bottle, hard, on the bottom. Nothing. I hit it again and a big load of ketchup shoots out.

Right on to Andi's chest and dress.

No.

I grab Andi's napkin. "I'm so sorry." I wipe at the condiment, but as I clean it off, the ketchup spreads all over her chest and cleavage. No. I drop the napkin. "Sorry I –"

I glance at Andi.

She's laughing.

Not a giggle or a chuckle. The sound that's coming out of Andi's mouth is howling and guttural. "It's fine. It's fine," she says. She waves one hand, holds her stomach with the other.

The sound is contagious. I laugh too, a little at first, then harder. I perch myself on the edge of my chair. "I can't believe I did that."

She grabs my napkin and wipes at the smeared ketchup. "It's all good, Matt. I think we know each other well enough by now that we can deal with a little ketchup on my chest."

"A lot of ketchup on your chest."

She pats at it with the other side of the napkin. "It's off now."

"Sorry."

"Stop. I'm glad it happened."

I bug my eyes out. "Glad? I'm mortified."

"You're human. Thank God you're human because I was starting to feel out of my league."

"Out of your league? Come on, Andi. You know what a screw up I am. You *know* me."

She gestures to me. "Well, right now, in that tux, you look like a romance movie love interest. You even smell incredible."

I blush. I'm not sure a girl has ever made me blush. It's embarrassing. "What about you?" I say, changing the subject. "Who knew how unbelievable you would look? When I caught a glimpse of you in the foyer, well –" I pause and recollect the moment when I saw her, the dress stretched across her body, hair cascading down her back – "you took my breath away. And you smell incredible too." I wink.

She laughs. "Well, aren't we just two good-smelling, incredible-looking buddies."

Buddies.

Right.

I have to remember that just because I feel one way doesn't mean Andi does. I gesture to our plates. "Should we eat?"

"Thought you'd never ask." Andi picks up a fish taco and takes a huge bite. She swallows. "So good." She looks at me. "Really, Matt. These are just like Bar Centrale."

I doubt that's true but the way she smiles makes me feel like it might be. "I'm so glad."

Andi samples the mac and cheese. I take such honest pleasure from her enjoyment of the food, it's ridiculous. I've been out to dinner with a lot of girls. I've been to five-star restaurants with world-renowned chefs. Yet this little dinner in the woods with Andi, a woman who might have no romantic interest in me at all, is my favorite.

She wipes her face with a napkin. "The food is incredible."

"And you haven't even tried the cake."

"I can't wait for the cake." The music on the speaker changes to a waltz. Andi inclines her head toward it. "A waltz. Classy."

"Do you know how to ballroom dance?"

"No." She laughs like I'd made a joke. "Do you?"

"Of course."

She slaps her hand on the table. "You do not."

"I do. My parents insisted. They had this woman come to the home a bunch of times to teach us manners and stuff."

She puts down her drink. "Like a tutor?"

"Yeah. Kind of like that. Her name was Miss Kay. Sometimes I still hear her in my head. Don't point with your index finger. Don't announce your bathroom breaks. Pass the salt and pepper together."

Andi lifts an eyebrow. "Sounds intense."

"Right now, I can hear her dance instructions."

"Seriously?"

"Yeah. Want to learn?"

"To waltz?"

"It's easy." I stand and hold my hand out.

She pauses a beat then slips her hand into mine. "Okay. But I might not be good."

I pull her to her feet. "I think you'll be perfect." I move so we are standing side by side. "This," I start, "is a box step. One, left foot backward. Two, step to the side. Three, step forward." I repeat the movements, recite the directions again. Andi moves per my instructions, her face adorable with concentration. I repeat the movements again. "That's right," I encourage. "One, two, three. One, two, three. One, two, three." I stop and watch her. Dancing in the forest, her face illuminated by candlelight.

She catches me looking, stops her own rhythm. "What?"

"Nothing. You look good, that's all."

"Would your Miss Kay approve?"

"Absolutely." I take a step toward the speaker and adjust it back to the beginning of the waltz. "Do you want to try with a partner?"

She steps toward me. "That would seem the most natural next step, wouldn't it?"

"That, it would." I face Andi. "According to Miss Kay, the waltz is mainly about posture. I'm going to hold your left arm up, you look straight over my shoulder, head tilted up. You put your right hand on my shoulder; I'll put mine on your back."

She mimes the movements in the air.

"Right," I say and hold my arms out.

She grasps my elevated left hand, puts her other on my right shoulder. Her face is inches from mine, angled over my shoulder as I'd instructed. I put my hand on her back, near the shoulder blade, and pull her close, but not too close. The inches between us are intoxicating, more than that would have been had we been touching.

"Here we go," I whisper. "One, two, three. One, two, three. One, two, three." We move, tentative at first, Andi's body erect with concentration. We repeat the steps and I keep up the mantra, my mouth near her ear. "One, two, three. One, two, three. One, two, three." Her shoulders drop, the movements become more fluid. "One, two, three. One, two, three. One, two, three." And we're in it. Waltzing in the woods, lanterns hanging all around us, an almost full moon overhead.

The music ends. Andi stops moving. She angles her face up and meets my eyes, her lips impossibly close.

CHAPTER 38

ndi

Matt's lips are on mine, gentle at first, then more searching. He pulls me closer, his body hard and muscular. He skims his hand down my dress; I grip his shoulders. The waltz continues and the lanterns flicker and sway in the breeze. The scent of our food infuses the air. I scarcely notice any of it. It's like time has stopped. It's me and Matt in a summer paradise.

He pulls back. "I have wanted to do that since the day I met you."

"You have?"

"Of course. I'm not insane."

He cups his hands around my face and kisses me again. I pull him tighter, whisper in his ear. "I've wanted to kiss you since the day I met you too."

He pulls back. "Really?"

"Yes. You were such a surprise. I thought you were going to be this fussy insurance person."

"I thought you were going to be a guy."

We both laugh but Matt's face turns serious. "This is okay with you?"

I know he's talking about Cole. He's putting me first. Again. "Matt," I say, looking up into his eyes, "you have made me feel a way no one ever has. Not Cole. Not anyone." I tiptoe so my eyes meet his. "This is absolutely okay."

His lips crush against mine. I'm consumed by him, his body, his lips, his hands all over me. I don't want it to stop and I'm not sure how long we're there, kissing in the moonlight, but, when we eventually pull apart, the music has stopped and all but two lanterns are out. Candles flicker on the table.

Matt slices two pieces of cake, puts them on plates, and sets one before me. He sits in the chair, his face framed in candlelight. His lips are swollen. Mine are too.

He smiles. "So. Do I win the bet? Did I pull off an epic date with just sixty bucks?"

"Hmm." I make a show of thinking. "I mean, the candlelight setting and the formal clothes and the gorgeous jewelry are all points in your favor. And the food was good. Fantastic, really." I stab a piece of cake with my fork and hold it up. "But I really think it all comes down to this cake."

"Down to the cake, huh?"

"Yeah." I put the fork in my mouth and bite the cake off. "This," I say, pointing the remainder of the cake with my fork, "might be the best cake I've ever had." I lift my eyebrows.

Matt shovels an oversized bite in his mouth and gives me a long look. "It's also the best cake I've ever had."

I tip my head. "I'm not talking about the cake, are you?"

He gives a wry shake of the head. "I wasn't talking about the cake, but I'm not as smooth as you think I am, so I'll go with whatever you were thinking." He stabs another piece of cake and holds his fork in the air. "To the best cake and the best kiss I've ever had."

I bump my own piece of cake to his. "To that."

We simultaneously pop cake in our mouths, and I'm struck by how fun it is. Romantic evenings with Cole were always serious. Candlelight affairs, not unlike tonight, but no levity. At all. We'd sit at some exclusive restaurant and Cole would look into my eyes, a heavy glass of expensive liquor gripped in his hand. He'd hold it up and we'd clink our drinks, and he'd say something entirely generic like "to us." The evening would have all the marking of romance, but it would never *feel* romantic.

Matt stands, walks to the table where he'd set the music and food and wine. He starts the music, grabs the wine out of the bucket, ice rattling in the wake. He approaches the table. I study him as he moves. He looks ethereal, like a supernatural, extraordinarily handsome being dropped from beyond. I want to kiss him again and, when he reaches the table, I stand. I extricate the bottle from his fingers and set it on the table. I encircle his neck with my hands, pull him close, and kiss him.

"I think you need to carry me back to the house," I whisper.

"For more cake?"

"For all the cake."

CHAPTER 39

ndi

A I wake up in my room at Liam's, my naked body tangled with Matt's. I feel like I snuck a boy into my room after curfew.

Matt rouses. His eyes flutter open and he shifts his head on the pillow. "Hey you." He smooths back my hair and kisses my forehead. "Good morning."

"Good morning." I prop myself up on my elbow. "You win the bet, by the way. Most epic date ever."

"Yeah? What put me over the edge?"

I smirk. "Definitely the cake."

"That is good news because I liked the cake the most as well."

He leans over and kisses my lips. What starts as gentle kissing morphs into a passionate repeat of last night. I fall into a half-sleep after, my head on his chest. Matt strokes my hair. "I love all the curls," he whispers.

I smile, too contented and too sleepy to comment. I fall asleep and am roused by the ping of the text message. Matt hands me my phone. A text from Mom. *Party starts at five.*

"Hot date?" Matt teases.

"Already checked that one off," I say. "Betsy's birthday party is today."

He sits up. "Betsy? Cinderella Betsy?"

"One and the same."

"Can I come?"

I glance over at him. "You can't seriously want to come. It's at Pizza Pals."

"I like pizza."

"The pizza is actually really bad. A Pizza Pals party is basically a bunch of kids, hyped up on sugar, running around playing video games."

Matt snorts. "What, exactly, about that does not sound like something I would like?"

I think a moment. "Crap. You're right. I was thinking about most normal adults. I forgot we are talking about you."

He bugs his eyes out. "Rude. Plus, Betsy likes me. And your mom."

This is an understatement. For weeks after the beef and beer, my mother kept asking about Matt, but she'd forgotten his name. She kept referring to him as the "tall handsome one." Chelsea asked about him too.

"Of course, you can come. But seriously, you're not bothered that Sawyer Hughes is coming Monday? You don't need to prepare?"

"He's presenting to us, remember?"

"Right," I say with more conviction than I feel. Something in my gut makes me nervous when I think about Sawyer. "Okay. Given your propensity for chaos and bad pizza, please come as my plus one."

He throws a slick smile. "I thought you would never ask."

We walk into Pizza Pals together, Matt with a secret, glittery gift bag in his hand. A gift he insists Betsy will love. The girl at the silver gate stamps our hands with an obligatory hand stamp, a picture of a cat with giant ears, one of the pals. He holds up his hand. "Catman."

I laugh and am so busy looking at the stamp that I almost ram into two boys running with plastic cups of game tokens.

"Watch it there, Catgirl."

"No. No. No," I say as we walk. "Not Catgirl. Wonder Woman. She's a friggin' badass."

"Fine. Wonder Woman it is. You'll need a costume though." He winks.

I slap his chest. "Stop."

Video games line the walls, a few boxy ones in the center. A series of colorful, connected plastic tubes line the ceiling with a big slide at the end. Kids crawl through. One whips down the slide with a soda in her hand. Video games beep and whir in electronic tones; bright lights flicker inside games. It smells overwhelmingly like pizza, and silver platters of half-eaten pies sit on tables all over the room, half-filled paper soda cups between them. Adults congregate in tiny groups around the edges of the space; kids sprint from game to game, prize tickets streaming from tiny hands.

It's so opposite of the woodland date that I almost laugh.

Mom waves from a corner, Jim affixed to her side like an appendage. "Andi. Over here."

We reach the party table. "You all remember Matt, right?" I'm pretty sure my face heats when I say the words, like there's a siren on my head blaring: yes, I had sex with this man three times in twenty-four hours, the last time just before we got here.

I don't have to worry because Mom completely ignores me and is all about making sure Matt has pizza. And a drink. And that he knows where the bathrooms are! It's not unexpected. Matt is THE MAN and, as such, in Mom's world, he gets absolute priority. I'm surprised she didn't suggest he sit in Betsy's birthday throne – a special, over-the-top chair for birthday girls and boys. Jim looks a little miffed, like he doesn't know what to do with himself without Mom cheering him on.

"Thanks so much for coming." Chelsea hugs Matt and me.

Two kids step forward, party guests, and hold up empty cups. "Off for tokens," she says.

"I'll get them," Matt takes the empty cups and makes his way to a token dispenser.

"He's a keeper," Chelsea declares.

"He is." I don't fight the suggestion. I can't pretend I'm not head-over-heels and completely infatuated with Matt Taylor anymore.

He returns with several cups that brim with so many game tokens, they look like they might spill over the edge. He sets them on the table. "Tokens for anyone who wants them."

I nod in the direction of the cups. "What did you do? Buy them all out?"

"No," he insists. "Just want to make sure there are enough for Betsy and her friends." He sweeps a cup of tokens off the table. "And for us. They have some seriously good prizes back there." He nods toward a booth crammed with cheap plastic items. Plush animals hanging from the ceiling over it and trays of candy sit in a covered case in front. "I'm going for the Nerf gun."

I peer in the direction of the prizes. "But what if I wanted the stuffed dog pal?"

He looks at me, his mouth in a smirk. "Well, you're on your own. I take my video game prizes seriously. This is no time for chivalry, Andi."

I smirk back at him. "Of course not."

He gestures toward a giant, upright wheel with sparkly numbers. "That looks like a good one. Should we try?"

We move to the wheel. He leans against the side of it in a way that looks seductive which, I know, is ridiculous given that we are in the middle of bleeping video games and screaming kids. My mind is still on the past twenty-four hours.

"Are you going to take it for a spin?" he asks.

"You bet." I reach up to grip one of the wheel's handles.

"Wait, wait," Matt says. "I think you need to grip it differently."

He moves behind me, puts his hands over mine, and adjusts them on the handle. His entire body is touching mine.

It's distracting.

"Now try," he says and steps back.

I pull the wheel. It spins around and lands almost exactly between 100 and 5000, the arrow slightly toward the latter. Tickets shoot out of the machine, a long strip of pink.

Matt holds up his hand. I high five it.

"Nice! Looks like someone's getting a stuffed dog pal."

We follow the wheel game by basketball shooting, throwing marbles on plates, a rousing game of Ms. Pac Man, and skeeball. Matt is a family star. Every time he passes Betsy, he gives her a fist pump. He waves at Mom when she's in his line of vision. He helps Brian and Chelsea distribute pizza on unicorn-themed plates and runs to find plastic forks when they run out. He slices cake, pours glasses of juice, and stuffs used wrapping paper into a giant plastic trash bag. His surprise gift to Betsy is an Elsa costume. She hugs it to her chest after opening and Chelsea is commandeered into the bathroom to help her change into it. Both of us give Betsy our prize tickets, and after she runs to the prize stand, a stream of tickets trailing behind her.

Matt and I stand the outskirts of the party room, remnants of cake and pizza strewn about the table. I lean into him. "You may have to calm down with all this helpfulness. My family may keep you hostage or something."

He makes a face like he's thinking. "Does that mean I'd get to attend more parties at Pizza Pals? Cause I could get into that."

I push at his shoulder. "You are too much. Thank you for coming."

"You're welcome." He kisses my cheek. "I had fun."

"I know. I love that."

My mind flashes to an image of Cole at this same party. He'd have stood in the corner, body language screaming "get me out of here," his long black hair pulled around his face like a shield. He wouldn't have played any games. He might have reluctantly stuffed a slice of pizza in his mouth. Instead of a gift she could open, he'd probably have given Betsy a gift card.

I grab Matt's hand. "We should go. Monday's a big day."

He agrees and we help with the final clean up and say goodbye to my family. Betsy, now in the Elsa costume, gives Matt a giant hug. I can't remember a more seamless family introduction.

All we need is for tomorrow to go well.

CHAPTER 40

M*att*
The day after the Pizza Pals party, Andi and I are in the toy store setting up for the meeting with Sawyer Hughes. Her arms are wrapped around a heavy chair; she's heaving it across the room. I extricate it from her hands.

"Hey. I had that." She tilts her head up and her ponytail shifts. "I've moved a lot of heavy things for sets, you know."

I put the chair down and give her a peck on the lips. "Sorry. Instinct." I look from her to the chair. "But I'd like to move it, if that's okay."

She scrunches up her face as if she's contemplating an immensely difficult question. "Okay. If it means that much to you."

"Thank you. It does."

It does actually. I don't want Andi to struggle with anything, certainly not a chair. I place it behind a long table in the front of the room, the place where we anticipated Sawyer would set up.

I look up and Andi's dragging a round table, way heavier than the chair, toward the center of the room. I don't interfere. She shifts the table to the left. "What?"

I hold my hands up. "Nothing. I'm just impressed you moved that."

She puts her hands on her hips. "I'm very strong."

"I have no doubt."

She eyes the table, shifts it back. "So. Are you excited for *Sawyer* to get here?" She emphasizes his name.

"Stop."

She crosses the room, picks a piece of lint off my shirt. "Come on, admit it. You have a little bit of a man crush on Sawyer Hughes."

I step back and look down at her. "Okay. Fine. Maybe a little."

She swats at my chest. "I knew it."

"The man's entire company is based on making boring places fun. I mean, come on." I don't add that I'm impressed by Sawyer's cool assurance, the fact that he doesn't seem to care at all about societal norms. In my research for today, I'd learned he had a yacht named *Last Laugh* and a racehorse, *All Horse and No Play*. And a New York City penthouse.

"It will be interesting to see what he came up with, that's for sure." Andi says. She moves the table a few inches to the right.

She's not as into Sawyer and Fun Overhaul as I am. It's one of the few areas where we don't feel aligned. We agree even on stupid things. Like, last night, we played *Would You Rather* with Liam and Ruth over wine and whiskey. We'd both rather be in a water balloon fight than a food fight. We'd rather find rats in our kitchen than roaches in our bed. We'd prefer wearing the same socks for a month over the same underwear for a week. We prefer to be excessively early over being a little late. We'd build forts on snow days rather than stay in.

Each time we'd turn over our papers with the same answer, Andi held up her hand for a fist pump. After the fifth time, Ruth exclaimed, "it's like kismet!"

I *know* a stupid game of *Would You Rather* doesn't mean

anything. It's less about the game than the feeling. With Andi, I can let out every piece of me. The parts where I can't sit still or have to ask her to repeat herself because I lost track of what she was saying. The parts where I'm quiet or loud. The times when I'm cranky. And the times when I can't keep my hands to myself. A lot lately.

I look forward to talking to or seeing Andi like it's the best part of my day.

It *is* the best part of my day.

She steps away from the table. A ping rings out. Andi slides her phone from her jeans and glances at the screen. An excited expression on her face morphs to an unreadable one.

"Everything okay?"

She looks at the phone like there's something on it she can't quite decipher. "It's for *A Walk in the Park*. It's down to me and one other person. They want to see one more design."

She looks at the phone again like she is checking to make sure she got the information right then lifts her head in my direction.

"Wow. Congratulations."

She shoves the phone back in her pocket. "I probably won't get it."

I whip my head up and look at her. "You probably will." But a selfish part of me hopes she won't. Long distance relationships are hard no matter what, but an overseas one would be particularly difficult. Especially since we are, just now, getting to know each other as more than friends.

Before either of us can comment further, the door swings open. Heels click on the floor. Bridget. She smiles in our direction. "Matt. Andi. I'm here for the meeting."

It takes me way longer than it should to process this statement. Probably because I did not invite her. And I know Andi didn't. Maybe Liam?

"Sawyer won't be here for another twenty minutes or so,"

Andi supplies. "I was about to get some drinks and food at the house. Do you want to come?"

Bridget sits down at the round table, the one Andi had just lugged across the room. It feels like she's emoting villain vibes, and I try to convince myself how silly that is. All she's said is that she's here for the meeting, a meeting she's fully aware I set up, and which is important to her father. It's not like before, when I was immersed in the highly uncomfortable double-agent dynamic. Bridget knows why we're here. There's no reason to assume a perverse intention.

"I'll stay here," she says and crosses her legs.

"Okay. Drinks on their way." Andi pushes open the door. It slams shut with a bang and I'm alone with Bridget for the first time since our confrontation about the fire.

"Well, Matt," Bridget says, "I've got to hand it to you, getting an investor to look at this property."

The words sound nice. They don't feel that way.

She fiddles with a pendant on her necklace. "I do hope Dad will have an open mind with respect to whatever Sawyer comes up with. It's not like this venue is teeming with possibility."

And there it is.

"It is teeming with possibility," I counter.

Before Bridget answers, the door opens. Liam and Ruth step inside, Ruth with a giant tray of Yuletide cookies covered in saran wrap. They're dressed in coordinating red shirts. I assume it's not planned, but who knows? They spend a massive amount of time together. Lots of baking. Last night they'd made banana bread.

"Dad." Bridget stands and strides toward her father. She embraces him, a full-bodied one, both arms wrapped around him in a tight squeeze. When she finally releases him, she looks to Ruth. "Nice to see you again."

Ruth throws her a broad smile.

Andi returns with drinks, Beckham and Emma behind her. We're all here. The original Santa Games committee.

"Sawyer just pulled in," Beckham announces. "Got a sweet ride too."

Nervous anticipation rises in my stomach. I have no reason to think things won't go well. Sawyer practically guaranteed a deal. Still, things *need* to go well. The other investors who'd seemed interested hadn't called.

Sawyer was it.

CHAPTER 41

Matt Sawyer saunters in wearing a black t-shirt with the Fun Overhaul logo in the center. He slaps his computer down on the front table. "Are you ready to have your mind blown?"

Beckham raises a fist. "Yeah, man."

I fist bump Beckham. "Show us what you got."

Sawyer slings a black bag on to the chair in front and pulls out a long, nylon sleeve. He reaches inside and produces a folded screen on a silver easel. He shakes it once; it pops open to full size. I'm stupidly mesmerized, like he's a magician and, next, a dove will fly out of his pocket, or he'll pull a coin from his ear.

He fiddles with the computer, grabs a remote out of the bag, and pushes his hair off his face. He doesn't talk and doesn't seem uncomfortable in the silence. He points the remote at the screen and clicks it. "Here we go." Green letters on a black backdrop fill the screen. The letters drip in what I think is supposed to mimic slime. The words: Welcome to Ghoultown.

Andi hits my thigh.

Sawyer grabs a pointer from the magician bag. "Surprised ya, didn't I?" He winks.

I laugh. It's a joke. Of course, it's a joke. I should have known any presentation by Sawyer Hughes would be fun.

"As you know," he starts, "Fun Overhaul is a company dedicated to amplifying fun. But we're also about profit. Massive profits for us. And for our clients." He moves to the screen and underlines the word "Ghoultown" with the pointer. "Halloween sells," he says seriously. "Fun Overhaul has done extensive market research and has found that Halloween outsells Christmas in every demographic except families with young children. And, even there, families with kids as young as seven still like a good scare."

He taps the pointer against his open palm, paces like a tiger in a zoo cage. "Fear is a massive money maker. Let me show you." He clicks the remote. The slide depicts a bar graph with two bars, a black one titled "Scare" and a red one titled "Cheer." Running across the bottom are category names: candy, themed-paraphernalia, decor, costumes. In each, the black bar is longer than the red bar. "Beyond this," Sawyer says, "there's the trend toward pop-up Halloween stores and interactive experiences like hayrides and mazes. Halloween is huge and has longer lasting power than Christmas. At least four months of the year are dedicated to Halloween, one for Christmas."

Andi squeezes my hand, hard, under the table.

"Wait," I mouth. I'm sure Sawyer is moments away from his big reveal: how Fun Overhaul would defy these compelling and lopsided stats. How Christmastown would somehow outpace the profits of Halloween and, possibly, all the other holidays put together.

He flips his hair back from his face. "And so," he says, "we pivot for profit. My design team has been hard at work on some initial prototypes for a Halloween themed park." He clicks to the next slide. Andi's original sketch of The Sky Ornament Ride appears on the left. I glance at the now familiar drawing of suspended baskets that look like Christmas ornaments hung by steel cables disguised as big red bows. Next to it, the Fun Overhaul drawing shows the same ride with its new Halloween theme: Andi's shiny ornaments replaced by frightening-looking pumpkin heads, the festive bows now spears.

Andi whips her head around and looks at me, eyes wide. "I told you so" blares behind her gaze. I glance around the room. Beckham leans forward with his thumb up likes it's frozen in place. Bridget looks impassive, almost bored. Everyone else looks shocked. Ruth's brows are knitted together as if she can't work out what Sawyer's talking about. Liam looks angry. Emma's mouth hangs open.

Sawyer either doesn't notice or doesn't care. He clicks to the next slide which depicts the Santa themed roller coaster modified so the cars look like reclining skeletons.

Click. The Merry-Go-Round features ghouls instead of reindeer.

Click. Mrs. Claus's Bake Shop is now Shelly's Spirits.

Click. The Toy Store is an Old-Time photo booth where groups pose for professional photos dressed as varied scary creatures.

Click. Click. Click. Each slide is worse that the last. My heart falls in my chest and sits like a boulder on the bottom of my stomach. No. No. No. It wasn't supposed to turn out this way. Sawyer was supposed to tweak Liam and Andi's ideas, not throw them out.

"Here's a good one, a big money maker," he says. "Ghoultown can serve as a venue for weddings with a haunted theme. There's nothing like that anywhere." He clicks a new slide which features a photograph of a zombie bride he must have pulled from the internet.

I can't even look at Andi.

Gratefully, Sawyer doesn't wait for a response and clicks the remote again. I sit up. The new slide lays out income projections. I stare at the numbers. Phenomenal income projections. Crazy income projections. Heart stopping, jaw dropping income projections. The kind that would be difficult to ignore.

Sawyer underlines the bottom number with his pointer. "I hope this figure is enough to convince you to look no further than Fun Overhaul for your investment needs." He leaves the number on the screen and looks around, expectant.

It's silent in a bad way. Stunned silence. Dismayed silence. Stupified, shocked, speechless silence. Beckham coughs; it's a relief.

Liam pushes back his chair, legs scratch on the hardwood floor. He crosses his arms. "I hate the idea."

"Dad." Bridget says his name like a warning.

Liam shifts. His back is to Sawyer; he's aligned directly with Bridget. "There's nothing about this your mother would want, sweetheart. She was all about Christmas and magic and happy memories. This is the opposite of all that." He sounds like he's talking to a small child.

Bridget shakes her head. "Mom would want you taken care of. She wouldn't want you sitting on a money pit."

"She would if this Ghoultown was the alternative." His face is red, his breathing slightly labored.

Ruth moves closer. "Are you all right?" she whispers.

He nods. Bridget doesn't push him again. Sawyer packs up his screen without speaking.

"Well, I'd go there," Beckham calls. "That idea is sick. That skeleton coaster man." He shakes his head.

Emma shoots her hand out and grips his forearm. "Read the room, Beck," she whispers.

Sawyer snaps his computer shut. I feel opportunity slipping away like water circling a drain. My brain spins and works for an angle, some way to get Sawyer to consider Christmastown. Nothing.

He produces a bound document from his bag and drops it on the table. "The slides in written form." His eyes find Liam. "If you change your mind, we can talk numbers." He slings the bag over his shoulder in a fluid movement and moves toward the door.

"Awesome presentation, man," Beckham calls.

Sawyer stops, points a finger gun in Beckham's direction, and moves his thumb like he's shooting. "Thanks, bro." He opens the door and slips out.

"Totally sick," Beckham reiterates, his eyes fixed on the doorframe.

Emma slaps his hand. "Really?"

"What?"

Bridget retrieves the bound document and flips to the profits page. She turns it around in the manner of a kindergarten teacher showing an illustration in a storybook. Her eyes rest on Liam. "I would not dismiss this out of hand, Dad. I know you had an idea –"

"Your mother's idea," Liam interrupts. "One I promised I would make a reality. Look, I know not every idea I've had is a winner, but this one is. This little pocket of joy in the world? I want this to be me and your mother's legacy. It's not about the money, Bridget. It's about the magic." He swipes a Yuletide cookie from the plate. "For me, it's Christmastown or bust."

Ruth puts her hand on his shoulder. "I'm with Liam. Christmastown or bust."

Andi smiles for the first time since the meeting started. "Christmastown or bust."

"Christmastown or bust," Emma echoes. She stares at Beckham who sits, silent, beside her. She slaps his shoulder. "Beck."

"Fine," he sighs, "Christmastown or bust." He pushes his bang back and adds, "but, for the record, Ghoultown is friggin' awesome."

There's momentary laughter, even from Liam. All eyes are on me. Bridget lifts an eyebrow. I can guess what she wants me to do: talk up Ghoultown and profits, make some smooth argument about why Liam should at least wait to say no. Part of me wants to. Part of me wants to work with Sawyer Hughes, a.k.a. the coolest man on earth, more than I want this venture off the ground. Ghoultown, Christmastown. They're both holidays. They'd both be original, epic, one-of-a-kind parks.

I catch Andi's gaze. She looks stunned, like she can't believe it's taking me so long to respond. My mind flies through all the conversations we've had about the park, to images of the two of us on the platform of the Sky Ornament Ride. I think about setting up The Santa Games and running all over the property in search of items on my scavenger hunt app.

And, even though today's Andi is right in front of me, I recall the other versions of her as easily as if there were multiple Andis in the room. Andi in the cat pajamas. Andi in the wedding dress. Andi in the incredible gown for our outdoor picnic. Andi when she's outside and the sun catches her eyes. Andi wrapped up in a blanket. Andi trying to win over Claus.

The answer is so clear, I'm not sure why I'd hesitated. I want to be with Andi, to see her be happy, so much more than I want to work with Sawyer Hughes. It's a no-brainer. I slap my hand on the table.

"Christmastown or bust."

CHAPTER 42

M*att*
Two days after the meeting, I'm on the front stoop of my brownstone, staring at my phone. I punch in the numbers. I know I shouldn't.

"Fun Overhaul." It's the dour receptionist. I can tell by her voice.

"It's Matt Taylor from Christmastown. I'd like to set up a meeting with Sawyer Hughes."

She says nothing for several beats. "You had a meeting with Mr. Hughes," she says curtly. "On Monday."

"Another meeting. Face to face. I can come there."

She exhales as though I've asked for something extraordinary. Maybe I have. Sawyer's a busy man. And Liam said no. But the thought of pitching more investors is depressing. The thought of the project being over is even worse.

"I'll see if he's available," she says.

I wait. A hot breeze blows at my back. A woman with two pugs makes her way across the street. An open-windowed car, vibrating with loud country music, passes.

It's been too long.

I stand and pace. I picture the receptionist, still at her desk, her phone facedown next to her. She's probably just waiting an appropriate amount of time before telling me to pound sand.

"Mr. Taylor."

I grip the phone to my ear, actually expecting the words "pound sand" to come out of her mouth.

"Can you come in Friday?"

"I can do that."

* * *

Convincing Liam to come to the second Sawyer meeting was a chore, not that I should have been surprised given that he now refers to him only as "the wanker." But I convinced him. Christmastown might not make as much profit as Ghoultown, but it wouldn't be nothing. And Liam's mantra – it's about the magic, not the money – was moving. We just had to get Sawyer to consider the idea.

We're in New York, the two of us, skyscrapers on either side of the crowded street. "I think we should go to that same deli after," Liam says. "You know, the one with the crusty rolls."

It's the only deli we've been to together, ever, so I know what he's talking about. "Sure, Liam."

He pulls at his shirt – he'd refused to get dressed up for the "wanker meeting"- as I pull into the parking garage. "We should get cookies this time," he suggests. "You know, those big ones, by the counter."

I maneuver my car into a tiny space. "Sure."

"I'm going to bring some back for Ruth. I'm thinking oatmeal."

I punch the engine button. "She'll like that," I manage, having no idea if Ruth would like oatmeal cookies or not. I'm frankly miffed that Liam is consumed by cookies ten minutes before the meeting for *his* park. I wonder, not for the first time, what the heck I am doing here.

But I know. Part of it is to see The Santa Games to fruition, proof that I can be successful without connections. The second part, the bigger one, is Andi. I want Chrismastown to succeed for her personally but I'm also afraid that, without it, things will change. She'll take that London job if she gets it.

"Maybe I'll bring some sandwiches home," Liam muses. "Do you think they'll keep?"

I don't answer, I can't, and thankfully Liam does not bring up food again. We enter the waiting room (still the coolest space ever) and are ushered by the sour-faced woman to Sawyer's personal office. Unlike the rest of the Fun Overhaul space, Sawyer's office is ordinary. Messy stacks of paper line his desk. Generic, abstract pictures, the kind that you might buy in a box store, hang haphazardly on tan walls. There are no framed photos, no trophies or knick-knacks or books. Even Sawyer looks different. His hair not hip but long, his clothes sloppy rather than chic. I feel like I caught the wizard behind the curtain in Oz.

"All right," he says, dark circles I'd never noticed prominent under his eyes, "you've changed your mind about Ghoultown?"

Liam stiffens.

"Actually," I say, "we'd like you to consider the original Christmastown idea."

"I did consider it." He leans back and taps a pen on his knee. "That was the whole idea behind Monday's presentation."

"I think there might be real commercial value in the back-story of Mr. Quinn and his wife," I say. "Their idea to create a little pocket of joy in the world after enduring some of life's more difficult experiences. The fact that they value people over profit, magic over money. It must mean something."

Sawyer twists the pen between his fingers. He says nothing but it looks like he's thinking. Liam seems to take his silence as an opportunity. He shares more details about tragedies he and Colleen had endured – lost jobs, miscarriages, cancer. Liam's bout in Vietnam.

Sawyer's eyes are intense, his head gently nods. The electricity in the room changes. And it feels like this is it. We're doing it. Story by story, Liam is gradually shifting Sawyer's perspective. I want to fist pump him.

"So," Liam concludes, "like I've said, it's always been about the magic, not the money."

Sawyer leans back, still twisting the pen. I imagine he's thinking about angles, about ways to market Christmastown. The longer he's silent, the more it seems this version of things is correct. It wouldn't take this long to say no.

After what feels like an hour, Sawyer jolts up. "It is about the money."

I stand with my arm extended before what Sawyer actually said catches up with what I thought he was going to say.

"Fun Overhaul is a business," he continues. "The company invests not to make some money, but the most money it possibly can." He glances at Liam. "Touching story aside, Fun Overhaul is about bottom-line profit. Ghoultown maximizes that." He picks up a plastic water bottle, his eyes still on Liam. "You may be in love with the idea of Christmas magic, Mr. Quinn, but our research shows most of the population has lost their faith in the goodness of people, in the love embodied by a holiday like Christmas. Fear is what people are accustomed to now." He takes a sip of water, points the bottle at Liam. "Fear is the new fun."

Fear is the new fun. What? We are so far off the trajectory I thought this meeting was taking, I can't form a coherent response.

Liam stands. He pulls his shirt over a protruding belly.

Sawyer points a finger gun at him. "I'll tell you what. I know, given your story and that of your late wife, that you don't want to be associated with a fear-themed park. I get it."

Liam remains standing, his hand gripped on the doorknob. Sawyer points toward the chairs. "Please. Sit. This will take a minute."

Liam moves and perches on the edge of the chair.

Sawyer leans forward. "So instead of partnering with Fun Overhaul," he starts, "why don't you let us buy the property?"

Buy the property? I'm floored. Liam must be too because he doesn't say a word. He's so still, it's like he's frozen in place.

"That way," Sawyer says, pulling open a drawer and retrieving a bright yellow pad of square sticky notes, "you're not associated with the park. Have to formalize this but," he swipes a pencil from an overstuffed mug, "I'd be thinking of a number along the lines of this." He scribbles on the pad, folds it, and pushes it across the desk to Liam.

Liam slides the paper off the desk and unfolds it. From my vantage point on the chair next to his, I can see the colossal number scratched out in Sawyer's messy scrawl. My first thought: I knew it. I knew the venue was worth something. My second thought: no way can Liam leave this offer on the table.

Sawyer puts his hands behind his head, his feet on the desk. He looks cocky. A long moment passes, then another. "You're making me nervous, Mr. Quinn," Sawyer says.

Liam stares at the number another beat, folds up the paper, and slides it back toward Sawyer. "Christmastown isn't for sale."

Sawyer jerks up, his chair reverberating with the movement. Surprise flashes across his features. He swipes the paper from the desk and tucks it in his open desk drawer. "Well, good luck to you both. You can see yourselves out."

I follow Liam out, not knowing if he's the stupidest man on the earth or the most principled one. We walk in silence to the deli, and when we reach the door, Liam says, "I think I'm going to go roast beef this time around."

I stop short. "How are you thinking about hoagies right now?"

"I think New Yorkers call them heroes, Matt."

My mouth drops open. "Are you kidding me, Liam?"

He shrugs. "I don't like that guy much."

I shut my eyes a moment, trying to comprehend Liam's rationale. I don't want him to sell Christmastown, but it seems like he's turned down a major deal with reasoning the equivalent to "he looked at me funny."

We step away from the door of the deli, stand at the edge of the sidewalk. "Look, Matt," Liam says, "I don't know how much time I have left. I do know I don't want to spend it working on a deal with that moppet in there." He flicks his hand toward the Sawyer's office building. "I want to keep dreaming about the property Colleen and I wanted to build. It keeps me feeling young and alive and, at my age, that's a hot commodity." He steps toward the restaurant, puts his hand on a thick silver handle, and pulls open the door. "Now let's get some food."

CHAPTER 43

ndi

A   Three weeks after what Matt has been calling *Sawyergate*, I lie on my bed at Liam's and flip through the theatre contract. I don't try to comprehend the dense legal language, but the payment amount jumps out at me, mainly because it's in all caps and bold, dollars spelled out as D-O-L-L-A-R-S. The amount is more than I have ever made at any job; the opportunity would be phenomenal exposure.

I should take it. It had never been my plan to spend my life as Liam's caretaker. I tried to take a chance with Christmastown. That seems to have failed. *This* is my opportunity. Live abroad. Work on a big-time production. Spread my wings.

Problem is, I like it here.

I like that Liam's house is nestled in the deep woods and that, every night, a rich midnight sky fills with stars. I like that lights don't flash outside my window. And that I can't hear the conversations from apartments with shared walls. I'm near friends and family and it's not ridiculously impractical to have a car. I like the nights Ruth cooks dinner with Liam and fills the house with the scents of comfort food. And I've come to look forward to the nightly Wheel of Fortune viewing, even though Emma teases me that it's a show for octogenarians. I enjoy Beckham and his surfer slang and the fact that he is, by far, the most laid-back person I have ever met. And though he still keeps me at a distance, I like seeing Claus curled up in sun patches all over the house.

I like walking around Christmastown, feeling the possibility still humming inside the desolate buildings and dormant structures. And, though it seems considerably less of a reality than a month ago, I still conjure plans in my head.

But Matt is the biggest reason I don't want to leave. I know how long distance relationships go. We'd have every intention of staying together but, slowly, we'd transgress into separate lives. One missed date becomes two. Two missed calls become three. We can't match up our schedules for a visit. Eventually, we can't remember when it was that we spoke last.

I don't want that to happen. But it doesn't seem mature or forward-thinking to stay at this job for I guy I only recently started dating, especially with my romantic history. If things with Matt are meant to be, they'll work out, right? No reason to turn down the opportunity of a lifetime.

All I need to do is sign on the last page.

I flip through the contract again, my eyes resting on the bolded payment amount. I pick up pen, set it down, and finally put the unsigned contract on my nightstand. I lie down and doze off. I dream about Matt in that half-awake, half-asleep mode where you know you're dreaming. We're on our woodland date again, Matt in his tux, holding his hands out for a waltz.

It's Bridget's voice that makes me fully wake up.

Bridget's voice.

Not in the dream.

Here.

She's yelling.

So is Liam.

I bolt upright. Bridget and Liam are yelling. I get out of bed and stand by the door. I can't make out enough words for the argument to make sense, but I hear enough that I'm concerned. Christmastown. Sawyer. Deal.

I bump open the door with my hip, tiptoe down the hall, and crouch at the top of the stairs.

Bridget. "You're giving me no choice."

Liam. "It's not your choice."

Bridget. "It's a generous offer. You won't get another."

I listen a few more minutes before piecing it together. Bridget wants Liam to sell the property to Sawyer. Matt told me the amount Fun Overhaul had offered; I wouldn't blame him. Still, it was his property, his decision. It's not like Bridget could *make* him sell.

Could she?

I stand and shake out my legs, slightly guilty that I'm eaves-dropping on a family disagreement. Claus passes by me on the stairs, tail in the air like a flag. Bridget's voice rings out: "I've prepared an application with the court for a conservatorship so I can accept this one-of-a-kind deal on your behalf."

"You can't do that," Liam insists.

"I don't want to, Dad, but you're giving me no choice. I'm looking out for you."

She sounds sincere, pleading, and I believe that she does, in fact, think this deal is best for Liam. Maybe it is.

"You have no proof that I can't manage things."

"I have proof," Bridget says, her haughty, lawyer-tone back. "There was a fire, first off, and I got a decent amount of infor-mation from Matt Taylor."

Matt Taylor.

I don't breathe. I'm locked in place, my face frozen in shock.

"What does Matt have to do with anything?" Liam asks. "He was here for an audit."

"He works for me, Dad, remember? I sent him here to get information that would help with the petition."

There's a long silence. Bridget's words ping in my head, their meaning plain. Matt was never here to audit Christmastown. Of course, he wasn't. I *knew* that was odd. I recall our conversation in Liam's kitchen about it, way back when practically the only thing I knew about Matt was that he could juggle. What had he said? I try to remember and the recollection comes to me in a burst. He said he was bad at his job. That's why Bridget sent him. Was that even true?

But it didn't all make sense. If Matt was trying to help Bridget, why did he help with The Santa Games? If the whole thing, finding investors, throwing an interactive event, meeting in New York, was a ruse to get information, it was an unnecessarily elaborate one.

My shock morphs. Anger, confusion, and betrayal whip through my body in its place. Bridget and Liam are still arguing, but I've lost track of where they are. I don't know what's been said in the last few minutes.

I start down the stairs, the reptilian part of my brain in firm charge of my psyche. I'll confront Bridget. I'll find out the truth.

I reach the bottom stair, step on to the hardwood floor, it's surface unforgiving under my bare feet. I stop.

What am I doing?

Bridget will only tell me her side, a side that I don't trust.

I don't need to talk to Bridget.

I need to talk to Matt.

CHAPTER 44

Matt
I stare at my computer screen, the list of emails I haven't responded to as long as my arm. I try to read one; my mind wanders.

Come on, Matt. Focus.

I try again. Nope. The cycle repeats itself in a loop: try to pay attention – don't – admonish myself - try again. I finally give up.

Today's score: ADHD, 10; Matt, 0.

I walk to the break room to get coffee because, obviously, *caffeine* is what's needed right now. I push open the door to the sleek room, all the furniture inside of it black and chrome. The only bits of color are the magnets on the fridge.

Kimmy stands at a black quartz counter tossing a green salad with so many vegetables it's like I've absorbed vitamins just by looking at it.

"Hey Matt."

"Hey." I grab a mug.

"The petition's done."

I don't know what she's talking about – par for the course – so I nod. "Yeah."

She angles her face toward me, a bottle of light salad dressing gripped in her hand. "I was surprised you were okay with it."

I grab a mug with the company logo and slip a k-cup into one of three coffeemakers that line the wall. I try to recall a petition I wouldn't be okay with. Nothing comes to mind. "I'm sorry."

"The conservatorship for Liam Quinn." She looks at me strangely. "Bridget filed yesterday."

"Bridget filed for a conservatorship?" A bolt of panic slices through my chest.

Kimmy's face freezes. She puts the salad dressing bottle on the counter. "I thought you knew. Your name is in it."

I take a step back, still processing. "What do you mean, my name is in it?"

"Things you told Bridget while you were at Christmastown. I mean, your statements are technically hearsay, but she has other stuff in there too. Like the fire."

"But that's not enough," I say in a tone that sounds childish even to me. "Liam would have to be disabled for the court to grant an application like that. The fire has nothing to do with anything. It's not like *he* started the fire."

Kimmy shrugs. "Bridget knows she won't win. She told me as much."

I'm numb with disbelief. The one redeeming quality Bridget had, in my mind, was the fact that she cared about her relationship with Liam. Filing for conservatorship would do nothing but stress the father-daughter dynamic. "If she knows she's going to lose, why did she file?"

Kimmy shakes her dressing and pours a minuscule amount on the green leaves.

I lean against the fridge. "Are you going to answer me?"

She sets the dressing down. "I didn't know you weren't in the loop."

"What loop?" I feel stupid asking the question. The whole conversation has been catch-up for me. It's clear there is a lot going on that I don't know about. Anger snakes up my chest; I tamp it down. Whatever is happening, Kimmy's the messenger. I reach out and briefly touch her shoulder. "Sorry to put you in this spot, but my name's being used. I need to know what's going on."

Kimmy moves away from me. She lets out a sigh so long it's like a balloon deflating. Normally, I'd take her obvious discomfort as a time to back off, but in this context, her reaction sets off alarm bells in my mind. What does she know that I don't?

She peeks her head out the breakroom door. Seemingly satisfied that no one is coming, she shuts it nearly all the way. "Okay," she says, "but you didn't hear this from me." She pauses. "Sawyer Hughes is our client," she blurts.

I want to ask "what do you mean?" but I know what she means. Sawyer Hughes is a firm client.

Oh.

I'm incredibly stupid.

I must be.

"He's our biggest client," Kimmy supplies.

This is no way makes me feel better.

She rattles on about all the areas in which Quinn Gifford serves as counsel for Sawyer Hughes. Real estate. Business. Horse racing. Divorce. I barely listen. I'm drowning in a sea of overwhelm. When she's done, I look at her, my mouth agape. I wish I had a better question than the one that comes out of my mouth. "How did I not know this?"

She shakes her head. "Everything is under SH Holdings, LLC. If you weren't working directly on the file, you wouldn't know."

I grasp this piece of information. Okay. So maybe it's not

entirely idiotic that I didn't know. But then a worse realization washes over me, and I feel the same as I might have had someone thrown a bucket of ice water over my head. "Was his interest in Christmastown a ruse?" I rush out the words because, right now, I can't think of many things more humiliating than finding out that Sawyer Hughes's enthusiasm about the project was pretend.

Kimmy opens the fridge door and places the salad dressing on a shelf inside. "No. The opposite. He wants it." She slams the door. "And Bridget wants Liam to take his offer. She sees it as a win-win. Her biggest client gets what he wants, and Liam gets a pile of money."

Pieces of story float, unmoored, in my brain. They don't connect.

Kimmy must sense my confusion because she motions for me to come forward. When I'm a few inches from her, she whispers, "Bridget thinks Liam will take the deal once he sees the application for conservatorship. He won't know it has no merit and he won't want to risk it succeeding."

I step back. "What if he brings it to a lawyer?"

"He won't. *She's* his lawyer."

I swipe my mug from the Keurig. "That's shitty."

Kimmy shrugs. "The price of success, I guess. Bridget's got to keep her top clients happy." She grabs her salad. "And it's not like getting a ton of money would be bad for Liam."

I shrug. She's not wrong. Still. Whether or not Liam sells the property is not Bridget's choice. "Can I see the application?"

"Come on, Matt." She looks at me like she wants to say no but says yes anyway.

I follow her to her office, and she hands me the document. I slump in a chair and start reading.

Shit.

I'm all over the application.

So's Andi.

I scan the words as fast as I can; Bridget's story emerges. Liam, an elderly man susceptible to suggestion, has been conned by his caretaker into investing his retirement in Christmastown. He was talked into renovating the property to host the The Santa Games and ended up having a dangerous fire which he himself had to fight off with a kitchen extinguisher. A committee of self-interested people talked him out of accepting an investment offer and, later, an opportunity to sell the property. Now he owns the dormant property but has no hope of investors or buyers.

The application is peppered with other unflattering images like Liam's nightly whiskey drinking. And the worst part of it? I'm the hero in this pretend saga – sent by Bridget to protect her father.

I throw the application toward Kimmy's desk with more force than I intend. It scatters to the floor, open to Exhibit E, the photo of Liam putting out the fire. "That's bullshit," I point to the application. "There's nothing true in there. It's a pack of lies."

Kimmy holds her hands up. "I didn't write it."

"I know." I stand, snatch the application from the floor, and set it on the desk. I start to pace, mind racing, my brain in a full-out panic. Liam can't see this. Andi can't see this. NO ONE should see this. I stop and look at Kimmy. "Did this go out?" My eyes, my voice, are wild.

"I don't know."

"Can you check?"

The firm has an electronic system used to check out court and other filings. Kimmy punches the keys on her computer, stops, and stares at the screen.

"It got filed this morning."

"Did Liam get served?" I practically yell the question. I'm flailing with panic and dread. The only way Liam and Andi would see the application would be if Liam had been formally served. If he hadn't, I still had time to intercept.

"This morning." Kimmy says the words gingerly, like she knows the bomb-like effect they are about to have.

No.

No. No. No. No. No.

My heart sinks deep into my chest.

I step out of Kimmy's office without speaking, my mind whirring with panic. I shut my door; it bangs closed.

There's no way Liam wouldn't look at the document. A lawsuit to take over your finances isn't the kind of thing you put aside to read later. He had to have read it by now. Had Andi? I pull out my phone to text her. My fingers freeze over the keyboard. What do I even say?

How are you?

Don't read the lawsuit?

I can explain?

No, no, and no. I can't text her because I don't know what she knows. So, I punch at her contact, regret forming in the pit of my stomach as soon as I do.

"Hey, it's Andi." Voicemail. I'm sane enough, barely, not to leave a message. I need to talk to Andi in person. I grab my keys, hurry down the hall, and the stairs. I race to the parking lot, spy my car, and stop short.

Andi is standing in front of it.

CHAPTER 45

ndi

Matt races toward me, his open coat suit jacket behind him like a cape. His tie is askew, his hair ruffled. He's talking. Too fast. I can't understand him. "I'm sorry," he concludes.

"Can we go somewhere else?" I'm not having this discussion in a parking lot.

"Sure." He moves toward his car.

"Walking distance?"

"Okay."

We walk down the crowded city block. The space around us fills with traffic noises and commuters talking, phones pressed to their ears. We reach a small coffee shop. Matt nods toward it. "Here good?"

I peek through the giant picture window. The space is arranged with a hodgepodge of old furniture in seating arrangements. The walls are muted, framed pictures of old movie posters hang with big hooks. Before, if we'd come here, the posters would have served as a fun conversation piece. Now they just seem like noise.

"Fine."

I snag a small table buttressed by two stiff armchairs. Matt places an order at the counter and returns with exactly what I would have ordered had I gone up myself: a black coffee with cream, no sugar, and an apple fritter. I stare at the steaming mug. Only a handful of people know my favorite breakfast pastry. Fewer know how I take my coffee. Matt knows both.

I grip my hands around the thick ceramic mug.

"I didn't know about the application for conservatorship," Matt blurts.

I draw back. "Ever?"

"I mean, in the beginning, yeah but, I changed my mind. I told Bridget Christmastown was a good idea."

I follow this statement with questions. Matt explains. And everything he says tracks. His change of heart. His discussions with Bridget. His interest in The Santa Games being a success. He explains about finding out, today, that Sawyer is a client. "Do you believe me?" he asks finally.

I do believe him. I'm not sure it matters. "I believe you." I pause and look out the window before looking back at him. "I know what Bridget said about me in the application isn't true. But it's almost true. Liam had forgotten about Christmastown until I put the idea back in his head. I've been selfish in all this. Maybe I wanted to see my designs get built. Maybe I was trying to prove something to Cole. I don't know." I pause. "I put in my notice to Liam. I'm leaving."

Matt's shoulders slump. "You shouldn't have to leave, Andi."

I shake my head. "Liam never needed a caretaker and Ruth is there almost all the time now. If I stay, it would be for Christmastown. I can see that's kind of silly now. And it wouldn't let Liam make the choice he needs to make. Unfettered, you know." I take a long sip of coffee, let the warm liquid slide down my throat.

"What are you going to do?"

"I got the job. *A Walk in the Park.*"

"The UK one?"

I nod.

A group of women, each with the same book in their hand, enter the shop and assemble in the seating area in front of ours. The space is instantly immersed with talking and laughter, the mirth contrasting gravely to the mood at our table.

"So, you're moving to London?"

"I'm moving to London." I say the words with fake confidence.

Matt leans back, seems to work something out in his head. "We can still see each other. Phone calls, visits. We can make it work."

My heart breaks at his assumption and I close my eyes for a long moment. When I open them, he's staring at me. "I'm going on my own," I say. "Unattached. I'm doing what I intended to when I took the job at Christmastown. Be on my own. Take a chance. Not be like my mother."

"You're not like your mother," Matt says quickly. "Not in that way."

"Aren't I though? I was infatuated with Cole. And I was infatuated with you. Honestly, Matt –" I shake my head – "if you had suggested we travel the world or join a circus or colony on the moon these past few weeks, I'm not positive I wouldn't have said yes." I dip my head and look at the table. "It took finding out the truth about your role to knock me to my senses. Maybe you changed your mind, but I was so wrapped up in you that I didn't even line up the inconsistencies." I look at him. "I can't let myself be like that."

He puts his head in his hand, pushes at his hair. He's silent for at least a minute and, when he finally looks up, remorse is written across his face as clear as if he'd used marker. Cackles from the table next to us fill the space.

"So that's it?"

I look down because I can't look at his face, at his expression, at the clear feelings for me reflected in his gaze. If I do, I'll lose my nerve. "That's it." I force myself to say the words. As I do, I conjure the phrase: if you love something let it go, if it's meant to be, it will come back to you.

The mantra doesn't help. Matt gets up and I watch the man I'm pretty sure I'm in love with walk out the door.

CHAPTER 46

F
ive months later
    Matt
    "Seriously, Matt?"

Steph stares at me from the doorway of our kitchen, shopping bags with thick handles clutched in her hands. It's exactly two weeks until Christmas.

I look up from my sandwich. Dirty dishes sit in a pile in the sink, remnants from my sandwich ingredients strewn across the counters. "I'll get it," I say, but the thought of getting up and doing something remotely productive makes me feel even more lazy. My body is lead.

Steph eyes me. "Nice outfit. Same as yesterday, I see."

I look down to check my clothes. She's right. I've been in the same old sweatshirt and sweatpants since Friday after work. "I was planning to change."

"Yeah. Right after cleaning up." She touches her face. "And shaving."

I finger my beard.

"And your computer class?"

I say nothing. In a flurry of stop-feeling-sorry-for-yourself-because-Andi-left activity, I'd signed up for Level II of Dane's class. I'd dropped out a few weeks ago. Ironically, I – the person who can't sit still to save my life -- didn't have the energy.

"And Liam Quinn? The guy you bent over backward for. You left him hanging."

In a surprise move, Liam called Bridget's bluff on the conservatorship. He's still looking for "the right" investor. He's contacted me a few times; I haven't called him back.

I wave my hand. Steph doles out the same cycle of negative commentary every few weeks. "All right, Steph," I say. "Enough."

She dips her hand into one of the bags and pulls out a flat, rectangular package. The box is wrapped in thick, red paper, a white bow at the top. She holds it up and I open my mouth to thank her for what I assume is an early Christmas gift. She throws it at me.

My hand shoots up and I catch it mid-air. "Jeez." I touch my head as if it had been hit. "What was that for?"

"It's a necklace for Andi. A nice one." She strides across the room and opens the fridge.

I stare at her. "Why would I get Andi a present?"

Steph swings her head toward me, the fridge door still open. "Because you've been a miserable asshole since she moved to London."

I roll my eyes. "As I've told you many times, she said she wants to be on her own. I'm not going to force myself into her life." I set the present on the table and push it away.

Steph pulls out a water. "Being on your own and accepting a gift from an old friend are two different things."

I say nothing. Steph slides into the seat across from me. "I'm sure she's going to be home for Christmas, Matt. Just go see her."

I shake my head. "No. She's probably doing great on her own. I don't want to mess her up."

I frequently picture Andi in London's West End with a rich

night life, a group of friends. I see her at pubs and drinking tea and going to touristy places like Big Ben and Stonehenge. She's doing it. Taking a chance. Living her best life. On her own.

Steph leans forward, water bottle gripped in her hand. "Do you want Andi in your life, Matt?"

I don't speak. I know the answer. Of course, I want Andi in my life. I miss her. And not in the way that's like, ah, that was a good time. It's guttural. And constant. The number of times a day I see something I want to share with her is absurd. Crazy thing, most of them she wouldn't even care about. Like the new hot dog cart on the corner. Or that fact that the woman down the street got a third pug. Or the Jake and Joe's pancake of the month. Still, I think of her. Mexican food, Wheel of Fortune, New York, trivia, Christmas, Santa Claus, blankets, plays, pizza, cats. All triggers straight to the ache in my heart.

"Well?" It's clear Steph won't let up until I answer.

"Yes, Steph. I want Andi in my life."

She bangs an open palm on the table. "Then goddammit, Matt, fight for her. Take a chance. Grand gesture the hell out of her."

I finger my napkin. "Isn't that disrespecting her wishes?"

She reaches across the table and puts both of her hands on my cheeks and squeezes. "I swear, little brother, you are an idiot. Have you even told Andi how you feel?"

"She knows."

"How would she know, Matt? Have you contacted her? Told her you miss her? Does she know that, since she left, you've been an unshaven, unkempt, monosyllabic man who's only redeeming grace is that you cared about her?"

I push at my plate.

"I'll take that as a no."

I push back my chair. "Look. I'm more of a man of action than words. I might not have told Andi how I feel but I showed her."

Steph slams her water bottle on the table. "Where's your action now then? All I see is you feeling sorry for yourself and putzing around." She takes a swig of water. "If Andi wants you in her life, she'll love that you fought for her. If she doesn't, she's a grown woman. She'll tell you. And *then* you respect her wishes." She leans back in her chair. "She can't say yes to a relationship with you if she doesn't know you want one, Matt."

"But—" I start.

Steph holds out a hand. "No buts. Put your cards on the table and let Andi decide." She sweeps up her water bottle and strides out of the room.

My eyes follow; her words stay in my head.

Is she right?

I push out of the chair, put the dishes in the dishwasher, and start it. I clean the remnants of my sandwich making, wipe the counters clean. After, I hop into a scalding shower and soap up, almost like I'm washing away the past months. I towel off and shave my beard. All of it. I stare at my clean face in the mirror.

Think Matt.

I need to do something big. But not something that would put Andi in the position of having to tell me (*again*) that she's not interested in a relationship. Something that would let her know how I feel but put the ball in her court.

I dress in clean clothes, discard my dirty sweats in the hamper. *No* thoughts come to mind.

Unless.

It would take more than just me. But it would mean everything to Andi.

I have an idea.

CHAPTER 47

ndi
It's Christmas Eve and I'm at home in my family kitchen, picking at a plate of Christmas cookies. I break each one in half, tell myself that a half is not like having another whole one.

Then I eat the other half.

Though I have been living an ocean away for nearly half a year, Christmas at home is the same. Our fat tree sits in the living room strung up with colored lights. Photos of me and Brian with Santa as babies are lined up on the foyer table. The hodgepodge of decorations we'd made as small children, including several papers trees decorated with stickers and massive amounts of glitter, are strewn across the mantel. Betsy, in tights with Christmas trees on them, skids across the hardwood floor. She is *very* hyped up on sugar.

I thought the sameness of home would bring me comfort. That the soul-crushing loneliness I'd felt in my tiny West End flat would miraculously disappear.

It hasn't.

Not that it's all terrible. The director loves what I've done so far with the sets for *A Walk in the Park*. And I've made a bunch of friends. Okay. Two friends. The girl in the flat next to mine, Claire, and the one who works on the lighting for the show, Suzanne. But they both grew up in London and have a significantly wider social network than I do. Plus, they've done everything. So, I do touristy things on my own. I've toured the Tower of London, St. Paul's Cathedral, the Roman Baths, several castles, and the Royal Botanic Gardens. I've ridden the London Eye. Twice. I took a long weekend in Paris and dressed like a Parisian, beret and all. I ate in outdoor cafés, toured the Eiffel Tower and the Louvre, and spent half a day trying to find the Pantheon. I go to pubs sometimes with Suzanne or Claire and I've seen a half-dozen West End shows with comped tickets.

I have more activity in a single day in London than I did in a week at Liam's. I'm almost manic about keeping busy because, when I'm busy, I'm happy. When I'm not, loneliness creeps in and worms its way around until all I can think about is Matt and Christmastown and those glorious couple weeks where everything was perfect. Sometimes, I close my eyes and pretend I'm back there, Matt and I on the platform of the Sky Ornament Ride, a sea of bright stars overhead.

"Hey Andi," Mom calls from the living room. She and Jim broke up and she is boyfriend-free for the time being. I'm grateful. I'm not sure I had enough energy in reserve to handle excessive fish talk. Or fish-inspired gifts.

I move into the room. Mom pats the couch cushion beside her. There's a giant bowl of popcorn on the coffee table. Next to it are strings with sharp needles tied to each end.

"I thought we'd string some popcorn for the tree." She holds a string in my direction.

"Sure." I grab the string and sink into the cushion next to her. Mariah Carey's *All I Want for Christmas is You* pings out of her phone speaker.

I grab a popped kernel, thread it on the needle, and slide it down. I pick up another and repeat the process until I'm in a steady rhythm. Mom does the same. "So, you're liking London?" she asks finally.

Mom has asked this same question in a variety of ways since I arrived home. I say what I always do. "It's good." Usually, I follow this response with a snippet of something touristy I'd done like visit Big Ben, but I don't add anything this time. Mom seems to take this as an opportunity.

"Do you miss the work you were doing at Christmastown?"

I give my best I-don't-care look. "It wasn't a job. It was a hobby." Reframing my passion for Christmastown as a hobby is something I have worked hard on the past few months.

"Right. But you were excited about it."

I shrug. Because as much as working on a West End play should be a dream, it doesn't feel like one. The spark of excitement I'd felt at Christmastown, the idea of finding latent magic, of creating a legacy that would last, isn't there. When *A Walk in the Park* runs its course, all my sets will be broken down and discarded, the only memory of them encapsulated in pictures.

"I like London," I say though I know it's not an answer to her question. I push a popcorn kernel over the needle with unnecessary force. It breaks. I do the same thing again. Bits of popcorn pieces settle in my lap in the aftermath. "I like being on my own."

"Hmm."

"What?"

"You can be on your own and still be with someone," she says, eyes glued to her ever-lengthening string of popcorn.

I swing my head to look at her, hoping for an explanation. None is forthcoming. "What do you mean?"

She puts down her string and looks at me. "I know I haven't been the best example of an independent woman, Andi. I don't know why." She shakes her head. "Maybe lack of confidence, maybe it was how I was brought up. For me, adopting a man's hobbies and interests, putting his well-being above my own, these are ways to show I cared. I get that it seems weak. Maybe it is." She looks away a long moment then turns back to me. "But you don't have to be like me. Don't feel like the antidote to getting absorbed into someone else's life is to stay alone. You can be with someone, someone like Matt, and not lose yourself."

Mom stands and drapes her popcorn string on the tree. "You and Matt are good together. And lightning rarely strikes the same place twice." She kisses my head and leaves the room.

Lighting rarely strikes the same place twice.

I know what she means. I may never find anyone who makes me feel the way Matt does.

I sit still, the popcorn string dormant in my hand, Christmas music still pings out of Mom's phone. I picture Matt at some posh holiday-themed event, the kind with tailed tuxes and floor-length gowns and flutes of expensive champagne. He'd hate it. I wished, like an ache, to be at his side, to be the person he'd said I was: the one who gets him.

My cell phone rings. I'm thinking so hard about Matt, I almost expect it to be him. It isn't. It's Liam. I switch on the phone.

"Merry Christmas, Liam!" I force cheer into my voice.

"Andi, are you near a television?"

"Yeah." I step into the family room. "Why?"

"I think there's something you're going to want to see on the news. Channel six, five o'clock."

CHAPTER 48

A *ndi*
At five o'clock, I gather my family and flip on channel six per Liam's instructions. Whitney Collins's face fills the screen. I'm confused. Liam wants me to see a feature anchored by Whitney Collins? Why? Then the camera pans out, the Chrismastown carousel clear in the background. Whitney, in a cute red hat and coat, grips her microphone.

"Hello. I'm Whitney Collins and I'm here this Christmas Eve reporting from a special place on the outskirts of Scranton, Pennsylvania. Christmastown." She gestures toward the carousel. The camera moves back to include Mrs. Claus's bake shop and the toy store. Both buildings look like part of a Nordic village, lit up and covered with bits of fresh snow.

"A decade ago," Whitney continues, "Liam Quinn and his late wife, Colleen, purchased this property. It was their hope to create a little bright spot in the world, a year-round haven for Christmas magic." She pauses; the camera zooms in on her face. "But tragedy struck the Quinns and it seemed their dream of a Yuletide sanctuary would not come to fruition." Whitney steps along the path of lit Christmas trees toward the lake. "Or would it?" She moves inside the gazebo, its edges outlined by white lights. "In an effort led by former Broadway set designer Andi Carter and Philadelphia attorney Matt Taylor, Christmastown held its first ever on-property event to attract investors, The Santa Games."

Mom squeezes my hand.

Pictures from the event flash on the screen. The first features a photograph of dozens of Santas marching on to the property. Then one of the tents, the balloons, and Liam and Ruth as Mr. and Mrs. Claus.

"The Santa Games attracted high-level investor Sawyer Hughes from Fun Overhaul and, it seemed, all would work out for this little park that could." Whitney puts her hand on the gazebo and the camera pans out to show the lake behind her. "According to an inside source, Sawyer Hughes proposed a plan with staggering projected profits. But there was a catch." Whitney pauses. "Christmastown was to become Ghoultown, a theme park not centered on love and joy but on horror and fear. In Mr. Hughes's own words 'most of the population have lost their faith in the goodness of people, in the love embodied by a holiday like Christmas.' Fear, according to Mr. Hughes, is the new fun." She waits a beat. "Liam Quinn formally turned down Fun Overhaul's offer because, in his words, Christmastown is about the magic, not the money. The problem is, without appropriate investors, the Quinns' dream of a holiday haven will be nothing more than that. A dream."

I move to the edge of the couch.

Whitney again walks along the lake; lit trees on the path reflect colored pools in the water. She stops suddenly. "We at Channel Six News believe in the goodness of people. We believe in Christmas." The camera zooms in on her face. "And we believe the world does too. Let's show investors across the globe that there's room in our hearts for a place dedicated to the love, joy, and the magic of the holidays. Use hashtag Save Christmastown and fill your social media with images of joy and love."

"Oh wow –" I start. But it's not over.

"And if you need a bit of inspiration," Whitney continues, "these men just might be able to give it to you."

The screen switches to one of the Santas I recognized from the event. He stands in front of the Rockefeller Tree in New York, a crowd around him. "Hashtag Save Christmastown."

Another image appears, this one of a Santa on decorated main street. "Hashtag Save Christmastown."

A Santa on a beach. "Hashtag Save Christmastown."

On a ski slope. "Hashtag Save Christmastown."

In a mall. On a farm. On boats, trains, cars, and, of course, sleighs. Dozens of Santas, all stating the same phrase: "Hashtag Save Christmastown."

After a dozen or more Santas repeat the sentiment, the feature returns to Whitney. She's on the carousel and, this time, it's moving.

"And so, for Channel Six News, this is Whitney Collins with a special message. Merry Christmas to all and to all a good night."

A commercial fills the screen. I stare at the television, my mouth open. Christmastown, the Christmastown I'd designed, the one we'd toiled over, was on television. And it looked every bit the magical winter wonderland I knew it would.

"That's unbelievable, Andi," Brian says. "Great work."

Mom rubs my back. "Looks like you might be heading back to Christmastown before you know it."

"I want to go!" Betsy shoots into my arms; I hug her tight.

"It's trending!" Chelsea holds up her phone. "There's already one hundred posts on Twitter under hashtag Save Christmastown."

One hundred posts? The segment had ended less than five minutes ago.

"More on Instagram," she adds.

I pick up my phone and scroll through the images. Some depict things: Christmas trees, stockings, churches, gifts, cookies. But most feature people. People in their homes, outside, in cars, in church. Young people, old people, families. All with the same sentiment: Hashtag Save Christmastown.

The doorbell rings. I look to Mom. She shrugs. I walk to the door, nervous anticipation in my gut. I pull it open.

A man dressed as Santa stands on the front step, an envelope in his hand.

"Ho. Ho. Ho. Special delivery for Andi Carter."

"I'm Andi Carter."

"Well, this, young lady, is for you." He extends the envelope in my direction. I slip it from his hand. He waves. "Merry Christmas!"

"Merry Christmas."

I shut the door and lean against it, the whole moment feeling surreal. I slip my fingernail behind the envelope seal and slide it across. I pull out a folded piece of paper. Matt's handwriting, not in crayon this time.

Dear Andi,

Merry Christmas! I hope this letter finds you well. Hopefully, by now you will have seen the television pitch Liam and I worked on to try to find an investor for Christmastown. I know how important the project was to you and Liam (and me), and I want it to have every chance it can to get off the ground.

On a different note, I miss you. I'd list all the reasons why, but I don't want this paper to turn into a scroll so, suffice it to say, you are a difficult woman to forget. I am not sure how you feel about me or where you are in your journey, but I will be waiting for you tomorrow at Christmastown at 6 p.m. I'll let you guess where. If you'd like to talk, please meet me. If you don't, no questions asked. I respect you, I care about you, and I wish you only happiness.

Love, Matt

PS--Regardless of your answer, I would like an update on how many cats you've traumatized in London. Catman needs to know.

I LAUGH, read the letter again, then a third time. Mom peeks her head over my shoulder. I extend the paper so she can see. An intake of breath; she squeezes my shoulders. "Andi, you have to go."

CHAPTER 49

M *att*
I lug the small Christmas tree up the stairs of the Sky Ornament Ride. The metal tree base, securely attached to the trunk, gets stuck on the third stair slat. I wrestle it out. This happens again. And again. It doesn't help that it's dark, the only light that from my phone flashlight.

I reach the top, breathing hard, sweaty despite the cold. The wind, reasonably gentle on the ground, whips freezing air on the platform. Something else I hadn't accounted for. I switch on the battery-operated pack and the tree lights up with colored flecks. It looks festive. At least that's good.

I hustle down the stairs and get the rest of what I need: the wine, the Yumcakes, and my gift for Andi. Not the gift Steph got; one I'd chosen. I set the items under the tree and play Christmas music on my phone. I check my watch. 5:50.

I open the box of Yumcakes, adjust the lights on the tree. I check my watch again. Still 5:50. I pull my coat tighter, wishing I'd thought to bring a heater or blanket or something. It's freezing up here. I stuff my hands in my coat pockets and scan for car headlights or some other indication Andi's on her way.

Nothing. I check my phone. Also, nothing. Wind rustles the tree branches. I jog in place for warmth.

There was always a chance she wouldn't come.

I knew that.

It's after six. I wait, half of me convinced she's on her way, the other half steadfastly sure of the opposite. I'm beyond cold; the wind's picked up. I try not to think about the fact that it's Christmas and I'm sitting alone on an abandoned amusement park ride. Holiday music still blares, almost like it's mocking me. I switch it off.

"Hey. I liked that song." A voice in the darkness. My heart leaps. Andi.

I stand. "Hey."

She steps into the light of the tree in a red jacket and a white hat, a ludicrously giant pom-pom on top. Her curls spill from under the brim; her cheeks are pink from the cold. She's got a present in her hand.

"I didn't know if you'd come," I say.

She smiles. "I'm not sure why you'd doubt it. I got a very compelling note from Santa Claus last night." She sets her gift under the tree. "He came right to my door." She looks directly at me. "It was, by far, the best gift I received this Christmas."

I take a step toward her. "Is that right?"

"That is absolutely right."

She puts her arms around me. I kiss her hat-covered head, inhale her scent. "I've missed you."

"I've missed you, too."

I brush my lips against hers. She pulls me closer; the kiss deepens. We draw back but don't separate. We embrace in the light of the Christmas tree. I don't know for how long. The wind picks up. Andi steps back.

"Matt."

"Yeah."

"I'm freezing."

"Me too." I shake my head, smiling. "I didn't expect these tundra-like conditions up here. Sorry."

She plants a kiss on my mouth. "Nothing to be sorry about. But should we bring this party inside?" She inclines her head to Liam's house.

"Liam's at Ruth's."

Andi winks. "All the better."

We gather our items, sans the tree, and head down the stairs.

"The news segment!" she says as we navigate the stairs and the walk to Liam's. "That was crazy. Hashtag Save Christmastown is still trending like mad."

"I know. I had no idea it would catch on like that. Liam's excited to see what happens with investment interest after the holiday."

"That was nice of Whitney," Andi acknowledges.

I shrug. "She did a good job."

I push the door open to Liam's and we step inside. Warmth envelopes us.

"So warm." Andi pulls off her hat, her hair wild with static. She puts an index finger on my chest. "Not a word about the hair. It'll take a second to calm down."

I smooth it with my hands. "Love the hair always."

"You're sweet," she says, unzipping her coat. "And you're lying."

I kiss the top of her head. "Nope. It's true."

We hang up our coats and move to the family room. I open the wine and pour us each a glass. I hold mine up. "Merry Christmas."

She clinks her glass to mine. "Merry Christmas."

"So, how's London? How's the job?"

She grabs the blanket she'd always wrapped herself in at Liam's and puts it over both of us. "London is the best thing I've ever done."

My heart falters. I was hoping she'd say the opposite. I lean forward and do my best to look enthused. "Yeah?"

"Yeah. I stepped way outside my comfort zone. I pushed myself professionally, personally. I figured myself out too. I learned what pieces of me are all mine instead of the ones I'd adopted to make someone else happy. I'm more sure of myself."

She pauses. I don't respond. I'm afraid the more sure of herself part involves a realization that I'm not the one for her. And I don't want to hear that right now.

"And you know what I figured out?"

"What?"

"I am okay by myself. Over the past months, I've traveled to six different countries and navigated everything I needed to, language, currency, transportation. I met new people, tried new things. I know that I am completely capable of having a fulfilling independent life."

I take a sip of wine; the liquid slides down my throat. I want to stop time because I know where this is going. Andi's not here to reconcile. She's here to say goodbye.

"I know I can be on my own." She grabs both my hands. "I don't want to be. I don't need a man to complete me, but I want to share my life. I want to be dependent and independent at the same time. That intersection where there's mutual love and respect but an appreciation for differences. I want to be with someone who lifts me up. Someone I can lift up."

I inhale a breath. Maybe Andi's not here to say goodbye after all.

"And if you feel the same way," she continues, "the someone I want to lift up is you."

I shut my eyes, open them, my heart lifting like it's full of helium. I squeeze Andi's hands. "I cannot tell you how happy you just made me. There is no one I would rather be lifted up by. I love you, Andi."

"I love you too, Matt."

We sit, hands gripped together. My love for Andi is something I'd known, but not fully admitted, for a long time. I'm not sure I would have realized the extent of it had she not been an ocean away.

She scoots closer and draws my face to hers. She presses her lips to mine, a tender kiss which quickly turns passionate. She leads me upstairs to her old room. We're a tangle of hands and mouths and discarded clothes. The pace is frantic, each of us, it seems, acting on instincts forced dormant for months.

After, Andi lies with her head on my chest. I finger her curls, kiss the top of her head. "I love that," I tell her.

She looks up and grins at me. "Good thing because you're good at it."

I smile, feel the warmth of her body next to mine. "You're not too bad yourself."

I drift off, contented, Andi in my arms. When I wake up, she's asleep beside me. She is not a pretty sleeper. Her mouth is open, her hair splayed out on the pillow. Covers, ones she stole from me during the night, are scrunched around her body, her arms gripping them in a life-lock. I kiss her cheek. I love this open-mouthed, cover stealing version of her just as much as all the other ones.

And I can't wait to tease her about it.

I creep downstairs, grab our gifts and the Yumcakes, and slip again into bed beside her. When her eyes flutter open, I'm eating one of the peanut butter cakes. She takes a few minutes to wake up fully.

"Are you eating a Yumcake in bed?" she asks, head still on the pillow.

"I was hungry. And they're good."

She props herself up on her elbow, teasingly slaps my chest. "Really?"

"What?"

"Seems a little extra."

I hold up the cake. "It's peanut butter. Your favorite. Too bad you have a thing against eating in bed." I pop the rest in my mouth and grab a second cake from the sleeve on the nightstand.

She sits up, covers pulled to her chin. "Hmm. Maybe, I can make an exception."

I lift an eyebrow. "Not too extra? Are you sure?"

"I'm sure."

I hand her the cake, and she bites into it. "Mmm."

"I know. They're better in bed. Something you wouldn't know if you didn't grow up around Yumcakes."

She laughs. "Thanks for enlightening me." She pops the rest of the cake in her mouth and leans over me to reach the box on the nightstand. She grabs another sleeve, pulls both cakes out, and hands me one. "I can never eat just one."

"Me either."

I grab the Christmas presents we'd brought each other from bottom of the bed. "Should we open these?"

"Absolutely." She grabs the one for her.

"Rude."

She rolls her eyes. "Like you would ever open yours first."

I smile because it's funny but, also, because she knows me. Even something simple like that. I would insist that she open her gift first. I nod toward the gift. "You're right. Go on then."

She rips off the wrapping paper and pulls out my gift, a framed picture of the map of the park, the one she had drawn for The Santa Games.

She stares at the map a long time and I start to worry that maybe Christmastown is not something she wants to be reminded about. "Do you like it?"

She hugs the frame to her chest. "I love it. Thank you. I can't wait to hang it up." She pulls it back and props it against her knees. "It looks like a real park map."

"It *is* a real park map. Or it will be." I point to the guy she'd drawn, running up the stairs of the Sky Ornament Ride, the one she'd said was modeled after me. "And remember, I'm right here."

"How could I forget?" She nods toward her gift, still in my hand. "Your turn."

I carefully unwrap the gift, lift off the top of the box. It's a ticket for *A Walk in the Park*. I hold it up.

"I don't know if you're busy," she says quickly. "But if you're not, I'd love it if you could be there for opening night."

I clutch the ticket. "Andi, there is nothing I would love more than to be there for opening night." I brush her lips with mine. "Thank you. I will be there."

We lie back. I kiss her again.

It's my favorite night with Andi so far.

CHAPTER 50

E ighteen Months Later
Andi
Matt and I walk past giant yellow construction
vehicles and towering dirt piles, the construction thanks to Big
Dog Investments, Liam's partner. Christmastown had been
deluged by offers after the hashtag save Christmastown
phenomenon. Even Sawyer Hughes had come crawling back;
Liam turned him down. Instead, he'd hired Kevin Richards,
owner and CEO of Big Dog Investments.

In addition to his strong company and sound plan, we all
liked Kevin personally. He was vocal about having ADHD and
supported scientific studies aimed to help those diagnosed with
the condition. He was committed to having Big Dog Investments meet Liam's vision, not the reverse. Plus, he came to
every meeting with his energetic brown dog, Bella.

I stop at a green post, my laminated drawing of a sleigh-
themed bumper car ride, Sleigh Slam, affixed to its side. On top
of that drawing, was a second, one of the map I'd designed for
The Santa Games. Kevin put a post like this in front of every

attraction. The idea: every person working on the site needed to keep Liam's vision in mind.

Six months after *A Walk in the Park* opened, I moved back to Scranton. Something I'd learned in my year-long London experience is that I'm a homebody. I like simple. I like predictable. I'd rather know a few people in a small town well than be one of a million in a glittery city. If this personality trait makes me a "complacent wallflower," so be it. It's who *I* am.

I gave up theatre design work and am employed by Christmastown full-time as director of design and marketing. I'm happy. Ruth and Liam married over the summer, and I'm renting out Ruth's place, at least for now. It's dated but homey, and in a strange twist of fate, I have Claus there. Ruth's dog, Rolo, and Claus didn't get along. I took the cat. He tolerates me now, seeing as I rescued him, I guess. Matt teasingly says it's Stockholm Syndrome.

Matt left Quinn Gifford. He's working on a degree in computer science at a school in Philadelphia. He comes to Scranton most weekends. Sometimes, I go there. Either way, weekends are for sleeping in, eating Yumcakes in bed (now a thing), and a healthy dose of lovemaking (it hasn't died down). We are regulars at Casa and even returned to Fun Time Escapes for a non-elevator themed adventure.

Now, at Christmastown, we stand in front the Sleigh Slam. I gesture to a thick bumper around the track. "Ooh. They added the rim. Do you see anything else?" I glance at Matt.

Finding what's new in the construction is a game we play most weekends. As an artist, seeing the tiny bits of progress, detail by detail, is a thrill. The construction feels akin to the process of drawing. What starts out as scribbles and lines or floorboards and beams eventually morphs into something real.

"Matt?" I poke his shoulder. "Hey."

He shoves his hands deep in his coat pockets. "Sorry. What were you saying?"

I point again to the bumpers. "See? The bumpers are new."

Matt strides forward and makes a show of hitting the rubber. "Sturdy."

"Right? I can't wait to test this one out."

Matt stands and smiles. "Me neither. I am the best at Sleigh Slam."

I lift an eyebrow. "You have lots of experience with sleigh shaped bumper cars?"

"Yes. It's a big thing on the Main Line."

I roll my eyes. "I'll bet."

We continue along the path in companionable silence. We reach a break in the path and Matt gestures to the Sky Ornament ride. "Want to go up?"

I glance at the nearly finished ride. The stairs, now stable, had been painted red, thick gold railings along the side. On the platform stands an ornate gold roof held up by poles covered with festive Christmas balls. The giant ornament carriages had been repainted, their insides now feature plush red fabric with stitching.

I squint at the ride. "I don't think they've added anything. It's pretty much done, right? Waiting on the permits?"

"Maybe we should we see?" He nods toward the ride. "Race ya."

He starts up the stairs. I follow. Matt sprints. He reaches the top and yells down. "Slow poke."

I trudge up the final stairs and on to the platform. Matt puts his arms around me, kisses my neck. "Okay," he says moving back, "now that I finally got you up here, I have a surprise."

"A surprise?"

"Yup. I'm up, right?"

We'd morphed into a tradition of surprising each other. Little things: movie tickets, Kit Kats (his favorite), a six pack of Chimay, the awful beer he loves. Matt's surprises included a bouquet of flowers from Marjorie, the woman who'd sold him that initial bundle from the side of the road. A new paint set. Cookies from the bakery with his promise he wouldn't eat them all. We'd fallen into a loose pattern of taking turns. I'd just gotten him a pack of Yumcakes so, technically, he was up.

"You're up." I crossed my arms. "But those Yumcakes will be hard to beat."

"It'll be close, but I think this might do it." He reaches into his pocket and pulls out a remote.

I eye it. "Matt?"

He holds the remote in my direction. "Do you want to do the honors?"

"No." I look from the remote, to the ride, my eyes resting on Matt.

Kevin had been working on getting permits for the rides.

Matt shrugs. "Why don't you press that green button and see?"

I slide the remote from his hand and press a giant green button. The carriages inch across the wire. Same as before but, *this time*, we can ride them.

"Cool, right?"

"So cool." The ornaments snake along in a line of festive cheer. I slap Matt on the shoulder. "Why didn't you tell me?"

"Because then," he says, kissing the top of my head, "it wouldn't have been a surprise." He slips the remote out of my hand and stops the ride. "Shall we? Now that there are permits, it won't be dangerous." He winks.

He opens the door of a gold carriage in the loading area. I slip inside and sit, my body sinking into the plush velvet. Matt takes a seat across. He presses the remote, and the ornaments start to inch again across the wire. I look over the edge at the construction equipment, piles of dirt, and half-built structures, but I don't see them. What I see instead is the finished version of Christmastown, a twinkling, magical mass of family-friendly attractions and dazzling lights. I squeeze Matt's hand. "I can't believe we are on this ride right now."

Matt doesn't answer. I avert my gaze from Christmastown and look at him, his face uncharacteristically serious. There's sweat on his forehead. "Are you okay?"

"I'm fine."

"Is it about the height? Because we can–"

Matt shakes his head. "It's not the height." He presses the button on the remote and the ride comes to a halt. Our carriage sways in the breeze.

What is going on?

Matt takes a deep breath.

My heart thumps with wild beats. Matt takes my hands in his.

"Andi Carter. I think I first fell in love with you when you fixed Liam's dishwasher and that feeling has never gone away. All day, I look forward to talking to you or seeing you or holding you. And, when I'm lucky, all three."

I squeeze his hands, my eyes fix on his.

He shakes his head. "Even when I'm not with you, I'm with you because I'm storing up all the things I can't wait to tell you about. You make me laugh harder than anyone. You make it feel safe to show you every part of myself. You make me feel loved and cared for in a way I never have. If I'm able to be with you every day for the rest of my life, I would be a happy man."

He bends down on one knee. My hands fly to my mouth. He reaches into his coat pocket, pulls out a black velvet box, and flips the top. He holds up a stunning solitaire. "Andi Claire Carter. Will you marry me?"

EPILOGUE

ndi

I stand in my wedding dress in the bridal suite at Christmastown, a room I'd personally designed. The ample space is themed white - white walls, giant puffy white chairs, white window dressings. One wall features large full-length mirrors trimmed in silver; another has a row of make-up tables. A grandiose crystal chandelier hangs from the center of the room.

"You're gorgeous," Emma squeals. She steps back in the off-the-shoulder burgundy gown I'd selected for my bridesmaids.

Steph, in the identical dress, shakes her head. "I'm not sure how my brother pulled this off."

I step back and take in my image. My wedding dress features a sweetheart neckline and a lace-covered bodice, narrow at the waist. The tulle skirt balloons out, ballroom style. My hair, long and curled, is held back from my face by a small tiara, a full-length lace veil attached to its back. I have on lace wedding pumps and no jewelry except for the diamond studs Matt gave me as an engagement gift.

My mother, still single and happily so, slips into the room.

Her hands fly to her face. "Oh sweetheart. You're stunning. You look like a princess."

"I feel like a princess."

Emma hands me my bouquet, a cascading mass of red roses, Queen Anne's lace, and greenery. "Are you ready?"

I hesitate. I was ready to marry Matt. I wasn't ready for the pageantry about to unfold. "Are there people out there?" I look toward the door.

Mom lunges forward and adjusts a tendril. "Lots of people, sweetheart."

I shut my eyes, nervous. When I open them, Steph is looking at me. She inches closer. "You own this, Andi," she says in her commanding Steph-like voice. "If anyone deserves the crazy romantic scene about to take place, it's you. It's *your* princess wedding package, remember. Show people how it is to be a Christmastown bride."

I meet Steph's eyes and squeeze her hand. She'd been an avid supporter since Matt and I got together. And she was right. I'd designed every square inch of this park. I'd planned the wedding package. I'd gotten the dream guy. If ever a moment was mine, this was it.

"I'm ready."

Steph knocks at the door and, almost instantaneously, a man in a gold and green uniform opens it. "Your carriage awaits." He holds open the door and makes a gallant gesture in the direction of the carriage. My carriage. I'd designed it to look as close as possible to Cinderella's famed pumpkin one. The circular structure is lit up and white, the seats inside are lined with plush velvet. Two horses with white coats stand in front.

The doorman assists my mother, Steph, and Emma into the carriage before extending his hand to me. I step inside and sit, my skirts billowing on either side, the bouquet still in my hand.

We are, right now, still in the back of the park, in the spot where we keep the parade floats when not in use.

The parade music, *Santa Claus is Coming to Town*, blares over the speakers. That's it, I know. The last song before the parade ends. The last song before I will be announced, and my carriage led down Christmastown's main street.

The song ends and our MC calls out. "Ladies and gentlemen, let's give a big welcome to our Christmastown bride, Andi Claire Carter, to be wed to our groom, Matthew Richard Taylor."

Cheers erupt. Our doorman, now on the carriage, gives the two white horses a gentle pat. *Beautiful Day* by U2, my song pick, sounds on the speakers. The carriage moves, slow at first. Then the horses turn and pull on to the main strip of the park.

"Oh." The word escapes, inadequate.

I'd seen Christmastown lit up a hundred times by now, but never like this. Illuminated buildings designed to look like a Swiss themed winter village line both sides of the street, three-pronged lampposts with festive winding greens in front of them. Every few feet, strings of lights designed with a Santa logo in the center stretch across the buildings. The lit gazebo stands at the street's end and, behind it, Christmastown Lake. Bright evergreens line the lake, their colored lights reflect pools of brightness in the water. The fountain, in the center, shoots out bursts of water.

Magic. That's what it feels like. The old buildings and piles of dirt had been transformed into this – an enchanted winter wonderland.

I wave at the onlookers as the carriage inches down the strip. People wave back.

"Congratulations!"

"Mazel tov."

"Merry Christmas."

A lump forms in my throat. I can't believe it's happening. Matt. The park. The wedding. Everything was coming together in a way that I would never have imagined.

A firework shoots up over the lake and, after a moment, a breathtaking cascade of silver embers float in the air. Two more fireworks shoot up; red and green lights illuminate the sky. Fireworks. I'd almost forgotten. Another part of the princess bride package.

Emma looks at the sky, wide-eyed. "This is incredible."

Steph leans forward. "Probably the wrong time to say this, but the park is going to make a shitload of money on weddings here."

I laugh, stare at the continued display of dazzling lights as carriage nears the gazebo. Matt at the altar! My heart literally leaps at the sight of him. He gives me a full-armed wave and his most dazzling Matt Taylor smile. I cannot wait to marry him.

The carriage turns right, and we circle the lake. Ruth had insisted we plant more Christmas trees; she'd been right. The pathway around the lake is a breathtaking display of Christmas cheer. The attractions, still lit up, stand behind the trees, adding a festive ambiance. We reached the gazebo on the other side just as a finale-level display of fireworks burst into the sky.

Brian, in a full tuxedo with tails, opens the carriage door. He helps our mother out, gives her a big kiss on the cheek. She takes the arm of Matt's friend, Potsie, who ushers her to her seat. Brian gives both Emma and Steph a hand and they wait at the end of the red carpet that leads to the altar. A small quartet plays *Prince of Denmark's March* by Jeremiah Clarke. Steph, then Emma, proceed down the aisle.

Brian holds his hand out. I slip my own into his and step out, the giant wedding bouquet cascading from my arm. I move to the end of the aisle. He kisses me on the cheek. "Go get him," he whispers.

I proceed down the aisle alone. An independent woman walking toward the man of my dreams.

The remainder of the actual ceremony is a blur. Later, I'd only remember Matt. How he looked when he smiled at me, how his hands felt in mine, the sound of him saying "I do." I'd remember the way it felt when he slipped the ring around my finger and the tender kiss, our first as man and wife.

"I now present to you, Mr. and Mrs. Matthew Taylor."

Our guests cheer. The organist starts Mendelsson's *Wedding March*. We link arms and march down the aisle. I can barely feel my face for smiling so hard. When we reach the end, Matt whispers in my ear. "First surprise of married life. Follow me." He grabs my hand.

"But –" I start.

He winks at me. "The guests know. I'll have their beautiful bride back in few moments. I just need this first memory to be ours." He kisses my lips. "Is that okay?"

I smile up at him. "Of course it's okay."

We stride toward the woods, reaching the edge. "Is this –" I start but I see it then, the lights and the lanterns exactly as they had been on that sixty-dollar date.

Matt picks me up and deposits me on to the very spot we'd stood all those months ago. He presses a button on his phone; a waltz sounds through a speaker. He kisses my hand, steps back, and gives a small bow.

"Andi, my beautiful bride, may I have this dance?"

THE END

ACKNOWLEDGMENTS

I am so excited for *The Santa Games* to be in the hands of readers! I have lots of people without whose help this book would not be possible.

My editing team: Shelly Alexander read the first chapters in an early version and pointed me in the right direction. Brenda Chin did a developmental edit of the novel and provided fabulous insight.

My beta readers: Terri Grant, Jody Giedraitis, and Katie Lippman. Thanks for your insight and encouragement.

My cover design artist: Jena R. Collins. Amazing!

Author Team: Maria Imbalzano and Sarahlyn Bruck. Thank you for your support.

My children: Kevin Treese for helping me frame this book on our COVID dog walks. Katie Treese for reading the numerous iterations of this book and giving me feedback. Cassidy Treese for your sense of humor, a major inspiration.

Jake: My biggest fan and without whose support I wouldn't have written any books. Love you.

A NOTE FROM THE AUTHOR

Hello! There are millions of books out there and I don't take it lightly that you took the time to read mine. Thank you! If you enjoyed *The Santa Games*, I would be deeply grateful if you would leave a review on Amazon or your retailer of choice. Reviews help other readers find my book.

I would also love it if you would consider joining my mailing list at www.leannetreese.com. I give share on my books (and some freebies) and, perhaps more important, include pictures of my dogs! I look forward to connecting with you.

ALSO BY LEANNE TREESE

Mother of the Accused

Their Last Chance

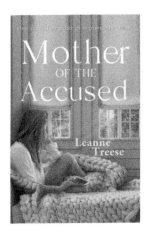

Made in United States
North Haven, CT
07 October 2022

25131049R00157